47 SORROWS

Thaddeus Lewis Mysteries

On the Head of a Pin
Sowing Poison

Editor: Allison Hirst
Design: Hailey Conner
Printer: Webcom

Library and Archives Canada Cataloguing in Publication

Kellough, Janet, author
    47 sorrows : a Thaddeus Lewis mystery / Janet Kellough.

Issued in print and electronic formats.
ISBN 978-1-4597-0928-7 (pbk.).-- ISBN 978-1-4597-0929-4 (pdf).--ISBN 978-1-4597-0930-0 (epub)

    I. Title. II. Title: Forty-seven sorrows.

PS8621.E558F67 2013   C813'.6   C2013-900834-9
                                    C2013-900835-7

1 2 3 4 5   17 16 15 14 13

We acknowledge the support of the **Canada Council for the Arts** and the **Ontario Arts Council** for our publishing program. We also acknowledge the financial support of the **Government of Canada** through the **Canada Book Fund** and **Livres Canada Books**, and the **Government of Ontario** through the **Ontario Book Publishing Tax Credit** and the **Ontario Media Development Corporation**.

Care has been taken to trace the ownership of copyright material used in this book. The author and the publisher welcome any information enabling them to rectify any references or credits in subsequent editions.

J. Kirk Howard, President

Printed and bound in Canada.

VISIT US AT
Dundurn.com | Pinterest.com/dundurnpress | @dundurnpress | Facebook.com/dundurnpress

Dundurn	Gazelle Book Services Limited	Dundurn
3 Church Street, Suite 500	White Cross Mills	2250 Military Road
Toronto, Ontario, Canada	High Town, Lancaster, England	Tonawanda, NY
M5E 1M2	L41 4XS	U.S.A. 14150

47 SORROWS

A Thaddeus Lewis Mystery

Janet Kellough

DUNDURN
TORONTO

For Catharine's birthday

Chapter 1

Thaddeus Lewis was splitting kindling in the back dooryard of the Temperance Hotel when he heard the children screaming. They came howling up from the direction of the shore — his granddaughter Martha in front, holding her side as if she had a stitch in it. Behind her were the two Carpenter boys and Michael Donovan, who, although he was far bigger than any of the others, was slow, the general opinion being that he was slightly addled as the result of being struck on the head by a large oak branch which had fallen through his roof one stormy night. Little Rosie Carpenter, wailing like a banshee, trailed the others by thirty yards or so. Thaddeus paused in his chopping and stood waiting until Martha reached him.

"On … the … beach. That way." She pointed with the hand that wasn't clamped to her abdomen, and then flopped, gasping, onto the ground.

"It's … a … monster," panted one of the Carpenter twins. Thaddeus could never tell which one was which.

"No, a big frog," said the other. He hadn't run as fast, and so had a little more breath.

"Uh uh. Dragon," said Michael.

Rosie had finally reached him, but she didn't stop to say anything. She just continued to wail as she ran past him toward home.

"Where exactly did you find this monster?" Thaddeus asked.

"On down the shore …"

"Not very far …"

"Yes it was, it was a mile …"

"Down the lakeshore …"

Thaddeus silenced them with a hand. "Wait here."

He walked across the yard to the hotel's back door, but just as he reached it, it opened. Martha's father, Francis Renwell, was there, a worried expression on his face.

"I heard screaming. What's all the excitement?"

"The children say they found something strange down by the lake. You'd better come along."

The Carpenter boys led the way, with Martha beside her father and Lewis and Michael a few steps behind. Fractured, irregular pieces of loose limestone and exposed tree roots made walking difficult along the shore. Thaddeus felt a familiar throb of pain in his knee as he stepped on a stone ledge that crumbled underfoot and caused him to slip sideways. As they rounded a bend in the shoreline, he could see a mob of birds — gulls, crows, and vultures — clustered around and on top of what looked like a mound of clothing. At the approach of the humans they shrieked and flapped out of the way.

It was obvious that there was no life left in the figure the birds had been picking at. The body was bloated, whether from being immersed in the water or from the natural gases that accumulate after death, Thaddeus had no way of knowing. He took only one quick look, then turned to Francis.

"Take the children back to the hotel, then go for the constable and the doctor. You'll go faster than I could."

He did his best to keep the birds from the corpse as he waited, but the crows, in particular, were persistent and sly. They darted in to peck away a morsel whenever they dared, then scrambled away, only to swoop down again a few moments later.

Judging from the tatters of clothing, this frightful figure had been a woman once. A cook aboard one of the lake boats perhaps? Or had some other disaster befallen her? It was no wonder the children had mistaken her for some sort of monster, Thaddeus thought. Her skin was a deep mottled burgundy, split in places, but he didn't know whether this was from the grotesque swelling that had taken place or if some marine animal had fed on her. One eye was little more than an empty socket. He suspected that the birds were responsible for this — they always went for the soft parts first. Her tongue protruded obscenely as her remaining eye stared sightless at the sky. The Carpenter boy had been closest in his description of what they had found. She had a distinctly froglike appearance.

Francis must have run. It was only a few minutes

before he returned with Constable Williams, though it seemed to Thaddeus that he had passed hours in the company of this macabre discovery.

"We'll have to wait for the doctor, but there's no question that she drowned," the constable said. "I haven't heard of any wrecks recently, but that doesn't mean nothing. She could have fallen off a wharf or a small boat just as easily as not."

After he arrived and had a chance to look at the body, Dr. Keough agreed with the constable's assessment.

"Poor soul. It's a dreadful way to die." He unfolded a canvas tarpaulin he had brought to serve as a stretcher. They spread the canvas out beside the corpse.

"I'm thinking we should just roll her over, don't you agree?" the constable asked. "If we try to lift her, she's likely to just pull apart."

Francis appeared reluctant to touch the body at all. He grabbed a piece of driftwood and poked it under her, levering the body up so the others could push her the rest of the way over. Lewis and the constable each grabbed a fistful of her skirts and hauled.

She must have been in the water for some time, long enough for the cloth to have weakened, for as they pulled, the fabric ripped and the body fell back down again with a soft whooshing sound. At the same moment a gust of wind lifted what was left of her skirts and blew them over her head.

They all gasped. In spite of the clothing, it was evident that this was not a woman after all. The wind had revealed that *she* was definitely and most unmistakably a *he*.

* * *

A drowning was no great novelty for the village of Wellington. Anyone who lived along the shore of Lake Ontario was familiar with the perils that attended the business of shipping, whether it was of goods or of people. Treacherous storms and shoals claimed many a ship, and the current could suck a body down to the lakebed, only to spit it up later in the most unlikely place.

What did have the people of the village talking, however, were the skirts and crinolines this body had been wearing when it washed ashore. A man masquerading as a woman was no common thing, especially not in the settled part of Canada West.

No clue as to the poor soul's identity had been found either, and no local vessels had reported a passenger or crew member gone overboard. There had been no purse in his pocket, no papers that might indicate who he was or where he might have come from. Nothing but a frayed piece of green ribbon that might have come from any one of a thousand places.

"Unless somebody's actively looking for him, I don't see how we'll ever know who he is," the doctor grumbled, "especially if he's an emigrant. The steamers are so overloaded, I'm not sure but that an entire boatload could go missing and no one would notice."

"Surely they have passenger lists," Lewis said. "Maybe we should check those."

"The ships all have lists when they start out, though I'm told half the people lie about who they are anyway.

And then so many of them die on the way over and so many more of them are held up in Quebec. By the time they get through all that and get aboard a boat that will bring them down this way, it's a wonder they know who they are themselves. I expect it would be easy enough to lose track of a man, if someone was disinclined to be careful in the first place, and by all accounts there's little care taken about anything in this whole sorry business."

Canada had been warned to expect a heavy influx of emigrants this year. The potato crop in Europe had failed again after several seasons of failures. According to the newspapers, most of the population of the green country of Ireland lived on nothing but potatoes at the best of times, and this latest disaster had put them into a crisis. The ports were full, they said, with anyone who could scrape together the passage money, all frantic to get aboard a ship.

Canadian authorities, mindful of the epidemics of cholera that had arrived in previous years, had directed port city officials to inspect each emigrant to determine which of these unfortunate travellers should be quarantined and which was healthy enough to continue the journey up the St. Lawrence River to Lake Ontario and beyond. Those fortunate enough to pass this examination were piled aboard lake steamers and shunted along to the next port, where again they were sorted. If someone was determined to conceal his identity, there was plenty of opportunity for paperwork to go missing in all this chaos, and Thaddeus could think of no other reason why the drowned man would have assumed his disguise.

"I expect it'll be up to us to bury this poor fellow," the doctor said. "I'll gladly donate the canvas we used to move him, and I suppose a couple of the local fellows might dig the grave, if asked."

Thaddeus nodded. It was an indication of his advancing years, he supposed, that the doctor had not asked him to perform such heavy labour, and certainly he was grateful on behalf of his aching knee, but at the same time he was a little annoyed that his infirmities had become so evident to others. Never mind, let the younger men dig. He would stand by the graveside and say the words if no other minister could be prevailed upon to officiate. But they should do it soon, before the smell from the putrefying corpse got any worse.

Chapter 2

Luke Lewis's backside had had more than enough of bouncing around on the seat of the mail wagon. He had been grateful when Benjamin Rumball offered him a ride down the long miles of the Huron Road to Galt. Otherwise Luke would had been faced with one of two equally daunting prospects — he could have walked the entire distance, or he could have asked his brother Moses for the use of the sway-back horse that was too old for plowing anymore. It would have been a plodding ride with the horse, who moved only a little faster than a walking pace and would need to be fed and watered, not to mention rested at frequent intervals. If he had walked, he would no doubt have been offered rides by farmers travelling the road, but none of them travelled far. Their assistance would have been sporadic and temporary and for long stretches of the way non-existent.

However, news of Luke Lewis's departure had spread surprisingly rapidly through the far-flung and sparsely populated settlement. He had pretty well resigned himself to shank's mare by the time word had gotten around that he intended to go all the way south to Toronto, where he would board a passenger steamer and be carried along the shore of Lake Ontario and beyond. And it hadn't been long before a solution had presented itself, or rather *himself*.

Luke had bumped into Benjamin Rumball at the general store in Clinton. "I hear you're headed south," Rumball said. "If you've no other way down the road, you can come with me. After all, I'm going anyways, and I'd be glad of some company along the way."

Once a week, Rumball drove the Huron Road all the way from Goderich to Galt, collecting parcels and letters along the way. At Galt, he picked up whatever post was waiting and then he headed north again.

"I go all the time," Rumball said, "so I don't care which particular time you pick. Just meet me here in Clinton."

Luke had immediately accepted the offer. It was far better than walking, certainly, and much better than riding the old horse, but Rumball's wagon was singularly ill-sprung and Luke's backside insufficiently padded to absorb the constant bouncing up and down on the rough wooden seat. Rumball, on the other hand, was shaped very like his name sounded, round and upholstered, and he seemed oblivious to the discomfort.

The road had not improved in the five years since Luke had travelled the opposite way in a wagon. He had been riding with his brother Moses then, and although he'd started the journey in a state of high excitement, he'd soon had the enthusiasm shaken out of him. By the time they had reached their destination — a tract of unsettled land that looked very much like all the other tracts of unsettled land they had just passed through — he had begun to realize the enormity of the adventure, and just how much work it was going to take before Moses's choice of farmstead would begin to resemble anything like a farm.

They had thrown up a shanty as fast as they could, neither of them keen on staying any longer than was absolutely necessary with their older brother, Will, who was homesteading on the next lot. Will had a two-year head start, but with two of them to do the heavy work, they had soon caught up.

The heavily forested land had provided more opportunity than just farming for the Lewis boys. Soon after they settled on their lot, the Canada Company's lands began to attract more settlers — just a trickle of them — from England and Scotland and Ireland, places where the trees had long since been chopped down and the lands turned into fields. These novice settlers had little idea how to proceed with a farm that was still wilderness. Luke found that he could make good coin as a chopper, and even Moses and Will abandoned their own work at times to help in the back-breaking work of cutting out small trees and brush and piling bigger logs into great heaps that could be safely burned. It was this labour that had provided Luke with the wherewithal for his current plans.

As the time approached for his departure, a number of his neighbours had besieged him with requests. It started with Jack Thompson two farms over, who asked if Luke could leave a message with a cousin whose farm was just a few miles down the road. This cousin had borrowed some harness months ago, Jack said, and now Jack needed it back. Luke thought this was a reasonable enough request and agreed that he could deliver the request "since he was going right by."

Then Mrs. Jack asked him to drop off a parcel of baby clothes to her sister who was farmsteading with her husband farther south along the road. "Just leave them at the inn at Mitchell. She's expecting her first come September," she said. "It's as easy for you to take them as it is for Jack to ride to Clinton and ask the mail."

It also wouldn't cost any money to have Luke carry them, he realized, but he didn't voice this thought. He would have to hide the parcel from Rumball, otherwise the innkeeper might demand postage for it. But the Thompsons were good neighbours, and had done the Lewises many a favour, so Luke felt he should oblige.

Then Ezra Miller asked if Luke could stop by his father's house in Galt and tell him to send his oldest boy north for the summer. The requests snowballed after that.

Almost everyone in the neighbourhood, it seemed, agreed that Luke was a far better choice of carrier than Benjamin Rumball, who was reliability itself with letters, but was apt to forget any verbal messages he was asked to pass on. Luke was charged with leaving news of engagements, announcements of births and deaths, and reports of the state of this year's crops.

He had protested that he was merely going home for a visit, and hadn't time to take care of all these things, but his neighbours, plus their neighbours (and, it seemed, everyone else within twenty miles), had pestered him until, in the end, he agreed that he would do his best to take care of their business along the way.

Luke had promised his brother that he would stay on the farm until the spring planting was completed. There was no point leaving before then anyway, Moses had pointed out, because the roads would still be a muddy morass from the spring rains. The planting was done, but then Moses had pleaded for help with one task after another, so that the year rolled around to the first week of July and Luke still hadn't left.

He had been in one of their back fields helping Moses remove a stump when he was hailed by a man standing by the fencerow. Glad enough of an excuse to stop working for a few minutes, Luke had ambled over to the man. It was no one he recognized.

"Good day to ye," the man said, tipping his hat, and Luke knew from his speech that he must be from the Irish settlement some miles away. "The name's Henry Gallagher," the man went on. "I don't believe we've met, but they tell me you're headed down to the front."

Luke nodded, his heart sinking, for he knew this man must have something he wanted him to do "since he was going anyway."

"I'm wonderin' if you might do me a wee favour. You see, my brother is on his way across to join me here. I paid for his passage on a ship named *The Syria*, and he should have arrived long since, but I haven't heard a word. You wouldn't mind asking around, just to see if he's there at one of the ports? And if he is, to give him this?"

Gallagher unfolded a greasy piece of paper, part of a letter long since received and memorized, for Luke could see cramped and blotted writing and the remnants of a seal. Inside this was part of a pound note, in Halifax currency. The bill had been sliced, not torn, and on a diagonal that slashed through the printing and the engraving in the middle.

"You see," Gallagher continued, "I don't know if Charley has the wherewithal to get hisself all the way up here. I'm hearing that things are terrible in the old country just now. He may have run out of money by the time he got to Toronto."

"I don't understand," Luke said. "What is he to do with a half-note?"

"That's so you know you have the right man," Gallagher replied. "After all, anybody could say his name was Gallagher and take the money, couldn't he?"

"But why?" Luke asked. "It's still just half a note and no good for anything."

The man beamed. "But he'll have the other one, you see. If he can produce the other half, you'll know it's Charley."

Luke had to admit that it was a brilliant means of identification. No two notes would be exactly the same — now that he looked closely, he could see that the cut had gone right through one of the numbers at the bottom. If Charley could provide the matching half, he could paste them back together and spend the money.

"How did you know that someone would be travelling all the way to the front?"

"I didn't really," the man admitted. "I'd clipped the bill in two and sent the other half to him last fall. I meant to send the other, but we had that early snow and I couldn't get to Clinton to mail it. But now that you're going anyway, the problem is solved, isn't it?"

"How do you know he was on *The Syria*?"

"I did that part of it through the Canada Company. They arranged to book him on the ship and get the ticket and the directions to him. They've been good about that, if not so much about other things."

Luke hadn't realized that the company that was responsible for selling land in the Huron Tract was willing to provide this service for their settlers. It only stood to reason, he supposed. It seemed that as soon as settlers had some success, they urged their friends and relatives back home to follow suit and come to Canada, and, like this man, often provided the wherewithal to make it happen.

"I didn't trust them with the cash money part of it though. I sent some English money through the church. But now that he's here in Canada, the Halifax will do."

"I'll certainly ask about him," Luke said. "But they say there's a heavy emigration this year. Shouldn't I just leave it for him at one of the shipping offices?"

The man thought about this for a moment. "No. One Irishman is just like another as far as they're concerned. They're apt to forget. I realize it's not likely you'll find Charley, but if you try, then at least I can tell myself that I've done what I could."

It seemed like a hopeless mission, but Luke didn't have the heart to turn the man down. "I'll do my best, but I can't promise anything."

The man nodded. "I know you will. And if something's happened to him, or you can't find him, maybe you could just drop a line to that effect if you happen to be writing to your brothers?"

"I'll do my best," was all that Luke could say. "And if I don't find him, I'll get the note back to you, just in case he turns up with the other half."

Satisfied with Luke's promise, the man had tipped his hat and gone on his way. It was no more irksome a request than any of the others that had been made, but the encounter finally galvanized him into action. That night after supper, Luke told Moses that it was time for him to go.

And having promised everyone to do his best, he now attempted to do precisely that. At every stop along the way, Luke left news that the innkeeper or storeowner or farmer could pass along, not only to the intended recipients, but to anyone else who cared to listen. It was hard to keep a secret on the Huron Road.

Chapter 3

Rumball kept them to a strict schedule, and each time they stopped it seemed to Luke that he was out of the cart for only a minute or two before he had to climb back up and continue their bumpy journey. The road had at one point been cleared to a width of sixty feet or so, but, except in the places where the settlers themselves kept the brush cleared back, bushy growth and spindly saplings had gained a toehold and threatened to reclaim the trail. The spring rains had left deep ruts wherever a vehicle had passed, and Luke feared for their wagon's axle every time a wheel slid into one of these.

After many hours on the road, however, they drove into Galt and across the bridge that spanned the Grand River. It seemed a very built-up and crowded place to Luke, after his years in the sparsely settled area to the north. The town boasted three-storey buildings, a towering mill, and a number of fine stone houses, odd contrasts to the log shanties and cabins he had become used to.

He parted company with Rumball at Shade's Inn, where he discovered that he had two options for continuing his journey. He could board the stage that left daily for Guelph, and go by land from there to Toronto, or he could find his way to Burlington Bay and catch a steamer from there.

He had arrived in Galt too late to catch the connection to either Guelph or to Dundas, where he needed to get in order to board a steamer. It was already late afternoon. Whichever he chose, he needed to find some place to spend the night. He was loathe to spend money on an inn. He had counted his money up carefully and calculated his costs as far as he was able, but wasting money now could result in hardship later on. He debated asking the local livery stable if he could bed down in their hayloft, but then he had another thought.

He stopped the first respectable-looking gentleman he met on the street.

"Excuse me, sir, can you tell me whether or not there might be a Methodist meeting house nearby?"

The man looked startled at the question, as though he had expected to be asked the location of the nearest tavern, not a church, and Luke became aware of his travel-stained coat and the dirt of the road that had settled on his trousers.

"Just over on the next street," the man said, pointing to the end of a substantial brick building. "As soon as you round the corner, you'll see the steeple."

Luke touched the brim of his hat in thanks, and headed in the direction the man had pointed.

He found a bit of luck when he reached the meeting house. A class meeting had evidently just finished, and a group of soberly clad women were filing out the front door, the minister just behind them.

"Excuse me, sir," Luke said when he saw the man. "I wonder if I might trouble you for a moment?"

All of the women stopped, eager to overhear what this young stranger might have to say.

The minister looked startled, but friendly enough. "Of course, of course, what could I do for you? If it's a private affair, we could go back inside." But he was already securing the lock on the door as he said it.

"Oh no, that's all right," Luke said, smiling. "I have no secrets." His purposes would be better met with the women there to overhear. "My father is a Methodist minister, and I thought that, as I was nearby, I would stop and pay my respects. I know he would want me to."

He had the minister's full attention, and that of the group of women as well.

"Now, that's fine." The minister beamed. "And what is your father's name then? I probably know him. There aren't so many of us that we're strangers to each other."

"He's retired now, of course, but he spent many years as an itinerant preacher. His name is Thaddeus Lewis." And then Luke held his breath. He had not been able to ascertain if this church was Wesleyan Methodist or Methodist Episcopal, and hard feelings over the failed union of the two denominations had yet to settle entirely.

He hadn't taken into account his father's notoriety.

"Oh, my goodness, Thaddeus Lewis. I haven't met him personally, of course, since we're a Wesleyan congregation, but everyone knows of your father, after all that unpleasantness a few years ago. Retired, you say? That's a shame. The church has lost a good man. Awfully good of you to pass on his respects. But tell me, what brings you to these parts?"

Luke was a little taken aback. He was perfectly willing to trade on his father's good name as a preacher. He hadn't expected to be welcomed on the strength of Thaddeus's reputation as a solver of crimes. He hoped that if he were indeed offered a bed for the night, he wouldn't be expected to regale his host with details of the infamous Simms killings, or his father's role in the discovery of a murderous wild boy in the sand hills of Wellington. Such lurid tales were novelties, he supposed, and apparently people had little else to talk about, but he had recounted what little detail he knew far too many times.

"I'm on my way to visit my father," he said in reply to the preacher's question. "Unfortunately, I seem to have missed the last stage. I could walk it, but I don't fancy navigating the way by moonlight."

"Very wise, very wise," the preacher said. "There's a rough crowd on the roads these days. All the emigrants coming in — they all say they're looking for work, but when they don't find it, they have no compunction about taking what they need."

Luke wondered if the brother of the man from the Irish settlement was one of these, and if the want of a few coppers was enough to turn him into a thief. He resolved to make every effort to find Charley Gallagher.

One of the women stepped forward then. She had had time to get a close look at Luke's cheap and travel-worn apparel. "Have you a place for tonight?" she asked.

"I thought I'd just ask the local livery if I could bed down in the straw," he said. "But from what you tell me, strangers aren't exactly welcome these days."

The woman turned to the preacher. "This boy can stay with us if he likes. It would be an honour to have the son of such a famous preacher." She turned back to Luke. "I'm afraid our little house is quite full, but you're welcome to a meal and the kitchen bed if you can find no better."

The other women looked quite put out. They hadn't spoken up soon enough and now they'd been trumped.

"I'd be much obliged, ma'am," Luke said. It might cost him a few tales about his father, and perhaps a prayer or two, but the Methodists had not failed him, bless their hearts.

Luke found not only a bed and a meal, but a ride. The Methodist woman, whose name was Mrs. Howard, was married to a book merchant who, as it happened, had business in the town of Guelph the next day. Mr. Howard was perfectly happy to accommodate a travelling companion, and they set off the next morning after what seemed to Luke a rather late breakfast. It was fully eight o'clock by the time Howard collected a horse and trap from the nearby stable.

The Guelph Road was very busy in comparison to the Huron Road, where he and Rumball had sometimes driven for miles without encountering another soul. Now Luke saw everything from coaches to smart traps, farm wagons, single horsemen, and pedestrians heading west toward Galt.

Mr. Howard obligingly deposited him at the coach inn, where he had only a short wait before he climbed aboard a stage for the final leg of the journey to Toronto. He found himself sharing the coach with a well-dressed man and an older woman. The woman snatched her skirts away from Luke's dusty boots when he climbed in to sit beside her, but the man seemed friendly enough and inclined to chat.

He was a lawyer, he said, on his way back to Toronto after trying a case in Guelph. "A nasty case of aggravated assault. It's a wonder the victim survived at all, and I'm sure he won't be quite right as the result of it. Culprit safely locked away now, of course."

"One of the Irish, I suppose," sniffed the woman. "They're causing trouble everywhere."

"On the contrary," the lawyer replied. "Boy from quite a good family, in fact. Just goes to show that you can never tell."

As they continued east, they were passed by a great number of wagons, carts, and drays piled high with luggage and household goods.

"Where is everyone going?" Luke asked. "It looks like the whole world is moving house."

"They are," the woman said. "Everyone who has somewhere else to go is getting away from the ports, because of the malignant fever. My daughter lives just on the outskirts of Toronto, but I'm not taking any chances. I'm on my way to collect her now. She and the children will stay with me until the contagion passes. It's the emigrants, you see. They've brought it with them and now it's spreading everywhere."

"Malignant fever?" Luke had heard of it, but only in passing. Cholera was the usual companion of emigration, and even in his short life there had been a number of epidemics that had raged through Upper Canada.

"That and ship's fever," the lawyer said, "although I'm not sure if they're one and the same. Any emigrant who looks ill is supposed to be held in quarantine, but it seems as though a dreadful number of them are slipping through."

As they passed the long miles, the traffic increased, although it began to change in nature. Those who were walking were, for the most part, respectable-looking enough — farmwives or labourers — but here and there they would pass knots of sullen-looking men who could have done duty as scarecrows placed in a field of grain to chase the birds away. These men would step aside and let them pass, but they grumbled as they did so. Occasionally, it appeared that there were whole families trudging along the road, wives and children straggling along in the rear, ragged, thin, and scowling.

They were like grey shadowy wraiths on the road, haunting the lanes with their cheekbones jutting in reproach. What work could these thin ghosts find in a land that was still being wrested away from the trees, and whose soil was so recently broken to the plow? No one would hire these men, Luke knew, even if there hadn't been fear of the diseases they brought.

It was well after noon when the coach halted at a stop in order to water the horses. Luke climbed down, weary from the ride, and walked across the road to where a large oak tree offered a shady place to sit. As he left Galt, the good Mrs. Howard had pressed a box on him. Now he opened it to discover most of a loaf of bread and a large wedge of cheese wrapped in cloth.

As he lowered himself down on the soft grass, he noticed a woman and a boy sitting in a heap beside the watering trough. The woman seemed exhausted and indifferent to their arrival, huddled into the tatters of clothing that hung off her. But the boy eyed him curiously, his eyes widening at what had been hidden by the cloth. Luke was ravenous, and stuffed a huge piece of the crusty bread into his mouth. But he was disconcerted by the boy's stare. He pulled another chunk from the loaf and held it out.

"Are you hungry?" he asked. "Would you like this?"

The boy jumped to his feet and ran forward, snatching the bread from Luke's hand. He returned to the woman, tore the bread in two, and handed her a piece.

Roused from her apathy, the woman looked up.

"*Go raibh mile maith agat,*" she called in a lilting cadence. "Bless you, sir."

"Is your name Gallagher by any chance?" Luke called. A woman and a boy travelling alone didn't exactly fit the description of Henry Gallagher's brother, but it was worth asking in case they knew of the missing Irishman.

The woman shook her head and turned her face away.

Luke returned to his meal, but he couldn't bring himself to eat it all. When it appeared that the coach was ready to continue its journey, he wrapped another chunk of the bread and a small piece of cheese in the cloth and handed it to the boy before he once again boarded the stage.

"You shouldn't have done that," the lawyer said. "If that's the way you're going to go on, you'll have every beggar in the Canadas following you about."

"It's only one boy," Luke said, "and he looks starved."

The lawyer grunted, but remonstrated no further. The woman glared at him, and pulled herself as far into the corner as she could.

Chapter 4

After an overnight stop in the town of Norval, where Luke spent an uncomfortable night in the open wood-shed behind the stagecoach inn, he and his travelling companions finally reached Toronto. Luke located the wharves without difficulty; most of the traffic in the city was headed either to or away from the waterfront. A burly man waiting with a wagonload of tanned hides directed him to a wooden building where he was told he could arrange for his steamer passage, but the agent who manned it was flustered and abrupt, and after he had sold Luke his ticket, he went rushing out the door.

Luke followed him down toward the water. There were numerous wharves along the front, protected by the long arching peninsula of land that kept the swells and winds of Lake Ontario from reaching ships anchored in the harbour. Each of these wharves was bustling with arrivals or departures or transfer of goods.

He watched for a time before he realized that there were three hours yet before his own vessel was due to leave, and now that he had his ticket in hand, he was free to explore at least a portion of the city.

It was by far the largest he had ever seen, and as he walked along the margins of the lake, he marvelled at the number of three- and even four-storey buildings of solid brick and stone beyond the jumble of wooden sheds and storehouses. As he turned to look north, he could see church spires thrusting skyward through a dense cluster of commercial buildings, manufactories, offices, and houses.

He wandered along the lakefront, unwilling to stray too far lest he become lost. As long as he could see the lake, he decided, he would know where he was. Farther along the shore there were more wharves, and as he walked a sailing steamer chugged into one of these and tied up.

Luke was a little taken aback when he saw the number of passengers that had been crammed onto the deck of this ship. He had been looking forward to his voyage down the lake. He had never ridden on one of these steamers before. Now he wondered if he had made a mistake and should have gone by coach instead, for this steamer carried far more bodies than he expected and it looked as though each was allotted little more than a couple of square feet.

As he drew closer, he was appalled at the state of these bodies, as well. Many of them were dressed in rags, and all of their faces were thin and pinched, their arms bony, their eyes glazed, but whether with exhaustion or

hunger or disease, he had no way of telling. They must
be emigrants, he realized, ferried up the lake to look
for work, like the haggard groups he had seen on the
Guelph Road.

A man in uniform boarded the vessel, evidently to
direct the disembarkation of the passengers. Only a few
at a time were allowed onto the pier, and these were
shepherded to an area that had been cordoned off.

They stood, confused and blinking, while a fussy-
looking man with a bushy moustache bustled over
to the group and, assisted by a woman in a nurse's
uniform, began peering into their eyes and feeling
their foreheads, directing them to open their mouths
wide as he looked for evidence of disease. When he
had finished, he would send each person to either the
right or the left, depending on what he felt about
their condition. Judging from the cries that greeted
each culling, husbands were being separated from
wives, fathers from sons, mothers from daughters.

Several of the women were waiting with ragged
bundles in their arms, and it was only when one of
these began to wail that Luke realized they were carrying infants. The women were required to unwrap the
bundles for inspection. When Luke saw how small some
of the babies were, he realized that they must have been
born during the long journey across the ocean, or after
their mothers had arrived in Canada. He didn't give
much odds for their survival under the circumstances.

The group that had been shuffled to the doctor's
right were herded away and loaded into carts. The
wailing increased as the carts drove away.

"Now, now, there's no need to carry on like that," one of the uniformed men said. "They're being taken to hospital where they'll be looked after. If you've friends or family in Toronto that you can go to, you're free to leave now. The rest of you will be fed directly and you can stay in the city for twenty-four hours. After that, you'll have to move on to another port."

Here and there groups of people detached themselves from the crowd and began to walk north along Simcoe Street.

Those who were left muttered their disapproval, but there appeared to be little real resistance to the directive. Constables walked up and down on the periphery of the mob, truncheons in hand, and this was enough to quell any protest.

Then Luke saw another man in uniform, although he didn't appear to be a constable, begin zigzagging though the crowd. Twice Luke saw him stop to speak to someone, and then he emerged with two young women in tow. He led them down a side street, little more than an alley, really. Curious, Luke followed them.

Tucked around a corner, where the alley intersected another street, a wagon was waiting. At first, Luke thought that a monkey had been given the task of holding the reins, but then he realized that the driver was a remarkably odd-looking man. He was very short and slight, with a great deal of coarse black hair and low-set pointed ears that framed a peculiarly wrinkled face.

The officer directed the women to board the wagon. "I've two more for you, Flea," he said to the waiting driver. "Go on then." He gave one of the women a little push toward the wagon. "You'll be looked after."

Luke was so bemused by the novelty of the man's name and appearance that he watched the scene for a minute or so before it occurred to him to wonder what was going on. It was possible, he supposed, that some benevolent organization, perhaps one of the churches, had organized some sort of relief system for young emigrant women separated from their families. Or maybe employment had been arranged for them at a factory or in domestic service. He hoped that this was the case, but the fact that the wagon had been waiting around the corner, hidden almost, lent a sinister air to the scene.

"Hans says he's a little short this week, but he'll make it up to you next," said the man called Flea. And he handed a package to the officer.

"Tell him he'd better. One more short week and the arrangement is off."

"Come on now, Badger, and who would you be dealing with if you don't deal with Hans?" Flea replied. "Ye'll take what he gives you."

"Irish bastard," the officer muttered under his breath, but he turned away as he said it. It was then that he noticed Luke. "And what do you want?" He pulled a truncheon from a loop at his waist and held it at the ready.

Luke had been curious, that was all, but realized that an excuse for his presence might be a provident thing to provide. He seized upon the first thing that occurred to him.

"I'm looking for someone," he said. "I just wondered if any of these young ladies might know him." He turned to the women sitting sullenly in the wagon. "Do you know anyone named Charley Gallagher?"

At the mention of the name, the man called Flea spat and fixed him with a glare.

"What do you want with Gallagher?" he asked.

Luke shrugged. "I don't want anything with him. I was just asked to make inquiries about him. Apparently he was expected some time ago by a neighbour of mine."

Flea's eyes narrowed. "And where does this neighbour of yours live?"

"A long way from here," Luke said. "You won't ever have heard of it."

He could see that the officer was puzzled by this exchange. Whatever the name Gallagher meant to Flea, it was apparently nothing to do with the man called Badger. "You'll have to move along," he said. "There's no loitering here."

Luke hesitated. Should he demand an explanation of what was going on? He had no real objection to make — only an uneasy feeling that the driver looked suspicious and that the women were vulnerable. Besides, Badger was evidently acting in some official capacity and he carried a very heavy truncheon.

"Thank you for your time," he said politely and turned away. He hoped he was doing the right thing. He headed back to the wharf, with the distinct impression that he had somehow narrowly avoided some serious trouble. Perhaps his imagination had run away with him. He hoped so.

The encounter did, however, remind him of the promise he had given. He would see if there was anyone at the wharves who kept a list of the emigrants who had arrived. With some difficulty, and a great deal of misdirection from the labourers who worked the docks, he was eventually directed to the emigration office.

There was a counter inside, behind which a clerk was scratching away at a sheaf of papers.

"I'm wondering if you could help me," Luke said. "I'm looking for someone."

"You and the whole rest of the world," the clerk said without looking up. "What's the name?"

"Gallagher."

The clerk sighed, and grabbed a pile of papers to his right, again without looking up. Quickly he scanned his lists.

"No Gallaghers today," he said.

"He was expected some time ago."

"He's probably been held back. You'd have to check at the other ports."

"Held back? Why?"

The clerk looked at him as though he was being deliberately obtuse.

"Because of the fever," he said. "Sick emigrants are held in quarantine. Where have you been that you haven't heard? The whole province is in an uproar about it."

Of course. The scene he had just witnessed at Toronto's harbour must be happening at other ports as well. "I'm sorry," Luke said. "I've just arrived from Huron. Do you keep lists of those who were kept back?"

"No. I have lists of those who have arrived here. I have no lists for those who didn't." The clerk finally raised his head to look at Luke. "The records are in a shambles anyway. There are hundreds of emigrants on every ship. Some of them die on the way over, some of them die in quarantine, the rest of them are piled on steamers and brought up the lake. We do our best to keep track of them all, but chances are nobody will find anybody until the season ends and the dust settles. Sorry." And with that he went back to his paperwork.

Luke wandered back outside, stunned by the notion of hundreds of people aboard each ship. Even in the backcountry, they had heard that there would be a lot of emigration this year, but hundreds multiplied by what? How many ships crossed the Atlantic in a season? Another hundred? The sheer number of people on the move was staggering, and what on earth were they all supposed to do when they finally got here?

At the wharf outside the emigration office, the steamer that had just deposited its load of passengers was being swabbed down, buckets of water thrown haphazardly over the decks, followed by a cursory mopping. Luke hoped that this was not the vessel he would be boarding shortly. This boat had just dumped a number of very sick people on shore, and he doubted that the random sloshing of water around the decks would do anything to disinfect the craft. He resolved to spend his coming journey outside, on the deck of the ship, and to avoid entering the cabin or going below decks. He wasn't entirely sure where malignant fever came from, but surely fresh air would do much to blow it away.

When it came time to board, he realized with relief that it was a different vessel entirely — one of the packet ships that offered regular passenger service around the lake. He should have realized this, he supposed. If there was fear of the malignant fever spreading, the packet steamers would lose a great deal of business if their passengers were made to sit in the same seats as infected newcomers. The overloaded ship he had seen must have been hired especially to handle the emigrant traffic.

Even so, once he boarded, he discovered that the passenger cabin was airless and fusty-smelling, so he held to his original resolve and found a place at the bow of the boat, where he could lean against the railing and watch the passing sights. He almost changed his mind once the steamer had left the shelter of Toronto's harbour and entered Lake Ontario, where the swell caused a steady thump beneath him. But then he became engrossed in watching the passing shore, marvelling at the number of settlements that lined the lake.

As they pulled in to the pier at Port Darlington Harbour, Luke could see that there were wooden sheds here as well, but not so many as at Toronto, which, after all, was a major town with nearly twenty thousand residents. That would be the preferred destination for anyone looking for work, and a natural way station for those who hoped to travel west into the farther reaches of the province.

He needed to stretch his legs and walk on solid ground for a few minutes. The constant pitch of the ship against the waves had made his legs stiff and sore. He wasn't used to being on the water. Perhaps he could also

find something to eat while he was ashore. He found the
purser and asked when the steamer would be leaving
again. The man assured him that they would stay in port
for at least a half-hour, and that he had plenty of time to
find a bite at one of the shops near the wharf.

He walked down the gangplank and picked his
way past the huge piles of cordwood stacked on and
near the docks, waiting to be loaded onto the steamers
in order to feed their insatiable boilers. He wandered
down the road that led away from the water, hoping he
would find someone selling pies or some other portable
fare. He didn't want to stray too far in case the steamer
left earlier than the porter had indicated — although he
had been told that the captain would blow the whistle
several times before departure.

Off in the distance he could see a gaggle of
people trudging toward the harbour. As they drew
nearer, the group resolved itself into twenty or so
ragged, exhausted-looking creatures who moaned
and grumbled as they walked. When they reached
the wharf, two women and a frail old man collapsed
beside a shabby pile of trunks, boxes, and carpet
bags. Some of the luggage looked as though it would
surely disintegrate in the light rain that had begun
to fall.

Luke walked over to them. "Are you waiting to
board a steamer?" he asked a man who was fingering
a gaping hole in one of his boots.

"That's what they told us." The man had a thick
accent that made Luke strain to understand what he
was saying. "They put us off further along because

they left our trunks here by mistake. We've had to walk back ten miles or more to get 'em."

"Why couldn't you have come back on a steamer?" Luke asked. "There are plenty of them going back down the lake."

The man shrugged. "They're willin' to take us one way, but not the other. And none of us have any money to pay for it anyway. They're grumbling enough as it is, because they're having to take us twice."

"Where is it that you you're headed?"

"Anywhere there's work. They say Toronto might be good. Or the area beyond." He looked up, his brow furrowed with worry. "There are farms to the west, aren't there? A man might get work there."

Luke thought of the bush farms he had left, where few could afford help, even when there was a crop to sell; and now that there was no market for wheat, even the successful farmers were too worried about the future to spend good money on a hired hand. It was true that the Canada Company offered land on easy terms, but even if these poor people could manage to get their hands on a lot of their own, he knew they could never manage the hardscrabble tasks of cutting and chopping. These poor souls were so rickety they looked likely to expire just from the thought of it.

"What's your name?" he asked, but it was apparently a touchy topic, for the Irishman grew wary.

"Who wants to know?"

"I'm looking for someone. My neighbour asked me to try to find him. Just anxious, that's all, because he's late. The name is Gallagher."

"Gallagher?" The man shook his head. "I wouldn't want to be a Gallagher, I don't think."

Luke was taken aback. "Why not?"

"There was some trouble with Gallaghers, as I recall." The man wrinkled his brow in thought. "No, I can't remember what it was exactly, just that there was some trouble over in the next county. Gallaghers and the law, you see."

Luke didn't really, but perhaps that explained the strange reaction of the carter in Toronto, who had spat at the mention of the name.

"Mind you, I'll be anybody you want for a day if there's a bed at the end of it." He cackled as he said this, as though it was some great joke.

"But you aren't, in fact."

"Well, no, not really. But you can't blame a man for trying it on."

"Well, never mind," Luke said. "I'll find him sooner or later." He fingered the coppers he had in his pocket. Just as the purser had indicated, there was a market of sorts near the wharf, not large, just a few stalls that offered bread, cheese, and meat pies, but he suddenly felt uncomfortable about purchasing a meal in front of this emaciated group. And yet, he had not enough money to feed them all. Finally, he pulled three coins from his pocket.

"I know it's not much, but it's all I can do at the moment."

The man practically snatched the money out of his hand. "*Go mbeannai Dia duit.* Bless you, sir," he said, and to Luke's astonishment he tugged at his forelock.

Chapter 5

The dead body on the beach at Wellington was a nine days' wonder. The Quakers offered a plot in the corner of their burying ground and Thaddeus, Francis Renwell, and the two men who had helped carry the corpse home turned up to help with the digging. If what Dr. Keough had surmised was true, and the man was one of the emigrants from Ireland, Thaddeus thought it most likely that the man was Catholic, and wondered aloud if they were doing the right thing in interring him in a Friends' cemetery. But Thaddeus's employer, Archibald McFaul, himself an Irish Catholic, pointed out that he could just as easily be an Irish Protestant, or not even Irish at all, but one of the many Scottish crofters who were also fleeing the dreadful conditions that the lack of potatoes in their homeland was causing.

"I think Quaker is a good compromise," McFaul said. "The Society is more or less acceptable to almost everybody. At least they don't seem to be outright offensive. And besides, they offered."

In any event, it was unlikely that anyone would ever know who the drowned man was, or why he had been dressed in women's clothing, so the chances of some relative objecting to the manner of his burial was remote.

Martha and the other children, with the resilience of youth, had seemed to recover from the shock of finding the body, and after the burial everyone settled into the routine of their days, the summer winds gusting from the lake.

Thaddeus luxuriated in this welcome breeze as he walked along Wellington's main street. The warm, fresh air was always such a lift to the spirits after the long grey days of winter, when the overheated rooms of his small house behind the Temperance Hotel seemed to close in around him. It was true that he had to be out and about every day in the course of his duties as secretary of sorts to Archibald McFaul, and he was thankful for the distraction these provided, but nothing could compare to the sense of freedom he had had while riding from village to village as a circuit riding preacher for the Methodist Episcopal Church.

Of course that was a thought that belonged to a summer day. When the blustering gales of February howled around his ears, his aging joints liked nothing better than to have him sitting by a fire. Still, the travelling life called to him now and again, though he knew those days were over.

It was noon, and he was just reaching the front steps of the hotel when he heard a shout behind him.

He turned and squinted in the direction of the voice. The man moving down the street seemed very familiar, but he couldn't quite place him. And then something in the way the figure moved jangled recognition loose. It was his son Luke.

It had been five years since he had sent his youngest child off west. When he left, Luke had still been a boy, gangling and unsure. The person who approached him now was a man, still rail-thin to be sure, but his shoulders had filled out and he walked with an assured air.

Thaddeus stuck his head inside the hotel's front door.

"Martha! Run and get your grandmother," he shouted, and then he walked back to meet his son.

Luke's face split into a grin as he reached his father. Then Thaddeus folded him into a bear hug before pushing him away at arm's length to inspect him.

"You look well," he said. "You've filled out and grown an inch or two. You must be as tall as your brothers now."

"I'm taller than Will. I still haven't quite caught up to Moses."

Luke turned as the door opened and Betsy came out on to the verandah. Thaddeus noticed that his son's posture suddenly stiffened as he saw his mother. Time and illness had worn Betsy down and she no longer resembled the woman who Luke probably remembered. She hesitated on the step, peering, unsure of why she had been summoned. Then, when she saw Luke and realized who he was, she sat down on the step and burst into tears.

Luke hurried over and sat down beside her. He put his arm around her. "Well that's quite a welcome for a long-lost son," he said. "I thought you'd be happy to see me."

"Don't tease," she said. "It's just such a shock. I thought never to see you again." And then she flung her arms around his neck, still sobbing with emotion. Luke let her sob, a bemused expression on his face.

They might have sat there forever, Thaddeus thought, if Francis hadn't appeared at the door. "Sophie's put the kettle on," he said. "I'm assuming you'd like this gentleman to come in and sit down?"

Luke stood, and then helped his mother rise, holding her arm carefully as she mounted the steps. She swatted at him. "I know I'm old, but I'm not entirely decrepit yet," she said. "You don't have to treat me like I'm porcelain."

"Yes, ma'am," Luke replied meekly, and Thaddeus laughed. Their son dwarfed his mother, but it was obvious that she still held the whip hand.

She led the way to the kitchen, motioned for Luke to sit down, and hurriedly set a cup of tea in front of him. Then she hobbled over to the stove where Sophie was dishing up the noon dinner. It was Saturday and they currently had eight guests staying over the weekend and another couple who had arrived just for a meal, but they had long since established an efficient routine. Thaddeus, helped by Francis and Martha, scurried back and forth to the dining room, while Betsy helped Sophie with the last-minute sauces and garnishes. That left Luke alone at the table, and Thaddeus could see that he was wide-eyed at the bustle around him.

The flow of the traffic changed as leftovers were brought back to the kitchen, used plates taken to the sink room, and dessert delivered to the tables. Thaddeus was the first to sit down beside Luke. He helped himself to a cup from the teapot in front of him.

"We'll have our dinner when the others are done," he said.

"Is it always like this?" Luke asked.

"Like what?"

"Are mealtimes always this hectic?"

"Oh, this? This is nothing."

"I must admit, I never thought to see my father wait at table."

Betsy joined them. "Oh, he's got quite good at it, hasn't he?"

Just then an older woman hobbled in from the sink room.

"Well, hello to you, young sir," she said.

"Eliza, this is my youngest son, Luke. Luke, this is Eliza Carr, Sophie's mother. And, of course, Sophie is the genius over there by the stove."

Sophie turned then and smiled at her mother, displaying two extraordinary dimples. Her glance took in Luke as well, a friendly welcome for unexpected family.

"It's actually Mrs. Carr who has bought the hotel, although Francis and Sophie run it," Betsy explained. "It's nice that we've all been able to more or less throw in together."

"Uncle Daniel has gone back to farming then?" Luke asked. It had been Daniel and his wife Susannah who had owned the hotel when the Lewises had moved to Wellington.

"Oh yes. Daniel decided that he wasn't cut out to be an innkeeper, and I think Susannah was quite relieved, since so much of the work seemed to fall to her. Sophie's a natural though, and it was fortunate that Mrs. Carr came into money just when Daniel wanted to get out. It allowed Francis and Sophie to marry, and it's provided a home for us all."

The dining room service had been completed, and now Francis and Martha returned to the kitchen and plunked themselves down close to Luke. Everyone had a question for him, and each was asked before Luke had time to provide an answer to the last.

"Wait, wait, wait, one at a time," Thaddeus ordered, and then promptly jumped in first with his own comment: "Why didn't you let us know you were coming? It's a wonder your mother didn't expire on the spot with the shock of it."

"I wasn't sure when I was going to get here," Luke replied. "I stayed to help Moses until after the spring planting, and of course that always depends on the weather. By the time I realized it was time to go, it was too late to write. The letter would have arrived long after I did. Besides, don't you like surprises?"

"Tell me about the children," Betsy demanded. "They must be nearly grown by now." It was a constant source of grief to her that she had no chance to see her other grandchildren.

"They're noisy," Luke said. "And mischievous."

"And how is farming in the west? Is it as good as they say?" Thaddeus asked.

"Better," Luke replied, "once you get the land cleared. The chopping is hard, but the wheat practically jumps out of the ground once it's sown. Wheat and potash, those have been the cash crops."

"Who are you?" Ten-year-old Martha finally found an opportunity to break into the conversation.

"This is your Uncle Luke," Thaddeus replied. "We've told you about your uncles who went west. Now this one, at least, has come back home. Do you remember him?"

She didn't. She had been too small when they left. "Hello," she said. "I'm Martha."

"I know," Luke said. "I figured you had to be, but I wouldn't have recognized you. I remember you being very small, but now you're all grown up."

Martha beamed. "You look like Grandpa."

"He does, doesn't he?" Betsy said. "He's a tall, dark stranger."

Sophie began dishing up the family meal, setting heaping bowls of early potatoes and snap beans in front of them, followed by a platter of fried chicken and a basket of crusty bread. Finally, when all of the food was on the table, she took her place beside Francis and waited expectantly for Thaddeus to say grace.

Luke was caught reaching for the platter of chicken. "I almost forgot," he said, pulling his hand back. "So many of my meals have been eaten in a hurry and standing up. I'm afraid grace is a nicety that has tended to slip away back in the bush."

"I believe it's a *necessity*, not a nicety," Thaddeus said. But he said it mildly. The mellowing effect of hard years had made him less inclined to judgment. And the boy had only just returned, after all. He said a few simple words of thanks, and then they all dove into the food.

"You haven't actually met Sophie, have you, Luke?" Francis asked as he began passing the bowl of potatoes around the table. "Sophie, this is the youngest brat in the original pack. Luke, this is Sophie, who for some reason consented to be my wife. We're still trying to figure out why."

Martha was indignant. "Because she loves you, that's why!" and they all laughed.

There was a hiatus in the conversation as everyone ate, which gave Thaddeus a chance to reflect on how much had changed in the years Luke had been gone. Francis with Sophie, instead of with Luke's sister, Sarah, who had perished at the hands of a killer. He himself no longer riding the ministerial circuits, but toiling at a hotel and assisting in the business of one of Wellington's important men. But the change that was the most profound, he realized, was his wife's physical condition. She was so frail. She had never fully recovered from the dreadful bout of fever she suffered so many years ago, but on her good days she had still been capable of a day's work that would exhaust a man. That would be the Betsy who Luke remembered, not the Betsy who had been prematurely aged by the apoplexy that had brought them to Temperance House, and which required a constant attendance from Thaddeus that had put paid to his preaching days.

Martha was the first to finish her dinner. She set her knife and spoon neatly across her plate. There was still dessert to come, but with the others still eating, she could now take control of the conversation.

"We found a monster down by the lake," she announced.

Luke looked surprised that this statement was apparently directed at him. "A monster? What sort of monster? You mean like a fish?"

"No, at first we thought it was a whale, or a dragon, but it turned out to be a man dressed like a woman, only drownded."

Luke turned to his father for verification of this astounding revelation.

"A dead body is hardly a topic for mealtime conversation," Thaddeus said.

"But why was it dressed like a woman?" Luke asked, and Martha shot him a grateful glance.

"We don't know," Thaddeus said. "But I'm not surprised the children mistook it for a monster. A drowned person is not a pretty thing. It was only after the doctor had a look at it that we realized that the dress was so misleading. Everyone thinks it must be one of the emigrants, and that he fell off a steamer."

"No one's come looking for him?"

"No. I suppose with so many of them arriving in such a hurry, it's not surprising that a few might go missing."

"I've been commissioned to look for one of them myself," Luke said. "There are settlements of Irish and Scots both, not too far from us. One of them asked me to keep an eye out for his brother, but it's unlikely I'll be very successful. There seem to be hordes of them."

"Poor souls," Thaddeus said. "I hear that half of them are sick and all of them are starving. I don't know that they're going to be able to find a better life here."

"I came across some of them on the road. They were hoping for farm work, but now that the tariff is lifted on wheat, I don't know anyone who can afford to hire them."

"Typical, isn't it?" Francis said. "Just when Britain has decided to destroy farming in Canada, they round up all their paupers and send them over with the expectation that they can farm."

The British prime minister, Sir Robert Peel, had changed the Corn Laws, as they were known, although "corn" in England apparently meant any kind of grain, and not just the yellow, husked ears that grew so readily in Canada. The tariffs that had been in place had given Canadian wheat preferential treatment in the British markets. Now this advantage had been wiped away with a stroke of the pen, forcing Canadian farmers to compete directly with the Americans, who produced far larger crops and enjoyed a much longer growing season.

"Everyone is wondering where we're going to sell our wheat," Luke said. "There's a lot of uncertainty about what's going to happen. Wheat is one of the few things that ever made money."

"It does seem very odd to me that Britain is rewarding the colony that rebelled while the one that has stayed loyal is being penalized," Thaddeus said.

"Kind of like the Prodigal Son, isn't it?" Luke said.

Thaddeus was about to retort, when he realized, for once, that he was being teased by one of his offspring.

"It's almost as if Britain is aiding and abetting their sabre-rattling," he grumbled. The United States was embroiled in a territorial war with the newly independent Mexico, insisting on America's right to expand westward to the ocean.

"Enough politics," Betsy said. "Tell us more about the children."

And with the arrival of the bread pudding, the conversation turned again to family.

Thaddeus could tell that Betsy was worn out, what with the excitement of Luke's arrival and the bustle of dinnertime. He knew he should shoo her off for her afternoon nap, but he also knew that it would be a waste of words — there was little likelihood that she would relinquish her lost lamb so readily.

Francis and Mrs. Carr rose from the table and busied themselves in the sink room, while Sophie was already organizing supper. Martha, bored by the conversation about people she had never met, ran outside to find her cohort of playmates.

"Let's finish the teapot and take our cups out to the porch," Thaddeus suggested. "It's a fine place to sit on a hot afternoon."

The Temperance Hotel had a wide verandah, and in the summertime the cool breeze that blew in from Lake Ontario wafted through it. The porch had been furnished with painted wooden chairs and rockers for the use of the guests, but it was here that Thaddeus spent most of his time when he wasn't wanted elsewhere. *I'm getting so old,* he thought. *Here I am sitting on the porch watching the world pass me by.*

They settled in one corner, well away from a cluster of patrons who had chosen to laze away the afternoon. Luke made a great show of stirring his tea while his parents waited expectantly.

"I don't bite, you know," Thaddeus said. "You can spit out whatever's on your mind."

"Is it a girl?" his mother asked. "Are you planning to get married?"

Luke blushed furiously before he answered. "No, it's nothing like that." And then when his mother's face fell, he added, "I just haven't met anyone, that's all."

"Plenty of time for that, Betsy," Thaddeus said. "After all, he's a young man yet, and needs to settle before he can think of taking a wife."

"I thought I was getting settled," Luke said. "But now that I'm here, I'm wondering if my efforts might be better spent in a different manner."

"Why don't you just tell me what you have in mind, and then I'll give you my opinion of it."

Luke nodded. "I think I want to go into medicine. I think I've saved enough money to take at least the first year of courses."

Thaddeus chuckled. "Luke the Physician? Apparently we named you well."

Luke smiled. "I'd actually thought of that, you know."

"A doctor?" Betsy said. "That would be wonderful!"

"After five years in Huron, I've decided that I'm just not cut out to be a farmer," Luke went on. "It seems to me it's just the same thing year in, year out, and you're always at the mercy of the weather or the markets or the insects or something. But after a while, I did find that I liked looking after the livestock — you know, dealing with their injuries and diseases. I was having quite a lot of success, too. Eventually the neighbours noticed and began calling me when they had an animal that was doing poorly. After a while they started calling about themselves as well. There aren't a lot of doctors along the Huron Road, and the settlements are so scattered, you see. I'd do what I could for them, but it was starting to make me nervous."

"I can see that," Thaddeus said. "After all, it's one thing if you lose a cow. Quite another if you lose a person."

"Exactly. I just don't know enough — I haven't had much experience with surgery, for example — and there are so many advances in medicine now, I'd like to know more about them. It seems to me that it's a profession where I'll never stop learning."

Thaddeus knew about this thirst for knowledge. He had had it all his life.

"They say a wise man is one who knows he doesn't know."

"Then I must be the wisest man on earth," Luke said.

"This all sounds wonderful," Betsy said, "but why are you talking about changing your plans now that you're here?"

"Because now I'm wondering if I've just been thinking of myself, and not you. I didn't realize how sick you've been, Ma. Maybe I should be looking to my responsibilities. I know you don't have to worry about Martha anymore, now that Francis is back, but I don't think the rest of us can expect him to take care of you as well. It's not really his place, after all."

Thaddeus felt a surge of pride in this boy who would stop to consider his aging parents, but at the same time had no intention of letting his dreams fall apart on their account. He was about to say so, when Betsy replied.

"You will not!" she said. "Your father and I are fine. We've long since sorted out our arrangements here, and everyone, including Francis, is perfectly happy with them. Don't you give us another thought."

Thaddeus seconded her opinion. "I know Francis is really only a son-in-law, but he feels as much a son to me as you are. We sorted out our differences a while back and, in fact, we owe each other a great deal."

Luke looked puzzled. After his sister had died, the name Francis Renwell had been enough to send his father into a rage. Lewis had never liked the man who had married his daughter, and, in fact, had held him responsible for her death.

"I was very wrong about Francis," Thaddeus admitted. "He was rash and headstrong — just like your sister — but he was in no way responsible for what happened to her. I've come to realize that he's a fine man, and now that he's married Sophie, he's settled down a great deal. And," he added, "I've mellowed some too. I'm not so quick to make judgments as I once was. Be that as it may, your mother is right. We're happy enough here. You go ahead. It sounds like a reasonable plan to me."

The relief on Luke's face was evident.

"So, where do you think you might go for the training?" Thaddeus asked.

"McGill has the best reputation. Besides, King's College is still too much under the sway of the Church of England. I was raised a Methodist, after all. I'm not sure I could stomach any leftover Anglican cant."

The old enmity between supporters of the Church of England and every other religion was slowly melting away now that the two Canadian colonies, Upper and Lower, had been refashioned as the Province of Canada, but the secularization of its institutions was not yet complete. McGill University in Montreal had had a School of Medicine for a number of years, Thaddeus knew, whereas the university in Toronto had only just established its program.

"I know you always hoped that at least one of your sons would follow in your footsteps," Luke went on. "I'm sorry. I'm afraid it won't be me."

Thaddeus thought of the long years he had spent riding from settlement to settlement through snow and rain and cold and heat, and of the responsibilities he had shouldered onto his wife while he was away

— responsibilities that had worn her down before her time. Of the poverty that even now plagued them. He had done it to save souls. Was it so different to want to save bodies? Luke and he were more alike than the boy knew.

"I'd say you've made an excellent choice," he said. "And don't you worry about us — we're snug enough here."

Chapter 6

Luke had planned to spend a week or so in Wellington before he continued his journey to Montreal, where he needed to register with the college and scout for an inexpensive place to live. After the years of chopping, ploughing, and cutting on his brother's farm, he found the gentler village pace relaxing, the conversation varied and informed, and the food superb. Sophie truly was a genius in the kitchen. He was still profoundly uneasy about his mother's health, however. She had the frail and fragile look that he had come to recognize as an indicator of more ill health to come. One of the reasons he had been so successful in treating animals, he realized, was his ability to sense when something wasn't quite right with them. But he scarcely needed any special talent to know that his mother was ailing.

More of a shock to him was the realization that his father was no longer in his prime. He had always seemed

invincible — as strong and unyielding as an oak tree.
Now he limped a little as he walked, and when he rose
from sitting for a long time he needed to steady himself
for a moment before he moved further. These infirmities were a result not only of long hours in the saddle,
Luke knew, but from the various injuries that Thaddeus
had suffered during the course of tracking down two
murderers. Near-drowning, a broken arm, and being
whacked on the head with a tree branch had all left their
mark. Luke hoped that both his parents had many years
left to them, of course, but it was obvious that they had
entered the twilight era of their years.

Wellington was a small enough village that news
of Luke's visit spread quickly, and many of his father's
friends dropped by the hotel to say hello. He had a long
conversation with Dr. Keough, the local physician, who
expressed approval of Luke's choice of career and his
plan for entering it.

"This country needs more good doctors," he said.
"There are a terrible passel of quacks around." And then
he launched into a long description of how the newly
formed Prince Edward Medical Society had threatened
prosecution against someone named Stewart who was
practising medicine without a licence. Luke counted up
the number of times he had attended patients himself
without benefit of a licence and resolved to keep this
information from becoming general knowledge.

In an attempt to divert the doctor from this long,
complicated, and essentially uninteresting discourse,
Luke asked about the dead body that had been found
on Wellington's shore.

"What are the physical manifestations of drowning?" he asked. He had only ever seen farm animals that had become mired in ponds, and those had been found within a day or so. He had no idea what long immersion would do to body tissue.

"It's not a sight I'd like to see often," the doctor replied. "The poor soul truly did look like a monster." Then, in great detail, he described the bloating and the change in colour.

"Is there a difference in appearance between someone who died from drowning and someone who died and then was immersed in water?" Luke wasn't sure that this distinction was in any way important, but it kept the doctor from returning to the previous topic of licensing issues.

"Not that I know of," Keough said. "I'm not sure what difference it would make anyway. The person would be equally dead regardless."

"Odd, the business with the clothing, though."

"Oh yes, very odd indeed. And nothing in the pockets to point us toward an explanation. Only a piece of green ribbon, and I have no idea what, if anything, that signifies."

Nor did Luke, but from there he was able to steer the doctor toward the latest developments in medicine, and a discussion of the current battle for public sentiment between the physicians of the traditional bent and the Thompsonians, who claimed that bleeding, blistering, poison minerals, and starving were poor substitutes for a sickbed regimen based on herbs and vegetables.

Many of Betsy's friends came to pay their respects to Luke as well. A number of these were from the Wellington Methodist community, their visits a reflection of the esteem in which his father was held. A handful of them were of a different connection, amongst them a Mrs. Sprung, who seemed to be a regular visitor, and with whom his mother spent a great deal of time drinking tea.

Each day after the noontime dinner, Luke found himself sitting on a chair on the verandah with his father, his mother having retired for a rest and the others busy with their various tasks. Sometimes the conversation was wide-ranging; at other times they sat in a comfortable silence, their faces lifted to the ever-hotter breezes blowing in from the lake. Luke enjoyed the silent days. He wasn't used to talking as much as had been required of him since his arrival in Wellington. For the last few years his world had been one of hasty consultation regarding which field should be cleared next, or what the price of wheat was likely to be.

His father appeared to enjoy the silence as well. They weren't so very different, Luke reflected. No doubt Thaddeus had grown used to silence, too, on his long rides between congregations. Silence was something that could be sorely missed when it wasn't there.

On one of these days nearly a week into his visit, Luke watched idly as a very stylish trap harnessed to a handsome horse trotted along the main street. As soon as it came into view his father sat up a little straighter. The buggy stopped in front of them, and Thaddeus stood as a very distinguished-looking man climbed down.

"Lewis! Good day to you, sir!" the man said in a booming voice.

"Mr. McFaul! Good day! I don't believe you've met my son Luke."

"Yes, yes, I'd heard he was here. Welcome to Wellington, young man." But unlike all the other acquaintances who had come calling, McFaul seemed little interested in chatting with Luke and got straight to the point of his visit. "I meant to talk to you this morning when you were at the warehouse, Thaddeus, but I got sidetracked with a shipment that came up a little short in the counting."

"Please, come and sit down," Thaddeus said. "Would you have tea?"

"Haven't time," McFaul replied. Then he turned to Luke. "I hear you're off to Montreal in a few days."

Luke had no idea how this man knew his plans. He hadn't mentioned them to anyone but the immediate family. But it was a small village, and he supposed that everyone's business was soon common knowledge.

"Yes, I need to get myself situated before I begin college in the fall."

"Excellent. Perhaps you'd like a little company for part of your journey?" He addressed Thaddeus again: "I have some business for you to attend to in Kingston. It appears that one of my business associates has fallen woefully behind in the payments on his mortgage. His interests were mostly in timber, I'm afraid, and of course he's come amiss now that the market has collapsed. I need you to take an inventory of his property and register some papers with the local court. I'll have all the details ready for you in the next day or so."

Thaddeus nodded, but Luke could see that he was puzzled. These were evidently matters that he attended to on a regular basis as part of his arrangement with McFaul. It hardly needed a special visit in the middle of the afternoon.

"I do have something else I would like you to do while you're there — and," he said, turning to Luke, "you could perhaps give your father a hand. The school has been short-handed since Father McQuaig passed on."

This reference was to the Roman Catholic boarding school, which Luke had been told was situated at Tara Hall, the magnificent brick house that McFaul had built for himself but subsequently bequeathed to the Church.

"I'd arranged for a replacement — a Father Higgins — to come from Ireland. The last I heard from him, he had successfully navigated the Atlantic and had got as far as Kingston. He should have been here days ago, but there's no sign of him. I'd like you to track him down. If he's fallen ill or something, you can see that he's looked after. If he hasn't, you can tell him to get his carcass moving."

"If you can get the paperwork ready, I could go tomorrow," Thaddeus offered.

"Monday or Tuesday would suit better, I think. And that would fall in with this young man's plans, I believe. Travelling is so much more pleasant with a companion, don't you think?" He nodded at Luke. "A pleasure to meet you, sir. Safe journeys, and perhaps our paths will cross on your next visit." And with that he leapt into his shiny buggy and drove off.

Luke found McFaul's manner very abrupt, and commented on it to his father.

"That's what I like about him," Thaddeus replied. "There's no nonsense. He just concentrates on the task at hand."

"I understood very little of what he said. There's no market for timber anymore?"

"None. And I'm afraid it's going to have repercussions here. Apparently, the bottom has fallen right out of the railway boom in Britain and now there's not so much demand for Canadian timber. And they've lifted the tariffs on it as well, so even if the market recovers, a lot of people believe we'll have to compete with the Baltic nations — Norway in particular — which, of course, we can't do, since their shipping costs are so much lower."

Luke had only the vaguest notion where the Baltic nations were, but gathered from what his father said that they were much closer to Britain than Canada was.

"So this gentleman in Kingston has come amiss because of developments in Britain?"

"Yes. The smart ones got out last year. But the demand has been so great that everyone else has been in the backwoods all winter cutting for all they're worth; but now that they've floated the timber down to the front, there's nowhere they can sell it."

This was disturbing news. Canada's most lucrative exports had always been timber and wheat, and now it appeared that neither could find a market. "I hadn't heard about the timber. The talk in Huron was all about wheat. I know a lot of the mills built along the border are going to be in trouble. The Americans can ship directly now, so why should they bother bringing it here first?" Luke shook his head. "Did our government even point out to Britain what their free trade policies would do to us?"

"Of course not," Thaddeus said. "It wouldn't do any good. When has Britain ever given a second thought to our interests? Sometimes I think we should have supported Mackenzie and his rebellion after all."

This was a surprising statement to Luke's ears. His father had never seemed interested in politics, other than those involving the Church. Now he was talking of free trade and tariffs and markets with an authority that spoke of working knowledge. It must be Mr. McFaul's influence, this interest in the complicated business of business.

And Luke figured that if anyone had been smart, and now stood to gain from others' miscalculations, it was probably Archibald McFaul.

It was a tearful goodbye. The entire family, as well as a number of the hotel guests, gathered on the front porch as Luke and his father prepared to depart for the wharf, where they would board the packet steamer that offered regular service to Kingston.

Thaddeus stood aside as Betsy fussed over Luke, brushing imaginary dust from his jacket and smoothing his hair — any excuse to touch him, it seemed. Everyone shook Luke's hand and wished him well, but just before he was able to disengage from the hugs and the handshakes and set off down the village's main street, Francis stepped forward with a wooden box.

"This is from all of us," he said. "I'm sure you'll find a use for it in your studies, but perhaps you might spare a page now and then for a letter, just to let us know how you're getting on."

Speechless, Luke opened the box to find a steel pen, a bottle of ink, and a supply of good-quality writing paper. Stammering a thank-you, he stuffed it into his pack and promised to write.

They only just made it to the wharf in time for their departure. The whistle was blowing as they boarded, and they had barely time to settle in the passenger cabin before lines were cast off and the vessel pulled away from the dock.

"I stood in the bow the whole way from Toronto," Luke remarked. "It seems odd to be on a ship and sitting down."

"Why on earth would you do that?" Thaddeus asked.

"I saw one of the steamers when it came into port. It was overloaded with emigrants and a lot of them were feverish-looking. I'm not sure how malignant fever spreads, but if it comes through the air, it would make sense to stand where the wind can blow the contagion away."

"I'll take my chances," Thaddeus said. "I don't think my knee can take standing all the way to Kingston."

Luke shrugged, but, as if to illustrate his point, a steamer heading west passed them as they pulled out into Lake Ontario. That it carried far too many passengers was evident from the way the vessel sat low in the water, and there seemed to be people festooned over every available surface. It was customary for the passengers of passing ships to wave at each other on the way by, but no hand was raised by anyone on the deck of the other boat. The passengers merely stared sullenly at the water.

"I see what you mean," Thaddeus said. "So the question is whether it's more dangerous to sit in the cabin where there might be a lingering contagion, or stand outside and let the wind blow it to you from any passing ship."

"Oh," said Luke. "I hadn't thought of that."

"Given that the two outcomes are equally likely, I'd rather be infected in comfort."

This question settled between them, they lapsed into a companionable silence as the steamboat chugged down the lake.

It seemed odd to Luke to be travelling with his father beside him. They had spent so little time together when he was growing up. Thaddeus would often be gone for weeks at a time, on the miles of road he was expected to travel as a minister for the Methodist Church. It had always seemed to Luke that the entire household would be disrupted whenever his father did come home for a few days, or a few hours, or simply long enough to get a dry pair of socks. He would shout orders at them, take them to task for something that hadn't been done to his satisfaction, and then ride away again. It would take a day or two for them all to settle again into the routine that his mother had established. Then later, when his mother had been so ill, after Luke's sister Sarah had died, there had been no routine at all, only Thaddeus, trying to keep the household together even when he wasn't there to make it happen.

The old man had softened later, after Sarah's murderer had finally been caught. Something had changed in him, and although Luke had been thrilled to ride off west with his brother, there had been a part of him that had wanted to stay, to find out who this father of his was exactly. He hadn't had the chance. And now he found that this man sitting beside him was a stranger.

Luke hoped he'd have a chance someday to change that.

Chapter 7

The lake began to spill into the St. Lawrence River as they passed Amherst Island, and before long they could see the buildings of Kingston in the distance. As they drew closer to the shore in preparation for docking at the commercial wharves that were clustered along the city's harbour, they passed a smaller set of docks that had been built to accommodate the brewery on the western outskirts of the town's limits. The docks were stacked with cordwood, as had been the case at Port Darlington, but lolling on top of these piles of wood was a ragged mass of humanity. Here and there children clambered over the logs; the rest of the people merely perched or, in some cases, were stretched out full-length in what seemed to be abject misery.

"Emigrant sheds," Luke said, and pointed them out to his father. "There were sheds like that in every port along the lake."

"Oh my," Thaddeus said, "I'd have to be in a bad way to find shelter there."

"I think they are in a bad way," Luke said. "Besides, what choice do they have?"

Kingston's public wharves were lined up along one side of the harbour, at the mouth of the Cataraqui River. Across the stretch of water were the shipyards that formed an essential part of the city's commerce. Beyond that was Fort Henry, overlooking the bay that was used by the navy.

As they disembarked, Thaddeus drew Luke's attention to Wolfe Island, which lay across the river from the city. "That's where I went through the ice that time, when I was chasing Francis."

"Yes, I know," Luke said. "You've told the story a dozen times, you know."

"Well, I learned a very important lesson that day."

"What was that?"

Luke expected to hear an impromptu sermonette on the evils of hasty judgment or the importance of trusting in God, but his father's response surprised him. "Always wear a scarf in the wintertime. It was Francis's scarf that saved me really."

Luke laughed. "Have you told him that?"

"Of course not. He's grown too used to being the hero."

As they walked away from the waterfront, they passed Kingston's new city hall. Luke was stunned by the size and appearance of the building. This was a far larger and more imposing edifice than anything he had ever seen before, even in Toronto.

Thaddeus noticed his awe. "Don't forget, Kingston was once the capital of the United Canadas, if only for a short time. They built a hall to house a government."

The decision in 1841 to pronounce Kingston the capital of the newly formed Province of Canada had met with the approval of no one but the residents of Kingston. Small, provincial, and too close to the American border were the chief complaints. There was not even anywhere for the Legislative Assembly to meet, although accommodation was eventually made for them at the local hospital. The larger Canadian cities were vocal in their dissatisfaction, so it wasn't surprising that the decision was soon reversed. In 1844, the capital moved to Montreal.

In the hope that they might somehow change everyone's minds about the suitability of Kingston, the city fathers went ahead with their plans for a building fit for a legislature. It was all to no avail, and now the building housed various businesses and offices, including the Board of Trade, the Custom House, a saloon, the Mechanics' Institute, the Orange Order, and a dry goods store.

Still, the hall was breathtaking with its dome and porches and portico. A market battery had been laid out in front of the edifice to replace the old shambles with its wooden stalls and constant danger of fire. Farmers now hawked their pigs and parsnips to the city's residents under the noses of the exalted personages within the hall.

Today, more than half of the stalls were empty, however. Thaddeus stopped for a moment, looking around with a puzzled expression. "It's July. These stalls should be heaped up with produce," he said. "Where are all the farmers?"

Not only were the farmers absent, but also missing were the neatly dressed maids and prosperous-looking housewives who picked through the vegetables and sniffed the fish in their daily haggles over dinner fixings. Nor were there the usual throngs of businessmen on their way to important appointments and their wives riding to festive social occasions. Instead the streets were filled with ragged children and scrofulous beggars. Luke and Thaddeus had to push their way past a knot of grimy men who stood on the corner eyeing a garishly dressed girl across the street.

Their destination was the courthouse on King Street, a block away from City Hall. It was easy to find with the gaol stretching behind it. Once inside, Thaddeus had no difficulty finding a clerk to file the documents McFaul had sent with him.

This business occupied them for only a few minutes, but as it was already late in the afternoon, Thaddeus judged that they should complete the rest of their business the following day. "First we'll find a place for the night and then why don't we see if we can find this priest that McFaul is so anxious about."

They walked along a curving road that led them to Brock Street, where Thaddeus stopped outside the Bay of Quinte Hotel. "I've found this pleasant on previous trips to Kingston," he said.

"A hotel? Is it expensive?"

Thaddeus waved away his objections. "Mr. McFaul is paying," he said, "and this is a Temperance House, so I have no objections to staying here."

There was a room available, they were told. "In fact, you could have separate rooms if you prefer," the innkeeper said. Business was apparently at a standstill in the city of Kingston.

Thaddeus indicated that one room was sufficient, and they stowed their bags in it before they set off for the harbour. Thaddeus hoped they might find the priest's name on a passenger list somewhere, but just as they were leaving the hotel, Luke thought to ask the innkeeper if he knew where else they might look.

"An Irishman you say? None of the steamers carrying emigrants are allowed to dock at the public wharves. They're all being sent down to the dock by the brewery." He waved his arm in a westerly direction. "You can just follow the road that leads along the shore. That'll take you past the hospital, and you might check there if you think he's gone down with fever. Although, if he's a priest and he's ill, he's most likely been taken to the nuns."

"The nuns? You mean a convent or something?" Luke asked.

"No, the other hospital, Hôtel Dieu, just up the street here. It's run by Catholic nuns. It's not really finished yet, but they're using it anyway. It's full of emigrants. At the rate they're being shipped over here, we'll all be down with fever before it's done. Either that or destitute."

He walked away muttering imprecations against disease, the Irish, Catholics, and life in general.

As it was by far the closest, they decided to ask at Hôtel Dieu first. They had no need to ask for confirmation that they had reached the hospital. A chorus of moans and groans, punctuated by the occasional wail, told them that they had arrived at a place of suffering. It was a building that was indeed not yet finished — Thaddeus could see from the street that part of the structure was still missing its roof. Nevertheless, it was apparent that even the unfinished section was being used to house patients.

No one took any notice of them as they entered, although there were plenty of people scurrying here and there, bustling into the rooms off the corridor or tending to patients who had been bedded down in the passageways. With difficulty, they edged down the crowded hall, stepping around those who lay whimpering on the floor.

The hospital was crowded beyond belief. Each room was stuffed with patients, two to a cot, others lying on the floor with only a thin blanket to cushion them. The stench from unwashed bodies and unemptied slop pails was a miasmic fog that threatened to overwhelm them. It was like a descent into the lower levels of hell, Thaddeus thought, where the brimstone had long since burned away and all that remained was decaying flesh and the filth it spawned. Surely no demons of Hades could inflict torment worse than this.

As they stood in the middle of the hall wondering who they should talk to, they were passed by a rather stern-faced nun. She appeared to be in a great hurry to get by, but Luke stopped her.

"'Ow can I 'elp you?" she asked. "Are you 'ere from the Benevolent Society?" She spoke with a heavy

French accent. As the name of their hospital signalled, this Order must have originated in Quebec.

Her face softened when they said they were looking for Father Higgins. "No, 'e is not ill," she said, "but 'e is a great blessing to those who are. 'E is assisting Sister Bourbonnière this afternoon, and I believe they are at the English 'ospital." And with that she swept away from them.

They retraced their steps to the market, and a man selling eggs at one of the stalls directed them to follow King Street, which would take them past the artillery parade ground. West of this, they were told, they would find the general hospital.

They soon left behind the brick walls of the market and the huddle of close-built houses. The hospital was located near the outskirts of the town, but as they passed the parade ground and turned onto King Street, they encountered a boardwalk, something that Thaddeus would have appreciated under ordinary circumstances as it was easier for him to walk on than the rutted road.

The scene that unfolded along this route was anything but ordinary, however. The parade ground, the lake shore, and the entire area around the hospital and the sheds that stood near it was covered with a sea of people. The boardwalk itself was awash with filth. Rats scuttled away from their feet. A number of people, both men and women, were clustered around a bucket in various states of undress, sluicing themselves in an attempt to get clean. Behind a tree, a man was openly fondling a woman.

As soon as Luke and Thaddeus were spotted, they were besieged with a cacophony of whining requests from beggars, pushing to get closer, their hands held out. They were gaunt and emaciated, their cheekbones jutting out, their arms thin and skeletal, and they were clad in rags that barely covered them. Hardest for Thaddeus to ignore were the children who crowded around, most of them with a lilt in their voices that betrayed their Irish homeland.

"A penny, sir, for the love of God ..."

"Have you food, sir? I'm starvin' ..."

"Please, sir, my mam is sinking fast ..."

Luke fished three coppers out of his pocket and shoved the money into the hands of three of the smallest children.

"Bless you, sir," one of them said, but the others merely clutched the pennies fiercely and ran before someone bigger and stronger could wrest their treasure away from them.

This generosity set off a melee as others crowded around. As gently as they could, Luke and Thaddeus pushed past the importuning children, but they were forced to be more aggressive as some of the men and older boys shoved the little ones away and stood in their path.

"That's all I've got right now," Luke said.

"Please, sir ..."

"Give us somethin' ..."

"I haven't eaten for two days ..."

They crowded closer, causing Luke to take a step back and bump against those standing behind him. He held his hands out, showing them to be empty. The gesture did nothing to make them move.

But Thaddeus wasn't prepared to be intimidated by such a ragtag mob.

"Out of the way!" he thundered. Startled, the beggars stepped back and he strode forward, Luke scrambling to follow.

The hospital was just a little farther down the street. It was an imposing limestone edifice, a dignified repository for the sick during normal times, but wooden sheds some ninety feet long had been built around it. As they drew closer, the stench was nearly unbearable. A number of makeshift privies had been erected nearby, but they appeared to be in dire need of a cleanout.

When they mounted the front steps of the hospital to make inquiries regarding the presence of McFaul's priest, their ears were again assaulted by sounds of misery and the stench intensified in the enclosed, airless space. As at Hôtel Dieu, it appeared that the general hospital was caring for many more patients than it had been designed to accommodate.

They were followed into the building by a well-dressed woman carrying a wicker basket. "Father Higgins?" the woman said when they explained their mission. "He's in the far shed with Sister Bourbonnière."

They retraced their steps and entered the shed she indicated, prepared to encounter even more misery, but they discovered that the smell was not nearly as overpowering as it had been in the hospitals. The open-sided construction allowed the ever-present breeze from nearby Lake Ontario to blow the worst of the stench away, although Thaddeus wondered how comfortable the patients would be on those rainy days when the cold and damp crept through the entire town.

Comfort had not been much of a consideration for the builders, he could see. A long line of wooden bunks stretched along the length of the shed, maximizing its capacity, but making medical ministrations difficult, the top tier difficult to reach, the bottom uncomfortably low. The structure had not been built with sickness in mind, he realized. The design had been intended to provide temporary shelter for healthy emigrants, who would spend only a few nights there before continuing their journeys or finding other accommodation.

One man, obviously a doctor, was examining a patient three beds along, while five people clustered around him, all of them asking questions at once. A nun moved down the row with a pail and a dipper, dribbling liquid into the open mouths of fevered patients, while another scurried in the opposite direction with a slops bucket. This nun stopped when she reached them, her eyebrows arched in enquiry.

"We're looking for Father Higgins," Lewis said. "We were told he might be here."

"I believe he is down at the end with Sister Bourbonnière," the nun replied. "Excuse me, I must hurry with this." And she bustled out the door, leaving them standing agape.

They finally located their elusive priest near a stack of wooden barrels that comprised a wall of sorts at the far end of the building. He, too, was carrying slops, but had paused to talk with a distinguished-looking man with an enormous pair of side-whiskers. Higgins, in contrast, was clean-shaven, a shock of wavy chestnut hair sweeping back from a wide brow.

"Father Higgins?" Thaddeus asked when the conversation appeared to be at an end and the gentleman departed.

"Yes, I'm Father Higgins. What could I do for you, sir? I sincerely hope you've come to help and not just to gawk at the misery."

"Not to gawk at it, but to take you away from it. Mr. McFaul sent me."

The priest's face fell. "I suppose he expected me some days ago?"

"Yes. He thought perhaps you'd fallen ill."

"I appear to be the only Irishman who hasn't. Come outside where the air is fresher and I'll tell you my story."

Luke and Thaddeus were only too happy to oblige, although several people nearby called for water, for a blanket, for a word of comfort.

"I'll be back shortly," the priest said. "Don't worry, I won't leave you."

They walked down by the shore of the lake. From where they stood, Thaddeus could see the buildings clustered around the harbour, and he realized how far away from the centre of the town the emigrants were being kept. The priest looked out at the water for a time before he spoke. Thaddeus waited patiently.

"I don't know what you've heard about the state of things in Ireland," he began.

"Only that the potato crop has failed, resulting in great hardship for the people," Thaddeus said. "The news we get comes only from the papers."

"Hardship is scarcely the word to describe it," Higgins said. "The poor in Ireland live chiefly on the potato. The farms are so small, you see, some of them no more than a couple of acres, but two or three acres planted in potatoes is enough to feed a whole family."

"That small?" Luke said. "That's nothing more than a kitchen garden here." Canadians were used to holdings of a hundred acres, two hundred acres, or more. Fifty was considered scarcely enough land to be called a farm. Two or three as a means to a living was unthinkable.

"So you see the problem," the priest said. "Without the potato, there's nothing else that can be planted that is so efficient." He sighed. "People are trying to live on nettle tops and seaweed. And they can't. Children are dying by the side of the road. Whole families have been found starved to death in their huts."

"Surely the government is doing something?" Thaddeus said. "Is there no charity that will take care of them?"

"Our charity consists of thin gruel and work-houses, eviction and indifference," Higgins said. "It's little wonder that so many are willing to risk death by coming to Canada. I boarded a ship in Limerick. I was one of the lucky ones — I had cabin passage, thanks to your Mr. McFaul. But the poor creatures who huddled in the hold sat in a sea of fever and filth. I buried ten on the voyage over. I left thirty more at

Quebec, twenty at Montreal. And when I arrived in
Kingston, I realized that half my parish was in hospital
or cowering in the sheds." He turned and looked at
them. "That was when I decided that I wasn't going
any farther. I will stay here and do what I can and I
will stay until I see no more sick being tossed off the
steamers. Tell Mr. McFaul that his well-fed schoolchil-
dren will have to wait."

This was said with a challenge, and there was a
long moment while Thaddeus digested what the priest
had told him. They had all read about the suffering
in Ireland, but the problem seemed remote and irrel-
evant until you saw the matchstick arms of a begging
child. He thought of the times when he had put his
own considerations aside to help in a crisis, and he
knew that were he in the priest's place he would do
the same.

"Yes, I'll tell Mr. McFaul," he said, "and I'll make
him understand."

The room the Lewises had been given at the Bay of
Quinte Hotel was clean enough and the bed was soft,
but Thaddeus was aware that Luke tossed and turned
for most of the night. The next morning they set off
to find the warehouse that no longer belonged to the
unfortunate man in the timber trade. As Thaddeus
took note of the details of McFaul's new possession,
he found that Luke was absent-minded and unfo-
cused on the business at hand. As a result, he was of
little help.

Even so, Thaddeus made short work of the task at hand.

"I'll be finished by the end of the morning tomorrow," he said. "All that will be left then is to change the locks. I'll be on my way in the afternoon."

"What do you think Mr. McFaul will make of his truant priest?" Luke asked.

"I can explain it to him. I don't think it will be of much concern. Mr. McFaul is a very practical man."

"I've been thinking about the situation here."

"It's a dreadful mess, isn't it?" Thaddeus said. "Before this is finished there will be more sick emigrants than there are people in all of Kingston. It's difficult to see how they can all be looked after."

"I'm wondering if I should stay too."

"Rather than go on to Montreal?"

"I'd learn a great deal of medicine here, I expect. And they could certainly use another volunteer."

Thaddeus was unsurprised by this announcement. He had already known what Luke was considering. He took a long appraising look at this son before he spoke.

"Yes, you could learn a great deal here, but it will also be far more dangerous for you. Surgery and physicking and leeching is a mild enough enterprise when you're sitting in a lecture hall with a professor. It's another thing entirely to dive into a mess and be up to your elbows in blood and filth."

"You've done it."

"Yes, I have," Thaddeus said, "when circumstances dictated. It's hard to turn your back when men are screaming in pain. But that was in battle, and their wounds were no threat to me. These people have a malignant fever. It's no contagion to shrug off with a poultice or a posset. You'd be taking a great risk."

"I can't in all conscience do anything else," Luke said. "Not after what I saw yesterday."

"Ah, the Lewis conscience. It makes itself apparent at the most awkward of times, doesn't it? Well, you're a grown man, Luke. I haven't made your decisions for you for quite a long time now. If you've truly considered the possible consequences, all I can say is that you have my blessing, and I have to admit that if I were a younger man I would do the same."

"Thank you."

"I would stay even so," Thaddeus said, "except that my duty lies with your mother now. That's a decision I made when she fell so ill."

"I know that," Luke replied. "And your decision makes mine all the easier. Besides, you've done more than your share over the years. Time to pass the banner on."

Thaddeus smiled. "At least I feel that I'm passing it to worthy hands." He felt a tremendous pride that his youngest son had such a profound sense of responsibility. But he had never before felt so old.

Chapter 8

Early the next afternoon, after having seen his father off on a steam packet that was returning up the lake, Luke walked along Brock Street to the Hôtel Dieu.

He wasn't sure who he should talk to, or why he was going to the Catholic hospital, except that he had been impressed by Father Higgins's declaration of commitment to his ailing parishioners and it appeared that the nuns had instituted a routine that lent at least a little organization to the chaos that engulfed them.

As he entered the building, he was once again struck by the sheer numbers of people the Sisters were looking after, and by the stench that resulted from cramming so many fevered bodies into one small space. He held his breath as much as he could while he searched the rooms for someone to talk to.

Finally, at the end of the hall, he found a black-clad nun in a tiny closet that had been set aside as the hospital's dispensary. Her face was wrinkled in concentration as she counted the very small number of vials on the makeshift shelves and then made a notation in a large leather-bound book.

"Excuse me," Luke said, knocking on the open door. "My name is Luke Lewis, and I would like to offer my services as a volunteer."

He was rewarded with a tight smile, although it did nothing to smooth out the worry lines on the nun's face.

"Good afternoon. I am Sister Bourbonnière. You are most welcome. As you can see around you, we 'ave far more patients than we ever expected." Her English was heavily accented, but easily understood.

"I have no formal training in medicine," Luke said, "but I do have a great deal of experience in rough and ready doctoring."

"No formal training is necessary, nor is it 'elpful," she replied. "The doctors appear to 'ave little idea what to do. Our function is to make our patients as comfortable as we can under the circumstances. The rest is in God's 'ands."

"I'll do whatever is required, but I would like the opportunity to observe the doctors, if that's possible."

She nodded. "We share our resources with the English 'ospital, although the Female Benevolent Society does most of the feeding and so forth there. Our primary duty is to the people in the 'otel, but the sheds are now full too. We share the nursing for these, and it is at the sheds that you would be most useful. There is a priest there …"

"Father Higgins? Yes, I met him yesterday."

"Then you must go to the sheds and ask for Father 'iggins. 'E will tell you what is most needed."

And with a slight smile, she turned back to her ledger.

Luke found that he was relieved to step outside the hospital again, and ashamed that he found its sights and smells so repulsive. Most of his sketchy medical experience had taken place in log sheds and barns where, it was true, the smells of blood and manure often intermingled as he struggled to safely steer a calf to the outside world, or to remove a piece of wire that had become embedded in a sheep's flank, but these seemed clean, natural odours in comparison to the funk that had choked his throat and stung his eyes at the hospital. Perhaps it was as well that he was being sent to the sheds first. At least there the wind had some cleansing effect as it blew in off the lake. And then he realized that Sister Bourbonnière had purposely sent him there. Past experience had no doubt shown her that even the most eager of volunteers were fragile and easily shocked, and that the sheds were marginally more acceptable to their sensitive noses and queasy stomachs. Still, he vowed to find some way to attach himself to any doctors who made the rounds of the sickbeds. He would keep his eyes open and learn as much as he could while he was here. Montreal could wait, at least until September.

His route from Hôtel Dieu to the English hospital, as the nun had called it, took him past a grassy common and through a neighbourhood of densely packed wooden buildings, more shacks than houses, although

even the term shack was too grand a term for some of
the structures. Every building that might have started
out with four walls had been added to or built upon
with old planking, bits of leftover roofing, canvas, and
in one or two instances chunks of driftwood. Ragged
laundry hung on nails to dry, flapping in the wind like
forlorn pennants from a derelict ship. The denizens of
the lean-tos and crooked cribs appeared to be spend-
ing little time inside them. Each tiny patch of packed
earth in front of a building held a ring of charred
stones, feeble campfires sending wisps of smoke skyward. Ragged children, gaunt men, and straggly
haired women huddled around them, although when
they saw Luke, the children sprang up and ran to him,
holding out their bony hands in supplication. He had
learned something, however, from his previous day's
experience on the boardwalk. He could never hope to
duplicate his father's authoritative command to let him
pass; instead he threw three coppers in the direction
from which he had just come, and when the children
chased after these, he quickened his pace until he was
within view of the general hospital.

He found Father Higgins bending over a man who
appeared to have only a breath or two left to him. The
priest was administering some rite that Luke guessed
was designed to help ease the man's passage into the
next world, but he was unsure what it entailed exactly.
He was unfamiliar with the ceremonies of the Catholic
Church, but reflected that the comfort of a clergyman
at the point of death was a need that was universal, no
matter what form it took.

He waited respectfully until the priest had completed his prayer, and then stepped forward.

"Father Higgins? Luke Lewis. You spoke with me and my father yesterday. I've decided to stay on for a time and see if I can give a hand."

"Every hand that comes our way is welcome. Have you spoken with Sister Bourbonnière?"

"Yes, she sent me here."

"Excellent. Here are two buckets. Empty one in the privy. Fill the other from the water barrel. Try not to get the two mixed up."

And with that, Luke's introduction to the fever sheds began.

As Sister Bourbonnière had said, there was little anyone could do to halt the progress of the fever, but an enormous amount to do in the effort of trying. There were four doctors who visited the sheds in rotation, he was told, but these four were also responsible for the care of patients at both the general hospital and at Hôtel Dieu. They advised giving the patients wine or brandy as a restorative, and occasionally tried bleeding to see if this could draw off the poisonous humours that afflicted the ailing bodies. Luke watched in fascination as one of the doctors drew a tourniquet around a patient's arm, causing the veins below it to bulge. He took a fleam then and inserted it into the largest of the veins. The consequent outpouring of blood was collected in a porcelain dish and disposed of with the slops.

Not all of the hospital patients were sick with ship's fever, he learned. There were any number of other feverish maladies that presented themselves, and only a close watch could determine which one was which. The emigrants also had their fair share of congestions, consumptions, confinements, broken limbs, biliousness, boils, quinsies, and hectic fever. Only the most dire cases were seen by the doctors. Everyone else was left to nurse themselves somewhere else.

Toward the end of the day, the man over whom Father Higgins had been praying finally gave one last shuddering breath and died. Luke was asked if he could help shift the body to the dead house, which had been set up under a canvas to one side of the shed.

"He'll be collected tomorrow and taken to be buried," Father Higgins said. "There are three others to wait with him."

The priest took one end of the stretcher, Luke the other. Already there was a smell coming from the body, different from the stench of blood and bowel and vomit that permeated the shed. This was the sour beginning of putrefaction.

They placed the man on a wooden platform with the bodies of two women and a young child. Just before they covered the corpses with the canvas, Luke took a long look at them. All four were little more than bones. He wondered what their lives had been like across the sea, and what desperation had made them risk the long journey to an unknown land. Who would mourn them? Who would miss them? Higgins mouthed a silent prayer and crossed himself. Luke could think of no appropriate benediction that he could give.

Chapter 9

That night, Luke returned to the Bay of Quinte Hotel —
but only briefly.

As he entered, the innkeeper was coming down
the hall. "I'm sorry, sir, but if you intend to stay
another night, I'm afraid I'll have to ask you for the
fee in advance. There are so many strangers in town,
you see."

"Excuse me," Luke said. "I understood that the
room was paid for."

"The room was paid for one night for Mr. Lewis
and guest," the man said. "Mr. Lewis has departed and
I have received no instructions regarding his guest."

"Oh." Luke hadn't considered this. Or rather, he
had hoped that Mr. McFaul's generosity had included a
second night. He should have realized that this wouldn't
be the case. After all, McFaul had assumed that Luke
would be travelling on to Montreal when he and his

father parted company. His afternoon with the sick and dying had left him exhausted, not only physically but emotionally. The room would be an expensive luxury, but he was too tired to even think about looking for somewhere else.

"Well, I guess I'll take the room for tonight anyway," he said, and reached into his pocket for the small satchel that served him as a purse.

The landlord came closer, to take the money, but when he was within a couple of feet of Luke, his nose wrinkled and he came to a stop.

"What's that on your coat?"

Luke looked down. His sleeve was covered with a sludgy stain. *Blood, urine … worse?* When he moved his arm to look at it, even he could smell the stink that emanated from it.

"I'm sorry; I was volunteering at the hospital this afternoon. I must have got something on me. If you would be so kind as to fetch me a bucket of water, I'll sponge it off before I go up to my room."

"At the hospital?" The landlord's face paled. "At the general hospital?"

"Well, more in the hospital sheds, really."

"With all those filthy emigrants?"

"Yes."

"Then I'm sorry, you can't stay here," the man said as he began hurriedly backing down the hall.

"Excuse me?" Luke said. "I don't understand."

"I won't have you bringing disease here. I've my other guests to think of, you know."

"But someone needs to help."

"Someone can do whatever they like. They just can't stay here and do it. Not even for one night. Not even for one minute. You'll have to wait outside while I get your bag."

And before Luke could protest further, the innkeeper turned and marched up the stairs. "Get out. Now," he flung over his shoulder. "Shoo! You can wait around back."

Luke knew that there was no point in arguing. He went out the front door and found his way to the back entrance of the hotel. As he waited for the innkeeper to reappear with his satchel, he did wonder if there was any point in looking for another inn. He was likely to receive the same treatment wherever he went, unless he cleaned himself up and then lied about what he had been doing. He debated with himself for a moment about employing this deception, but in the end he decided that it would be unfair. The innkeepers, in fact the whole town, were probably fearful of the contagion spreading. If he were running a business he would feel the same way, he supposed, and as no one had any idea how the disease was transmitted, he had no way to judge how great the risk was.

A few minutes later the innkeeper appeared at the back door and tossed the bag out into the dooryard.

"There you go — take your bag and go somewhere else."

Luke wandered back in the direction of the hospital. If bad came to worse he supposed he could curl up in a corner of one of the sheds for one night, although he would like to get away from the smell for a while. Still, he had slept in rougher places.

His route took him to the huddle of wooden dwellings that he had passed through earlier that day. He wondered if he might find a corner of one of them to rent, although it was too late to start looking that night and he expected there would be few vacancies. These sorts of cheap lodgings would be a magnet for any emigrant who had a few pennies in his pocket, not to mention the regular working-class inhabitants of Kingston. Still, he could ask the next day.

Only a few ragamuffin children accosted him as he walked. Most had likely bedded down for the night, even though the late evening light of summer had only just started to wane. As he drew nearer to the sheds, he could see that some emigrants had opted to sleep underneath bushes or trees, a patch of grass a more inviting pillow than a few square feet of hard-packed earth. Now and again, a child cried, but without much vigour.

He walked down to the lake so he could sponge the mess off his coat sleeve. Now that the smell had been brought to his attention, he was aware of it every time he moved his arm. The shallow water at the lake's edge was greasy and green, but even though the water was fishy-smelling, it served to sluice the smear away.

In the end, he was unwilling to face the nightmare of the sheds. Instead, he found an unoccupied corner where two limestone walls of the hospital met to form a sheltered spot. The rock felt warm to the touch — it still retained much of the heat of the day's sunlight, yet faced away from the ever-present and merciless west wind.

He opened his satchel and retrieved the heavy winter coat he had packed in anticipation of Montreal's frigid winter. It would keep the damp of the earth from seeping into his body during the night, although it might well be stained beyond redemption if he used it in this manner often.

He had only just made himself comfortable and closed his eyes when he sensed someone staring at him. He opened his eyes to find a girl of perhaps nine or ten years — it was difficult to tell the ages of any of these emigrant children as so many were so small — but this one was so slight and pale and insubstantial that she appeared more like a wispy wraith than anything of flesh and bone. Her face shimmered strangely in the fading light and it was only when she moved that Luke saw that her face was covered in a yellowish-white scaly rash that reminded him of the discarded skin of a snake. Her odd visage was framed by thin, fine, almost white hair, and her eyes were so light that they seemed to have no colour at all. She regarded him solemnly for a moment before she spoke.

"You was at the sheds today," she said.

"I was," Luke agreed.

"Are you a doctor?"

"No, not yet. I hope to be someday."

"But you know something about doctoring. You wouldn't be at the sheds else, would you?"

"I know a little," Luke admitted. "Are you feeling sick?"

The girl's eyes widened in alarm, and Luke realized that he had said the wrong thing. None of these children would ever admit to being unwell, he realized, for fear that they would be whisked off to disappear like so many of their family members. In their world, weakness brought only calamity.

"You don't look sick," he said quickly. "Is there something else amiss?"

"A lady's cut her thumb and now it's festering. She asked at the hospital, but they chased her away."

"I could look at it, if you like."

The girl nodded and waited until Luke packed up his makeshift bed before leading him back to the rundown neighbourhood he had just passed through. The path snaked through a warren of tiny, unpainted hovels that appeared in imminent danger of falling in on themselves.

The girl stopped in front of a figure who Luke at first mistook for another child. On closer examination, he realized that it was a woman, but he could scarcely hazard a guess at her age. She was tiny to begin with, but hunger or disease or misery had wizened her to almost nothing. Her face was a mass of wrinkles, punctuated by a sharp, beaky nose. She had what appeared to be a herd of ragged children at her feet, although as Luke approached they rose and resolved themselves into six small bodies, the smallest perhaps three or four, the oldest a little younger than the girl who had brought him here. As to their genders, it was impossible to tell.

"This here's nearly a doctor," the girl announced. "He can look at your thumb."

The woman mutely held out a bony hand, loose skin flapping as she moved her arm. There was a gash just beneath the thumbnail, not deep, but the flesh was open from the cuticle to the knuckle, greenish ooze collecting in the cut.

"This is infected," he said. "It's not serious right now, but it needs to be cleaned up. Have you any salt?" He had often found that cleaning out a wound with warm, salty water worked wonders on those occasions when a cow or a pig had been ripped by a wire or stone, and he had no reason to believe that this method wouldn't work equally well for a thumb.

The woman shook her head. "I have nothing but what they give me at the shed."

"Well, let's clean it out as best we can tonight, and I'll beg some salt for you tomorrow." At least there was a supply of warm water nearby. There was a small fire still burning in the yard, with a tin pot of water beside it. He tested the temperature and judged that it was warm enough for his purposes.

He looked around the tiny encampment, but he could see nothing that he could use as a swab. He pulled his handkerchief out of his pocket, dunked it into the water, then wrung it out over the woman's outstretched hand. He would have preferred to have her soak the thumb for a few minutes before he began cleaning it, but he guessed that the pot was used for cooking, or to hold their drinking water, and he hesitated to foul it with a septic cut.

The children clustered around him, rocking back on their haunches as they watched. The smallest one thrust a filthy thumb into its mouth.

"I'm Luke Lewis by the way," he said as he worked.

"It's a fine thing to meet such a distinguished gentleman as yourself, nearly Dr. Luke," the woman said. She didn't volunteer her own name in return.

Luke poured some warm water into the palm of his hand, trying to dip his handkerchief in it and clean out the wound at the same time, but he couldn't keep the water from leaking out onto the ground. The ghostly girl suddenly appeared at his side with a battered and dented tin bowl to use as a makeshift basin. He hadn't even noticed her leave the yard. As she handed him the bowl, her sleeve fell back, exposing a thin wrist. Like her face, it was covered in a whitish scale. He thanked her and, after immersing the thumb, began coaxing the crusted matter away from the edges of the cut.

"That's as clean as I can get it now," he said, after working away at it for a time. "I'll find some salt tomorrow, and we can go at it again. Try to keep your thumb as clean as you can in the meantime, and I'll look at it again in the morning. Will I find you here?"

The woman peered at him suspiciously, as if confirming her future whereabouts would be a perilous and foolhardy thing to do.

"I'll come looking for you," he said finally.

He was about to head back to his makeshift corner when the girl tugged on his arm. "There's another lady wants to talk to you," she said, and she led him to where two women were waiting by the hospital sheds.

They were both young, and although their clothing hung in rags around them and there were hollows under their cheekbones, they had obviously made attempts to keep clean and had taken some pains with their hair. They brightened when they saw Luke, sitting up a little straighter, and one of them smiled a little. The other held a wailing bundle.

"Deirdre won't stop crying," the woman said. "Do you think it's the fever?"

Luke swept back the rags that covered the child's face. A year and a half old, he judged, maybe two, small and thin, but not starving. And then he noticed the rosy red patches on the infant's cheeks. He had seen this before, with his brother Will's children.

He smiled at the woman. "It's not the fever. I think she's just teething and having a miserable time of it." He hesitated and then decided to sacrifice his second handkerchief. He ducked into the nearby shed. No one was there to ask permission from, so he went over to one of the oak casks that were stacked up in the corner and poured a little brandy onto the cloth. He took it outside to the woman. "Let her suck on this. It will help relieve the pain and send her off to sleep. She should be fine in a day or two."

She offered the infant a corner of the handkerchief. The child latched on and sucked vigorously, with only sporadic intervals of hiccupping wails until finally it settled down for a good long pull.

"Bless you, sir," the woman said. "I'm sure she'll be fine now."

"But perhaps you should come back tomorrow and check on her," the second one said.

"Yes, that would be a grand idea," the first woman agreed. "You'll do that, won't you?"

Luke assured them that he would, and, satisfied with his first foray into the world of doctoring, he returned to his makeshift bed.

Chapter 10

Luke awoke the next morning to the unpleasant sensation of a toe being poked into his ribs. He opened his eyes, squinting against the light from a sun that was already quite high in the sky.

"Wake up, you lazy Protestant whelp. It's time to go to work." It was Father Higgins, who again applied the toe of his boot to Luke's side, not ungently, but with a grin. "What are you doing here?"

Luke sat up and yawned. "The innkeeper wouldn't let me back in the hotel when he discovered where I'd spent the day yesterday."

"Well, that won't do, will it? How can I get a navvy's work out of you during the day if you've no place to rest your head at night? Leave it with me, and I'll find you someplace better. Now come on, we've got work to do."

Luke bundled his belongings back into his pack and rose to follow the priest, who had marched off in the direction of the newly completed emigrant shed at the foot of Emily Street. "Have you had anything to eat yet?" he called back over his shoulder.

"Not unless I ate it in my dreams."

"You'll have to lump in with the poor folk then," Higgins said, "although it's not so bad. You'll have to serve it up first though."

Already there was a lineup just outside the shed. Luke and the priest pushed past the waiting emigrants and entered. Two rather nicely dressed ladies bustled around a large iron pot that had been set to simmer on the stove.

"This is the footman," Higgins said to them, pointing at Luke. "Just save a little at the end for his wages."

One of the ladies promptly shoved a nest of tin bowls into his hands, while the other stood poised with a ladle.

"I'll get you to take the pot to the table outside, if you don't mind," she said. "Then you can give out the bowls. After we've fed thirty or so, you'll have to go and collect their bowls; otherwise we won't have enough dishes for the rest. Besides, we'd never get them back otherwise."

This was undoubtedly true. The bowls that sat beside the stove were remarkably similar to the one in which Luke had soaked an infected thumb the previous evening.

He stepped outside to the waiting emigrants, handed out the bowls as instructed, and gestured for those first in line to begin filing past the table where a woman ladled out a soupy stew. As soon as the first bowls had been filled, he handed out ten more, and then ten again, and when the bowls were gone he was sent off to chase down the first lot, retrieving their dishes and depositing them with another woman who stood perspiring over a pot of hot water. She promptly washed them in readiness for another round. They were licked so clean, Luke thought that they scarcely needed a wash at all.

For the next hour he repeated the dance again and again, until the entire line had filed past the servers. By this time his mouth was watering and his stomach was grumbling, and he hoped that there would, indeed, be some of the stew left. He was vaguely ashamed of himself. He had gone only twelve hours or so without food. Many of the emigrants appeared to have gone days or weeks, maybe even years, without enough to eat.

"We need some more water," the ladle lady said when he had brought the last of the bowls back. "Have your share first though." She scooped up the last bit of stew that was left in the pot and handed it to Luke. "I'm Mrs. Thompson, by the way."

"Luke Lewis," he said through a mouthful of food.

"Father Higgins says you've offered to stay with us for a while."

Luke nodded his agreement with this statement. The meal that had been served up to the emigrants was quite tasty, although a little on the thin side. It was mostly a sort of gruel, but here and there were actual pieces of meat, along with some vegetables — he could taste peas, potato, and possibly turnip, although these last two items had been boiled to a mushy pulp. They must have been from last year's crop and had spent a winter in someone's root cellar.

"We give out bread later in the day," Mrs. Thompson said. "And you could help with that, if you like, although I'm sure there will be plenty of other things for you to do."

"I'm happy to do anything you need, although I would particularly like to be here when the doctors come around. One of my reasons for volunteering is to learn a little medicine before I go off to school to study it in earnest."

"That's fine as long as the doctors don't chase you away. They're a little short-tempered as it is, and now one of them has the fever as well."

This was ominous news. Everyone had hoped that the fever was killing so many emigrants as a result of their malnourished condition. But if it was spreading to the doctors, it could spread to anyone.

"Whatever you can do, Luke, is a boon," Mrs. Thompson said. "Help when you can, sleep when you need to, eat when you have time. We're not even at the end of July and there are still two months left in the shipping season. We can't look after the number of people who are here now, and by all accounts there are as many again on the way. I have no idea what we're going to do."

"I'll do my best," Luke promised, as he slurped up the last of his stew.

"And now, could you bring me a bucket of water?"

In the wintertime, Luke learned, carters drew water straight from Kingston Harbour to supply the residents of the town who had no wells. In July, however, the water in the harbour was covered with a green, foul-smelling scum. Then the carters drew instead from the lake, at a place a little west of the hospital, away from the privies and where there was a current that kept the water reasonably clean. Even so, when Luke opened the spigot of one of the barrels that were lined up just outside the shed, the water that gushed into his bucket was warm, with a fusty, stale smell.

He delivered two buckets of water, and then went to help the carter, who was collecting the dead.

The wagon lumbered its way from the nuns' hospital to the sheds at the brewery wharf, along to the Emily Street shed, and then to the general hospital, where an open pit had been dug on the grounds. Luke was directed to help lift the shrouded bodies up onto the wagon, only to lift them down again when they reached the pit. They were then placed side by side and covered with a little dirt and lime, so that the next day another wagonful of bodies could be laid on top.

As he did this, he watched the area around the hospital grounds carefully. As soon as he saw a man striding toward one of the sheds, he followed so he could observe the medical rounds. This doctor appeared not to hold with bleeding fever patients. Instead, he directed that they be given extra rations of brandy and wine from the casks stacked in the corner. Two patients had deep lacerations, one of the leg, the other of the arm, and Luke watched carefully as the doctor sutured the edges of the cut together with catgut.

The doctor must have been aware of Luke hovering over him as he worked, for when he came to the next patient, he asked Luke to help. The man sat at one end of the shed, moaning and holding his arm. His right shoulder appeared to have slid down his arm, so that there was an unusual protuberance in the upper part. There was nothing but a flat area where the crown of the shoulder should have been.

"*Hmph*, dislocated," the doctor said. "Give us a hand, will you, lad, or rather a foot."

The man was laid down on the dirt floor and Luke was directed to place his foot in the man's armpit and to pull steadily on the arm while the doctor massaged the shoulder and steered it toward its normal seating. With a faint "pop" that was felt, almost, rather than heard, the joint slipped home. The man fainted, but the doctor seemed little concerned by this.

"Give him a sip of wine when he comes to," he said, and moved on to his next patient.

Farther down the row of bunks moaned a woman whose foot had turned black and gangrenous and a man who had recovered from the fever, but who now seemed unable to digest any food he was given. By the end of the day Luke felt that he had had an interesting start to his medical education.

By seven that evening, the pace had lessened somewhat as the patients slipped into restless sleep. Sister McGorrian, one of the nuns from Hôtel Dieu who had worked in the sheds all day, was relieved by Sister Bourbonnière and a local priest named Father Phinney.

Luke was weary beyond belief; nevertheless, he found a cleanish rag and a small packet of salt by the stove. He was about to set off in search of the woman with the infected thumb when he was waylaid by Father Higgins.

"Where are you going with that?" he asked.

"I'm doing a little doctoring on the side," Luke said.

"Good Lord, aren't these poor souls dying fast enough as it is without your help? Never mind, here's a place where you can rent a room. It's just turned up vacant, according to Father Phinney. Ask for Mr. Rattigan." He handed Luke a piece of paper with directions written on it. "You can read, can't you?"

Luke grinned. "A little."

"Well, that's a relief then. The last thing we need around here is another illiterate doctor."

Luke tucked the paper in his pocket and left in search of his patient, who he found sitting in her small yard, the little ones curled up beside her.

"I'm back," he announced.

"Dr. Luke!" The woman beamed.

"I'm not a doctor," Luke protested.

"No, that's right — you're better than a doctor, for at least you tend those who stand a chance of getting better."

"Let's take a look at your thumb."

She held it out for him. It was looking pinker and healthier already.

He poured some salt into the battered bowl and added some water from the tin pot over the fire. "I want you to soak it in this for ten minutes or so," he said, "and then we'll dry it off as much as we can. While you're doing that, I'll just slip off and see if I can find my other patient."

"I know where they are." The girl with the scaly skin showed him the way to the next street, where the two young women sat outside a tiny house. One of them rested her foot on a chunk of firewood. They smiled when they saw him, and busily tucked stray wisps of hair into place.

"How's the baby?" he asked.

"Oh, she's fine. You were right, it was just her teeth. She's sleeping now." The child was lying on a thin blanket in a corner of the yard, evidently asleep, but still emitting a low whimper. "But Mary here has a problem with her foot," the woman continued. "Maybe you could have a look?"

Mary leaned over and untied the scuffed leather boot she wore. "It hurts when I walk," she said, and she flexed her foot, showing a brief glimpse of her ankle.

There was not a lot he could do for her. She had an angry-looking bunion, the result of wearing extremely ill-fitting shoes.

"It might help if I could cut that section of the shoe away," he said. "At least it would relieve the pressure."

"Oh, but they're new!" Mary protested. "One of the ladies at the shed gave them to me. Who knows when I might ever get another pair."

"I know, but your foot won't improve until the shoe stops rubbing against the sore spot. I tell you what — let's make the hole and I'll try to find you another pair that fits better."

She nodded her assent. Luke took his penknife and began working a slit along the seam where the upper met the sole. As he worked, the baby's whimper became a low keening sound.

"Does she always do that?" he asked.

"Oh yes," Mary replied. "She never seems happy. Rennie named her well, didn't you Rennie?"

"What do you mean?" Luke asked.

"Deirdre. Deirdre of the Sorrows. She's the most sorrowful baby I've ever seen."

The reference meant nothing to Luke, but he understood the gist of what Mary was saying.

"Where are you from?" he asked while he worked.

"Ireland," the sister named Rennie said, as though it weren't obvious from her accent.

"And how long have you been here?"

"Too long," Mary replied. "I'd fancy going somewhere else, if someone would take me." They both giggled at this.

Luke refrained from further questions and concentrated on the modification he was making to Mary's boot.

"There, that should do it," he said when he was finished. "Leave it off as much as you can."

"Thank you, doctor."

"I'm not a doctor," Luke said. But he found he didn't mind being called one, not even by two giddy girls who were so obviously in the market for beaus.

"Will you come back and check it again?" Mary asked.

"I doubt it will be necessary, but if it makes you feel better, then of course I will." He wasn't sure why he agreed to this, except that it was a chance to practise his bedside manner.

As soon as he finished attending to his first patient's soaking finger, he retrieved the piece of paper Father Higgins had given him from his pocket. But he was perplexed by the instructions that were written on it. The neighbourhood was crammed with houses, some of their entrances fronting on the narrow streets, some of them at the side or the rear of the buildings. The lodging he was looking for was apparently two-thirds of the way along the street and unpainted, but there was no indication as to whether it was situated north or south of where he now stood. He turned to the ghost girl, as he had begun to think of her.

"Do you know where this is?" He read out the instructions he had been given.

She nodded. "Follow me." She led him around the corner and pointed to a large wooden house. Then she seemed to vanish into the streetscape. Luke knocked on the front door, and almost immediately a huge man in a rumpled shirt opened it.

"Mr. Rattigan? I was told to see you about a room." The man merely nodded and led him inside.

Like many of the other buildings in the warren that comprised Stuartsville, as Luke learned the area was called, the house he entered had been crammed onto a lot that was far too small for it. Only the narrowest of alleyways divided it from its neighbours. The back-yard consisted of a few feet of hard-packed ground, and even a corner of this had been commandeered for a small hut-like structure that appeared to house rather a large family.

From the window of the tiny second-floor room he had been given, Luke could see similar structures stretching in all directions, many of their occupants hunkering down in whatever outdoor space they could find. There were no trees big enough to shade the wooden buildings — there was no room for anything to grow, other than a few scrubby elders and weedy-looking bushes.

It was a neighbourhood for mechanics and labourers, whose employment could vanish in an instant or be transplanted to some new place on the morrow — cheap, cheerless, and not conducive to dreams of anything better. It had been made more dreary by the arrival of so many emigrants, for it was obvious that a number of the little stall-like structures that had filled in the corners and alleyways had been thrown up recently in response to the numbers arriving at Kingston's wharves. These were temporary accommodations, built of old planking and canvas tarps scrounged from the docks or the dumps. The inhabitants of these hovels were the lucky ones; either those with enough money to pay the tiny rents or perhaps helped out by the emigration agent. Luke was unsure which, but he could see that their situation was better by far than those in the sheds, which now overflowed with the sick and the dying, or the streets, where orphans and beggars reigned.

As tired as he was, Luke found it difficult to fall asleep in the closet-like cell that held nothing but a cot and a chair, so he stood at the window, which would open only a crack, and surveyed the scene below. The moon was bright and full, and here and there he could see figures moving along the streets and through the yards, small fires gleaming and flickering in the dark. He suddenly realized that he looked directly down into the little encampment that sheltered the woman with the festering thumb and her brood of children. They were still sitting in the yard where he had left them, probably hoping, as did he, for some breath of wind to blow sleep their way.

Chapter 11

August 12, 1847

Dear Ma, Pa and everyone in Wellington,

I am well, but find that I am very tired most nights from labouring with the fever patients. What seemed like complete chaos at first has slowly resolved itself into a routine of sorts, although the numbers of emigrants who continue to arrive constantly threaten to overwhelm the organization that has been put in place.

There are four nuns who visit the sheds in rotation, all members of The Hospitaliers of St. Joseph under the direction of Sister Bourbonniere, whom we met at Hotel Dieu Hospital when we arrived here. The other hospital, down by the lake, is staffed by volunteers from the community, spearheaded by an organization with the rather exalted name of The Female Benevolent Society. They are almost universally referred to as "The Benevolent Ladies" — a name that for me conjures up an image of Greek Goddesses or Chinese Empresses gracefully descending to earth in order to minister to the mortals! This is not as fanciful as it may seem as their ranks include the women of some of Kingston's most prominent families, among them the Mayor's wife and a Miss Macdonald, sister of the current member of the legislature.

Many of the local priests attend the hospitals and sheds every day as well, and Father Higgins is tireless in his efforts. I spend many days working at his side and truly admire and like the man. He has a wonderful hearty manner about him that seems to set the Irish (and me!) at their ease.

Local churches of various denominations help with providing outdoor relief to the indigent family members of those who have been admitted for care. These now number in the many hundreds and the contingent grows with every steamer full of emigrants.

I do not know how many more can be looked after here, and yet we have still to get through the rest of August and the month of September, which are, I am told, the heaviest months for emigration.

I can be useful to them only in the smallest of ways. The doctors seem perplexed as to the proper treatment for ship's fever and our efforts consist of trying to keep our patients as clean and comfortable as possible. This disease takes a fearsome toll — some days we bury as many as ten or twelve people, and their beds are filled as quickly as they are vacated.

Nonetheless, I am content with my decision to stay here and do what I can for them. I would make a poor physician indeed if I were to turn my back now on such a pitiful scene of suffering.

Hoping you are all well and content. I sometimes dream about sitting down with you all at one of Sophie's dinners.

Your loving son,

Luke

Luke had become as familiar as the doctors were with the signs and symptoms of what he learned was formally known as typhus fever, although it had many names: ship's fever, camp fever, jail fever, famine fever. Whatever its name, it began with the victim becoming pale and lethargic, obviously unwell and feverish. It was this symptom that the emigration agents at the ports looked for, and the sorting that Luke had witnessed in Toronto was the separation of those who showed these early signs of infection and those who didn't. Soon after, the patient would complain of headache, and be unable to stand bright lights. Five days or so after the initial symptoms, a rash would erupt on the chest, or black spots would appear on the tongue, after which time the sufferer would descend into the typical stupor and delirium of the disease. It was this stupor that gave the disease its name: typhus was Greek for "mist." After the disease progressed this far, recovery was in the hands of God. Patients either survived or they died, and no one seemed to know which would be which, although Luke rather suspected that the general health and condition of the patient had some bearing on the outcome.

The fever itself generally lasted for about two weeks, but the patient was by no means out of danger when the bone-racking chills subsided. Often, Luke noted, the sufferer might develop a pneumonia, or a dropsy, or blood in the urine. In a few, the fingers and toes would turn black with gangrene. And in all too many cases a patient who was seemingly on the mend might suddenly collapse into a precipitous death.

"Some of these patients must already have had the disease, but were passed through quarantine and sent up the river anyway," Luke observed to Father Higgins one morning as they carried pails of water into the shed where the outdoor relief ladies were beginning preparations for the daily stew. "Nearly all the people who arrived yesterday had evidence of pretty advanced symptoms."

"I'm sure you're right," the priest said. "When I came through Grosse Isle the ships were lined up waiting to be inspected. I'm not sure how thorough any of the inspections could be, given the numbers involved."

Luke wasn't entirely sure where, exactly, Grosse Isle was, although he assumed from the name that it was in Quebec, and from the context that it was on the river.

Higgins rolled his eyes when he asked about this. "You're a bloody uneducated heathen, Luke Lewis. I know more about the geography of this country than you do."

This was becoming typical of Luke's exchanges with Higgins, who treated him to the same sort of banter he adopted with his countrymen. Luke took no offence to anything he said; in fact, he was used to this sort of treatment. It was the way his brother Moses had always talked to him.

"I've been in the bush for five years," he protested. "Information is a little hard to come by in the Huron."

"That's no excuse. For your information, should you choose to retain the knowledge, Grosse Isle is just downriver from Quebec City. It's the first quarantine station in the St. Lawrence River. I don't know how many have been taken off there, but I'm sure it's more than anyone was prepared to look after. They probably ran out of beds and just sent on whoever they couldn't manage."

In fact, it seemed that no one had been prepared for the thousands of people who had arrived. Quarantines had been set up at every port between Quebec and Toronto, and yet the fever slipped through each inspection, gathered force as it sped along the waterways, and at each stop spat out a detritus of skeletal, walking dead.

"We're just fortunate here that Sister Bourbonnière agreed to break cloister when the Bishop asked her," Higgins went on.

"What's cloister?" Luke asked.

"It means they don't normally go out into the community to minister to their charges," the priest replied. "The charges, instead, come to them. You really are a little Protestant pagan, aren't you?"

"I can't help it. My father's a Methodist preacher. What did you expect?" He was learning to give back as good as he got when it came to conversations with Father Higgins.

A thin blond man in a bunk nearby overheard this comment and shifted his weight up onto his elbow. He was feverish and covered in rash, but had not yet descended into the peculiar mental fog of typhus. "A Methodist preacher," he said. "Will he come to visit here, do you think?"

Luke went over to the man and helped him lie back down again. "I'm sorry, he doesn't live here. Are you a Methodist? Would you like me to try to find someone for you to talk with?"

"That would be grand if you could," the man said. "I'd rather not have the priest. We're not Catholic, our family. We're not Methodist either, mind you, but it would be a little closer to what we're used to."

"What church do you attend?"

"The Church of Ireland."

Luke looked to Higgins for clarification of this, for he had never heard of the church. The priest's eyes were narrowed as he regarded the man; then, when he realized that Luke was looking to him for an answer, he shrugged.

"Basically transplanted Church of England."

"The Methodists are close to that, aren't they?" the man said worriedly. "It's the same thing really, isn't it?"

Luke wondered what his father's response to that statement would have been, given the longstanding enmity between the Methodists and the Anglicans in Canada, but it wasn't his place to lecture anyone on the doctrinal and political differences of Canadian faiths. "There's Church of England proper here in Kingston. Should I ask someone to come?"

"Please, if you could. I've lost my children. Do you think there's someone there who could look for them?"

It was a plea that Luke had heard before: parents looking for children, children looking for siblings, orphans looking for any kind of kin at all. Families had been ripped apart at every quarantine station, but Luke knew of no church or charity that was in the business of reuniting them. It would be cruelty itself, however, to point this out to a sick man.

"What happened to them?" he asked.

"Jack was held back at Montreal," the man said, "and I fear he's dead, but I'd like to know for certain. Our trunk was put on the wrong steamer there and no one could tell us where it was sent, so my wife and I went to Bytown and my daughter Margaret travelled down the river looking for our possessions. The other daughter is here. Don't worry about her — she'll be fine — but I'd like to find the other two."

"I'll see if I can find someone to help you," Luke promised, although he was not at all optimistic. Nevertheless, he would do his best.

The male volunteers on hand each day tried to rotate among the sheds and the hospitals as much as possible, sparing the nuns the heavier tasks of lifting bodies and lugging water.

As they were walking toward the brewery wharf and its adjacent sheds, Luke questioned Higgins about the man who wanted a minister. "Do you know him?" he asked.

"I know who he is," the priest replied. "His name is John Porter. He's from a village in my parish. He was never in my church, of course, but I know of the family. They're small farmers who rented their land from the local Lord. I expect they were encouraged to emigrate when the estate switched over to grazing cattle."

"Does that happen a lot?"

"Oh, yes. There were a lot of estates making the change even before the potatoes failed. The landowners can't make any money from the farmers they rent their lands to — not even from the ones that ever grew anything besides potatoes. Some of them make a little from wheat, but not nearly enough to pay the landlord's debts." His face showed a bitterness that matched his voice. "All those people dying of hunger while wagonloads of wheat are shipped across the Irish Sea."

"Farming is in a sad state here as well," Luke said. "Everybody's pretty worried."

"But Canada is supposed to be the saviour of the Irish peasant," Higgins said. "Acres of land just waiting to be settled."

Luke snorted. "You have to understand what it's like, starting a farm. You can't just stick a spade in the ground and throw in a few seeds. You have to clear the forest before you can even begin. It's back-breaking work, and I've seen it defeat well-fed English farmers with years of experience. The idea that these scarecrows could do it is ludicrous. And even the established farmers who can afford to hire help aren't going to hire a man who looks like he could be knocked over by a brisk wind."

Higgins was listening intently, with narrowed eyes. "Isn't that typical," he said. "No one's thought anything through, and in the meantime the paupers are being shovelled out of Ireland by the boatload."

"What do you think is going to happen?" Luke asked.

"In Ireland? There will be no one left. They'll all have died or gone off somewhere else."

"And here?"

"I don't know. You'd be a better judge of that than I, Luke Lewis. It's your country, after all. Even if you don't seem to know anything about it."

"All I know is that there's precious little work right now for anyone," Luke replied, "and precious little spare money either. It's a bleak outlook, all right."

They had reached the brewery shed and the conversation came to an end as Luke busied himself with the lifting of bodies and Father Higgins with the elevation of souls.

***

When Luke returned to the hospital sheds later that afternoon, the scaly ghost of a girl who had fetched him the first night was standing by the side of one the bunks gazing down at the man whose name was John Porter. He was having a fitful sleep, and was unaware of his visitor. Now that he saw the two together, Luke realized that there was a strong family resemblance. Porter, like the girl, was very fair. He had almost no beard, and was thinly built and narrow of face. Unlike his daughter, however, he showed no sign of the scaly skin that reflected the light so strangely. The girl turned when she heard Luke behind her. There was no sign of any emotion on her face.

"That's my Da," she said. "He's dead." And then she left the shed.

The girl was nowhere to be seen as Luke made his private rounds that evening. Word had spread that there was a doctor, or at least someone who was nearly one, who would attend to the minor complaints that the hospitals had no time for. A red-haired man who was camped out on the parade ground had rammed a large wooden splinter into the palm of his hand. Luke removed it and cleaned out the puncture. A broken finger needed a splint. Many of the emigrants suffered from sunburn, the result of sitting on the decks of steamers or the docks, and of being unaccustomed to the merciless sun of a Canadian summer.

Another man complained of headache. Luke took one look at this bloodshot eyes and shaking hands and suggested that he sluice some cold water over his head. "You might stay away from whiskey for a few days, too," he suggested.

At least the man had the decency to look sheepish, although he had a novel explanation for where he had come by the money for liquor. "The fairies left it under a rock for me, I swear," he said. "They were always partial to me on account of I say hello to them every time I cross a bridge."

"Well, tell the fairies from me that after this, they should be leaving it for bread and not the booze," Luke said. The man began to laugh, then stopped abruptly as the movement hurt his head.

Luke then went to check on the lady with the festering thumb. It no longer appeared infected; in fact, the cut was beginning to grow over with clean, healthy-looking skin. He set her off into a high dudgeon, however, when he made the mistake of addressing her as Mrs. Porter.

"I'm not Mrs. Porter. I'm Bridie Shanahan! What on God's green earth would ever make you think I'd be a Porter?"

Luke reddened and stammered an apology. "It's just that I saw your daughter, or at least the girl with the white hair, at the fever shed. She said that John Porter was her father."

"And so he is," Mrs. Shanahan said, as if that explained everything.

"But ... oh well, never mind. I'm sorry."

"Now don't you be sorry, Dr. Luke. There was never any good to be gotten out of being sorry, was there? You can be sorry all you like, but it won't be bringing Mr. Shanahan back, will it? Nor Bridget, nor Dorey, nor Sheena, nor any of the others. Nor me ma, nor me da, nor Charley Gallagher, come to think on it."

This last muttered name hit Luke like a slap. "Wha … what did you say?"

"I said there's no promise in being sorry, that's what I said. It doesn't do any good."

"No, what was the last name you said?" But Mrs. Shanahan just looked at him fiercely, her dark eyes snapping defiance.

"Charley Gallagher. You mentioned Charley Gallagher." He had all but forgotten his promise to the man from the Irish settlement, made so long ago and before he realized the scope of what he was being asked to do.

"Poor Charley Gallagher shot down. I'd never be a Porter." She shuffled around her little campfire, stirring at the tin pot with an old wooden spoon. "Still and all, I have to have seven, don't I? It all comes to naught unless there are seven."

"Seven what?" Luke struggled to understand what this woman was saying.

"Seven girls, of course," she said. "There have to be seven, otherwise there's no meaning to any of it."

She stirred the pot again, with an air of having explained herself perfectly. *She's quite mad*, Luke thought. Still, she had reminded him of a duty that he had neglected. He vowed that he would make more effort to inquire after Charley Gallagher. He had promised after all.

He left Mrs. Shanahan with another small twist of salt and made his way around the corner toward his lodging. Just as he reached the front step, he was hailed by the two young women with the fussy baby. They were sitting on the front stoop of a building across the street and three houses down.

The woman with the sore foot, Mary, smiled at him. "It hardly hurts at all now," she said. "Slitting my shoe really did the trick." She thrust her leg out and waggled her ankle.

"And Deirdre's tooth has come in," the other woman said. "I'm Rennie, by the way. Rennie Doyle." She smiled at him coquettishly. Luke was amazed that anyone would saddle a child with a name like Deirdre Doyle, but then he was finding many of these Irish names outlandish and exotic in the extreme. Sister Bourbonnière's carefully kept lists were full of names that Luke had never heard before — Connors and Calums and Liams; Ionas and Oonas and Bridgets.

"I hope you meant what you said when you promised to find me a new pair of boots," Mary said. "Otherwise, I don't know what I'll do, with a great slit in the side. Does it rain a lot here in the winter, do you know?"

"Worse than that," Luke said. "You'll be knee-deep in snow come January. I'll find you a stout pair of boots before then, don't you worry." Another promise. He was starting to lose track of the promises he had made.

This one he would have to keep, otherwise Mary's foot would be frostbitten before the year was out. "In the meantime, could I ask you a question?"

"Of course," Mary said, and smoothed her tattered skirts back over her legs.

"Do you know Mrs. Shanahan over on the next street?"

"Bridie Shanahan? I think everybody knows Bridie. And all her children."

Rennie Doyle confirmed this with a nod of the head.

"Did you know that the oldest one, the one with the funny skin, isn't hers?"

Mary looked at him with astonishment. "Of course she isn't. She's Anna Porter. She's a merrow."

"A what?"

"Well, her grandmother was anyway," Rennie said. "And Anna's a throwback."

"What's a merrow?" Luke had never heard the term before.

"A seamaid," Mary said, "a sidhe. Anna's grandmother was covered in scales, too. They say she brought riches to the Porters."

"She foretells doom as well," Rennie pointed out. "Don't forget that part. People are frightened of her because of that."

"That's true," Mary said, "but it pays to catch one, because of the money she brings."

"How do you catch a ... what it is it, a merrow?"

"She has to take off her red cap to come ashore," Rennie said. "If you can find the red cap and hide it, you can keep her."

"Until she finds it again."

"Or gives it to someone else. Merrows are fickle creatures," Rennie said, and then she and Mary began to giggle.

Luke began to suspect that the women were pulling his leg. "So how did the girl end up with Mrs. Shanahan? Isn't she frightened too?"

Mary and Rennie stopped giggling and shifted position, a little uneasily, Luke thought.

"Now, that's a long story," Rennie said, "and I'm not sure I've got it to rights."

"Mrs. Shanahan said there had to be seven."

"Did she now? Poor thing." Rennie thought for a moment. "Yes, that would make sense, I suppose. There were seven of them."

"Seven what?"

"Why, seven girls, of course!" Rennie said with astonishment. "She had seven, but she lost them. Now she's got seven more."

Luke was finally beginning to make a little sense of this rather silly conversation.

"So, none of the children are actually hers?"

"No," said Mary. "All orphans."

"But the Porter girl isn't an orphan," Luke pointed out.

"No, but the mother died of fever a few days ago and the father's in the shed, as well, so I don't expect his chances are good, are they? And Anna would know that, being a merrow and all."

This all seemed to make perfect sense to the two women, but Luke was still confused. Finally, he said,

"And what does Charley Gallagher have to do with all this?"

Rennie shot Mary a quick glance, then waved a dismissive hand. "Oh, that's all an old story. It doesn't really matter now that we're all in Canada, does it?"

"Doesn't matter at all," Mary echoed.

"Well, thank you for the conversation," Luke said, although he was little the wiser for it.

"If you need to know something, just ask," Mary said.

"We'll be here," Rennie added.

Luke nodded his good night and walked back to his lodging, bewildered at the difficulties of trying to get information out of the Irish.

Chapter 12

The next day brought five more steamers to the brewery dock and over a hundred new patients to the hospitals. Even though there were twelve bodies waiting to be buried, Sister Bourbonnière directed the carters to concentrate on moving fever patients from the wharf to the hospitals and sheds, although she confessed to Luke that she had no idea where they were going to put them all.

When Luke arrived at the wharf, the emigration agent was in a great state of agitation over the numbers of emigrants that had arrived. Again, Luke witnessed the inspection process, with a doctor separating those who were supposedly healthy from those who showed signs of typhus. The ill were taken to the wagons for transport. The healthy, rather than being shepherded toward the nearby sheds, where in the past they would have been fed and allowed to rest for a time, were instead funnelled onto a waiting lake steamer. The agent appeared to be moving as many along as quickly as he possibly could, but the hollow-eyed and exhausted passengers were protesting. With good reason, Luke thought. They had already travelled long miles and had been sitting for hours in the hot sun. It was a long journey to the next port, and in the meantime they had likely had nothing to eat and little opportunity to sleep. But Kingston could accommodate no more. The sheds were full, the hospitals bursting, and the city's resources strained to the breaking point.

Some of the patients were so sick that they were unable to walk. Luke helped to carry them on stretchers to the wagons, and as soon as they had crammed in as many as they safely could, the wagon would pull away, to an accompanying wail from relatives left behind.

They had nearly filled the fifth wagon when he heard shouting.

"I demand to know where you're taking my brother," yelled a large black-haired man who was attempting to push past the agent.

"You'll have to get back on the steamer," he was told.

"I will not!"

"Unless you have friends or family in Kingston, you'll have to go on to the next port." The agent held the man by the arm and tried to pull him away from the gangplank.

Then a man on the shore stepped forward. "I'm his brother. He can come with me."

This man, too, had dark hair, but there the resemblance ended. Whereas the first, under ordinary circumstances and not half starved to death, would have been a tall and handsome specimen, the second was tiny and monkey-like, with a thin, wrinkled face and protuberant ears. Luke found it hard to believe that the two men were related. The agent obviously didn't believe it either, for he maintained his grip on the first man's arm.

The man had stopped struggling, however. Now his face opened in an incredulous grin. "Flea! I thought never to see you again, boy!"

"Pierce! *Dia duit!*"

At this, the emigration officer let go, and the man named Pierce rushed down to the dock to embrace the monkey-like man. It wasn't so much an embrace, Luke thought, as a lift. The smaller man's feet left the wooden planking below him and dangled in the air as his brother spun him around.

The agent shrugged and turned to the next emigrant.

Suddenly, Luke realized where he had seen the dark little man before. He was the wagon driver from Toronto wharf, the man who had handed the constable a paper packet and then driven off with the wagonload of women. *Flea.* There was no mistaking the name. But what was a Toronto carter doing in Kingston?

Pierce released his brother from his smothering embrace and set him down again on the dock. Flea scanned the crowd. "Where's Dermot?" Luke heard him ask.

"They've taken him off to hospital. He's not looking too well. It may be the malignant fever, I don't know. I need to make sure he's being looked after."

"We both will, and let's hope for the best, eh? We'll go and find him by and by, but first you can help us load up some barrels."

Together they walked around to the far side of the brewery.

The doctor had not yet begun his inspection of the second of the steamers. Luke would not be needed for a few minutes. Curious, he followed the two men.

There was another dock at the western end of the building, sheltered in a small cove and out of sight of the main wharves and the entrance to the brewery itself. It had obviously never been built for anything as large as a steamer; nevertheless, a steamer was tied to it. As Luke watched, a man rolled four barrels along the planks and onto the ship. Luke knew that they were empty from the ease with which the man could handle them.

"That's it then, Mr. Bellwood. I'll have more for you in a couple of weeks."

"You'd better," a man growled in return. Luke could only assume that he was Bellwood. "Hans don't like it when there's mistakes." Flea and Pierce scrambled aboard as the lines were cast off and the steamer prepared to chug away. "There you are, Flea," Bellwood said. "And who's this sad-lookin' pup you've got with you?"

"This is my brother, Pierce," Flea replied. "Recently arrived from Ireland, he is, but ready and able to assist us. There was another brother with him, but he's been hauled off to the hospital."

"That's all I need is another lazy Mullen. Never mind, with any luck the third will die and we won't have to bother with him."

"We thought we'd go and find out what happened to him after we dock at Kingston wharf."

"As long as you're back in the morning. We take another load of dogans up the lake tomorrow."

Just as the steamer pulled away, the man called Flea happened to look up. He saw Luke standing by the edge of the building. He stared for a moment, then his eyes narrowed. He turned to say something to Bellwood, but whatever he said was blown away by the wind.

Luke walked slowly back to the main wharf, unsure of what he had just seen, and unsure of why he was even interested, except that it had struck him as so odd to see the man called Flea in Kingston. What was the last name he had heard? Mullen? And there had been another name as well. "Who else are you going to deal with if it's not Hans?" Flea had said to the constable in Toronto. "Hans doesn't like it when there are mistakes," Bellwood had said to the man loading barrels. Who was Hans, and why did he have such influence? And why did it niggle at Luke, when he had so many more pressing matters to attend to?

His speculations were soon shoved to the back of his mind as he returned to his duties as the sorting of emigrants continued. To his dismay, and to everyone else's, he was sure, there were far more sent to the wagons than were loaded onto the boats.

* * *

Late that afternoon, as Luke followed the last of the wagons toward the hospital, he met Father Higgins, who was going in the other direction.

"That's all of them," Luke said. "For today anyway."

"I'm looking for one in particular," Higgins said. "A brother of one who was taken to the sheds. I was told that he stayed behind."

"There's only a handful of the healthy ones who were allowed ashore. They all claimed to have family here. Whatever the truth of that may be, they left the wharf as soon as they could so they wouldn't be forced back on a boat."

"Well," Higgins seemed a little nonplussed at this information, "I guess I'll just have to tell Dermot Mullen that his brother has gone on."

"Dermot Mullen?" Luke said. "Is his brother's name Pierce?"

The priest nodded. "How do you know the Mullens?"

"I don't," Luke said, "but Pierce made a fuss, and then another brother stepped forward to claim him. I think his name was Flea, although it seems an odd name for a man."

"Florence Mullen is in Kingston? How strange. Do you know where they went?"

"They boarded a steamer that was loading barrels. I think they were headed to the public wharves at the harbour." For some reason, Luke didn't tell Higgins that he, too, found it odd that Flea, or Florence as his name apparently was, had turned up in Kingston.

The priest turned around to fall in step beside Luke. "It's off to the wharves we go then."

"How do *you* know the Mullen family?" Luke asked.

"They're from my parish. Troublesome bunch, actually, with Flea the ringleader and the other two just following along. Nevertheless, I'll do what I can to reunite the wild brothers. At least then we'll know where they all are."

"Wild in what way?"

"Oh, it doesn't really matter now, does it? It doesn't matter who anyone was in Ireland, they're all in the same boat now. Or off it, I suppose, for Dermot and anyone else who's being held in quarantine."

They parted at the general hospital, where the wagons had deposited the dying and were now lumbering off to collect the dead.

As the afternoon wore on, Luke began to realize that Higgins had been gone for a long time, longer than it should have taken to make his inquiries. When the priest did return, he was boiling with anger.

"These steamer captains should be brought up on charges," he fumed. "The conditions on board the boats are bad enough, but the attitude of the crew is unacceptable."

"What happened?" Luke asked.

"I was manhandled. I was obstructed. I was the subject of foul language and insult. I was treated with contempt. They act as if my presence is the greatest imposition."

"Perhaps you should lodge a complaint," Luke said. He could think of nothing else to suggest. The local authorities might do something, but in all probability they wouldn't. Resources of all kinds were stretched as thin as a strand of spider silk, and no one was likely to take notice of a disgruntled priest.

"Am I being unreasonable?" Higgins asked, although Luke was relatively sure that he expected no answer. "Do I not have the right to inquire about any one of the thousands of people they transport? It's not as if they're over careful about keeping track themselves. And the conditions are deplorable. There should be an investigation."

"Did you find the Mullens?"

Luke could see that Higgins had almost forgotten his original errand in the heat of his anger, but now that he was reminded of it, he began to calm down.

"No, I didn't. And you're right, much as I hate to admit it. But I'll go to the town hall only as a last resort. I'm going to go back and talk to the captains. I shouldn't have to put up with such foul-mouthed invective when I'm making a simple inquiry. Come with me, Luke, to back me up and tell me which steamer the Mullens were on."

Luke agreed to accompany the priest. He would have done anything Higgins asked him to do, even though he couldn't fathom how his unprepossessing form could be any sort of backup to anyone.

The harbour was its usual sea of masts, and to Luke's eye all of the sailing steamers looked the same, but he was sure that the name of the steamer had been a play on its captain's name — *Bellwind* or *Bellwater* maybe. He tried to bring the name to mind by visualizing the scene beside the brewery. *Bellweather.* That was it.

"It's that one," Luke said. The steamer was tied up with four other vessels at the public wharf. A very dirty and dishevelled-looking man was coiling a length of rope on the deck. Higgins hailed him.

"I told you before, priest, the captain is in his cabin and he'll not see you," the man said. "You're not to step foot aboard this vessel."

Higgins stepped closer. "Excuse me, but we would like to hear that from the captain himself."

"Oh you would, would you?" The man spat over the rail, the wad landing on the dock a few inches in front of them. "Well you can like whatever you like, that doesn't mean you're going to get it."

Just then a man emerged from the cabin. Luke recognized him as Bellwood.

"What's the trouble here, Neddy?"

"This papist and his friend want to hear you speak. They think I'm lying to them."

Now that Luke was closer to the man, he realized that Captain Bellwood was every bit as dishevelled and quite a lot dirtier than the man he had addressed as Neddy.

"I believe I have the right to inquire after a passenger," Father Higgins began.

"You have no rights here at all," the captain replied. "This is my ship, and what I say goes."

"The man we're looking for is Pierce Mullen. He's

believed to be aboard your ship. He met up with his brother Flea earlier today."

"Those are heathenish names. Can't say I've ever run across 'em before."

"Nevertheless," Father Higgins continued, "their brother Dermot is in one of the hospital sheds. He has the fever, and he'd like his brother to know where he is."

Bellwood shrugged. "What's that to do with me?"

"Could we come aboard and look for him?" Higgins said.

"Are you calling me a liar? I'm tellin' you, he's not here, and you will not set foot on my boat."

The captain was yelling now, and his loud shouts had begun to attract a crowd. These were the usual sorts who hung around the docks — hands from the other vessels, some of them, but a goodly number of time-wasters and drunks as well.

"Let 'em aboard!" one of them shouted. "He's only looking for someone."

"He will not set foot on this ship!" the captain shouted again.

Father Higgins had had enough. "I really don't wish to involve the law, but if I must, I must. We'll see what the constable has to say about this." And with that he turned and walked away.

Luke scrambled to keep up with the irate priest. "Is this really necessary?" he asked.

The priest was white-lipped. "This is not the first time I've been denied access by the steamer captains. I know for a fact that people have died while I stood arguing on the dock."

Luke knew very little about the Roman Catholic faith, but understood that it was, for some reason, vitally important that a priest be present at the moment of death. He understood this man's frustration — he was duty bound to ease a follower's passage into the afterlife, and yet was being denied his purpose.

"Why won't they let you on the ship?" he asked.

"Because of the conditions on board, I expect. The poor souls are crowded as badly as on the ocean-going vessels. There's filth everywhere, the water is bad, the food is non-existent, and if one of the passengers dies, they're left where they fall, no matter that the still-healthy are sitting beside them. It's a wonder the fever sheds aren't twice as full as they are now."

"Lies! Those are all lies!" Bellwood was not content to let them carry their tale to the constable without extenuation on his part. He was following a few feet behind them, spewing invective as he walked.

"You and your Papist horde can all rot in hell as far as I'm concerned," he shouted at them. "Filthy Irish Catholics don't deserve any better treatment, and you know it as well as I do. They live like animals, so I'll treat them like the beasts they are." He had obviously overheard Higgins's rant about steamer conditions.

Luke spun around to face him. "You're making good coin carting filthy Irish up and down the lake," he said. "How much of the money you're given for decent food and water have you skimmed off along the way? I'm no Catholic, but I wouldn't do to any animal what you do to your passengers."

"Slander! Defamation! I'll see you in court over this."

Father Higgins pulled Luke away, and from then on he maintained his silence until they reached the gaol at the rear of the courthouse.

The constable, when they found him in a small office on the second floor, seemed loathe to get involved.

"Now, now," he said, "I think everyone should just calm down."

"No," Father Higgins replied, "I would like to register an official complaint against this captain."

The constable sighed and pulled a sheaf of papers toward him. He began to laboriously take down the details of the complaint while the captain muttered and grumbled. Luke occupied himself by admiring the view from the window, which encompassed an excellent vista of the harbour, with Garden Island beyond it and Wolfe Island in the distance. From this vantage point he could see what an excellent harbour it was, and why Kingston had always been strategically important. There was abundant shelter here for ships, and from the heights overlooking the scene, it would be possible to see, and therefore control, any traffic approaching the river where it narrowed on its exit from Lake Ontario. His admiration of the location was interrupted when he noticed a knot of people on the dock. The ships seemed small from here, and hard to identify, but it seemed to him that the crowd was gathered around the steamer that belonged to the rude captain standing behind him. He nudged Father Higgins, who followed his gaze to the scene below.

"Sir?" The constable was still wrestling with writing down what he had been told so far and seemed disinclined to brook an interruption.

Luke raised his voice. "Sir? There seems to be some altercation down on the wharf."

This gained the captain's attention. "Bloody hell, my boat!" he yelled and in an instant he was out the door and on his way back to his vessel.

His departure finally got the constable's attention. He rose and looked out the window, then turned and ran after the captain. Luke and Father Higgins scrambled down the stairs after him.

It was only a short distance from the courthouse to the wharf, but both the constable and Bellwood were wheezing and gasping as they ran, and Luke and Father Higgins very shortly caught up with them. And then they all stopped, aghast at what was transpiring in front of them.

News of Father Higgins's difficulties must have spread like wildfire through the town. There were at least fifty people, by Luke's reckoning, gathered around the steamer yelling at Neddy, the first mate, who was yelling back. His words, however, were lost in the uproar from the crowd. And then a rock, thrown by someone on the dock, hit him squarely on the chest. He abruptly closed his mouth and awkwardly fell back.

More rocks flew then. Luke could see Flea Mullen cowering behind the shelter of the wheelhouse. The shouting from the crowd grew louder, and then they surged forward, scrambling onto the deck of the steamer. Two stout men picked Neddy up by the arms and legs and threw him onto the dock. Flea was apparently unwilling to wait for similar treatment. He jumped into the water. Luke could only hope that he knew how to swim, for his abrupt departure was unnoticed by anyone else.

One of the stout men was apparently the leader of the mob, for he now stepped forward and addressed the captain. "You have infringed upon the rights of a right-fully ordained priest of the Roman Catholic Church," he bellowed. "And you have denied fellow human beings any comfort in death. You'll not recover your ship, sir, until you undertake to remedy the situation."

The captain shifted from foot to foot uneasily. "Bloody dogans," he muttered under his breath. Father Higgins merely looked stunned by the turn of events.

"I think we can all agree that Father Higgins has a right to search out lost relatives, but this isn't the way to assure that right." The voice came from behind Luke, and he turned. But by then even more people had gathered, whether from curiosity or because they wished to join the fray, and he had no way of telling who had spoken, although he recognized several members of the Board of Health, several other steamer captains, and a handful of ministers of various faiths.

The captain had also turned at the sound of the voice. "Now we'll get some satisfaction," he said. "Mayor Kirkpatrick, you can see for yourself that these ruffians have seized my vessel. What are you going to do about it?"

Just then a rather large number of uniformed soldiers came marching down the street. The mayor had called in the army.

These were well-disciplined troops from nearby Fort Henry. As soon as they reached the wharf they fanned out to enclose both the wharf and the ship, bayonets fixed and pointed menacingly at the crowd.

"Any man who disperses now will be allowed to proceed peacefully," Mayor Kirkpatrick announced. "I promise you that this incident will be investigated fully, and a solution found. But in the meantime, you all need to go about your business."

Luke noticed that two of the ministers moved up to stand beside Kirkpatrick, as if to lend support to this statement. Several gentlemen, businessmen from their appearance, followed suit. One of the steamer captains spat noisily onto the dock.

The crowd who had seized the ship stood stock still for a moment, as if weighing their options, and then slowly three of them moved to the gangplank and descended to the dock. It was enough to galvanize their compatriots, and one by one they left the ship and melted away through the forest of bayonets. The last to leave was the stout man who had addressed the captain. The spectators on the wharf departed, as well. Neddy, the first mate, lay groaning on the dock, but no one paid him any mind, least of all his captain.

"I want satisfaction for this." Again, the captain addressed Kirkpatrick directly, and Luke wondered if there was a prior acquaintanceship that would impact on the consequences of this melee.

"That's a shame, because you're not likely to get it," Kirkpatrick said. Whatever claim the captain thought he might have was to be denied him.

Instead Kirkpatrick turned to the constable. "I'll leave you to sort this out," he said. "Sit the captains and the Father down and come up with some sort of a solution that will suffice for the future. I don't want to hear any more of it."

"And the men who seized the boat?" the constable asked.

"I gave a promise of impunity, and I mean to keep it. This town is like a tinderbox as it is. The last thing we need is to deliberately ignite it with heavy-handed retribution."

"Help! Help me!" The cry was punctuated by noisy splashing. Flea could not swim after all, apparently. Luke rushed to the side of the wharf. Mullen was clinging to the bow of the ship, but was unable to gain a secure handhold, so was at intervals bobbing beneath the surface of the water. The captain, who had re-boarded his ship, ambled over and threw a barrel into the water. Luke made to help pull him in, but the captain stopped him. "He can paddle himself to shore, the cowardly bastard. He's unlikely to drown as long as he has something to hang on to."

Flea clung to the barrel, but seemed confused about what to do next.

"Kick your feet!" Luke called. "Go between the docks and you can get ashore."

Mullen finally seemed to understand that he needed to propel himself to where the shore sloped down to meet the water. As he kicked away from the ship, he nearly lost his grip on his lifeline as it bobbed up and down and slowly began to turn. Luke was able to read only ILLERIES, TORONTO before Flea clutched the barrel more firmly and steered his way to land.

Father Higgins had by then entered into what appeared to be a very earnest discussion with the mayor and the constable, and Luke judged that his small part in the drama was at an end. It was time he returned to the sheds anyway. With all the new arrivals that afternoon, the Sisters would be struggling to keep up with the work.

As he left the wharf he realized that the crowd that had gathered had well and truly dispersed, frightened no doubt by the presence of the soldiers. Kirkpatrick's quick action had effectively prevented a riot, but it was a reflection, Luke supposed, of the tensions that had arisen from the influx of so many poor and sick newcomers. He was not sure how many had passed through Kingston's sheds, but he guessed that it must number in the thousands, the tally rivalling the number of people in the town itself. And Kingston was but one port. How many fevered thousands could Canada be expected to minister to?

As it turned out, Father Higgins's inquiries had been a wasted effort. When Luke entered the shed where Dermot Mullen had been bedded down, in a space at the end of the bunks, there stood the man who Luke knew to be Pierce Mullen. Higgins returned a few minutes later.

"Pierce! I've been looking for you!" The priest greeted Mullen with a grin. They were obviously old friends.

"Father Higgins! Oh, now I know Dermot's in good hands, with you here."

"Dermot is in God's hands, as is every other poor soul in here," said the priest. "But, yes, I'll do my best by him."

"You could start by finding him a real bed. I thought he was being taken to a hospital, not a cattle shed."

"The hospitals are full. Everywhere is full. No one expected this, and no one was ready for it. I hear you've found Florence, though, and that's a good thing, isn't it? You can help each other out. A new start in a new country for the three of you, eh?"

There was a puzzled expression on Pierce's face, as if he was trying to work out how Father Higgins knew that the brothers had been reunited.

For some reason, Luke hoped that Higgins wouldn't let slip the source of his information. He wasn't sure what, if anything, he had interrupted, either on the Toronto waterfront or at the brewery. But Luke was sure that Flea hadn't been pleased with his appearance at either.

He noticed that the buckets beside the stove were empty again, so he decided to haul some water and leave speculation about the Mullen brothers for another time. Besides, he felt awkward overhearing the conversation between the priest and Mullen, as though he were intruding in some way. The exchange had been full of implication and innuendo.

It was so crowded in the shed that he had to tiptoe over Dermot and shoulder past Pierce and Higgins in order to get to the buckets. Pierce turned right around in order to get out of his way, and then he seemed to freeze. Luke realized that he was staring at a patient a few rows away. It was John Porter, who stared back wide-eyed for a moment, then turned over and drew his blanket closer around him.

Chapter 13

Luke had little time to reflect on Porter's reaction. The next day another four steamboats full of emigrants arrived at the wharf and fully forty passengers were ordered to hospital care.

As the wagonloads arrived, it was clear that there was nowhere to put them. He looked for Sister McGorrian to ask what they should do, but when he located her he found that she was in no condition to make decisions of any sort. She was leaning against the wine barrel at the far end of the shed, dabbing at her forehead with a damp cloth.

"Just give me a moment, Luke," she said. "I just need to rest for a bit."

"Have you a headache?" Luke asked.

Her eyes widened as she realized what Luke was implying.

There was no doctor in the shed at the moment, but

Luke knew that Sister McGorrian was suffering from the early stages of typhus. She needed to return to Hôtel Dieu, but in the meantime there was a wagonload of sick patients waiting outside. He called to Father Higgins, and together they spread whatever available blankets they had in the aisles between the bunks. It would make tending to those in the beds even more difficult, but there was nowhere else to put anyone.

"Is there room in any of the other sheds?" Luke asked the wagon driver.

"No. They're full up. We left twenty at the brewery already." The carter wrinkled his brow in thought. "There might be some room at the Hôtel. There were a bunch died there last night. We just haven't had time to move 'em yet."

Luke's stomach turned at the thought of newly arrived fever patients being whisked into beds barely vacated by the dead, but a bed was a bed, he supposed. "Take the rest to the hospitals then. And can you take the Sister as well? You'll need to let Sister Bourbonnière know that she's unwell."

The carter's alarm was evident when he saw the sheen of sweat on the nun's face. Not even God, apparently, could protect them all from the fever.

Luke dragged his weary body back to his airless room that night, but sleep wouldn't come to him. His mind kept replaying the day — the look of fear in Sister McGorrian's eyes as she realized her likely fate; the moans of those around her, already held in the grip

of fever; the fetor of the sheds; the dead bodies he
had carted to the pits. He tried to lighten his mood
by cataloguing his personal medical triumphs: Mary's
bunion, the splinters he had removed, the pus-filled
eyes he had bathed, the supply of grease he had found
for those whose skin had gone chapped and dry in the
summer heat. But these were minor complaints that
paled in comparison to the suffering of the typhus
victims, about whom, it appeared, he could do nothing. And again, his mind's eye would return to the
lifeless forms he loaded on and off the wagons. It was
hours before he could force his eyes to close in sleep's
surrender, the eastern sky already reddening as he
drifted off.

His spirits were lifted the next day when Sister
Bourbonnière handed him a letter, the address written
in his father's hand. He stuck it in his pocket, but after
he had helped with the outdoor relief, he walked down
to the shore and tore it open.

August 22, 1847

My dear Luke,

Thank you for your letter of August 12.
I am well, as are the rest of the people here,
with the exception of your mother, who finds
the heat trying. I am sure that she will begin to
feel better once we are into September and the
nights are cooler.

We think of you every day and trust that
God will keep you safe as you tend to the

poor souls who have been deposited on our shores. The newspapers report that Kingston is not the only city that is overwhelmed with the numbers of emigrants they have been expected to accommodate. Conditions at the quarantine station at Grosse Isle are dire, they say. Montreal is nearly as bad, and Toronto is overflowing, although the papers claim that the City fathers were slow off the mark because so many of them are Orangemen and so many of the emigrants are Catholic. It was Bishop Power, apparently, who insisted that they act before it was too late.

The situation between the United States and Mexico remains worrisome, especially since the Americans are now promulgating a policy of "Manifest Destiny," whereby they seem to think that they have a God-given right to take over the entire continent. I know more than a few people who would take issue with that view, and, like myself, have in the past taken up arms to thwart it. One wonders, however, whether or not they will turn their armies north once they have defeated the Mexicans. I fear we can expect little aid from Britain should that occur. Perhaps we should teach the Irish to march.

I am expecting that Sophie will have some news for us soon — she has dark rings under her eyes — but as she has had several disappointments in the past, is waiting until her condition is obvious before announcing it.

I'd look forward to dandling a little one on my knee again, but that may just be the sentimental caprice of an old man. Besides, I have no notion of who would replace her in the kitchen.

Please let us know when you are planning to depart for Montreal and I will endeavour to manufacture an excuse to come to Kingston. I would like very much to see you again before you begin your studies.

With the greatest respect,

Your loving father

That night, as the sultry air of a late August evening hung like a pall over Kingston, Luke knew that sleep would again be difficult, in spite of the fact that he was exhausted. His father's letter made him realize how claustrophobic his life was at the moment and that the world continued to turn whether he was aware of it or not.

He grabbed a handful of newspapers from the bundles that were stacked in the corner by the casks of wine and brandy. The Benevolent Ladies collected old papers from family and neighbours, and even from the newspaper offices themselves, and brought them to the sheds. They were more useful than rags for cleaning up the worst of the messes. They didn't need to be washed. They could be used once and then burned in the stove.

Luke would sit outside, he decided, like the other inhabitants of Stuartsville, eat his supper, read the papers, and hope that there was enough of a breeze to keep the worst of the mosquitoes away. As he neared the market, he could see a thin white-haired child bobbing and weaving among the stalls. He had to squint in order to focus on her movements. She was so slight and insubstantial that at times she seemed to float through the jumble of stacked firewood, the hanging carcasses, the baskets of produce. And then, like a flash, he saw her hand shoot out and grab a pear. The hand retreated and the pear disappeared. He blinked. It had happened so quickly that it was almost as though he had imagined it. No one else seemed to notice, and why would they? Luke thought. The girl was like a spectre caught out of the corner of one's eye, dismissed as a moment's imagining.

She chose her moments, waiting until a farmer's attention was diverted by a customer or one of the urchins who was not so adept at petty thievery. Then the small white hand would flash out and an item would disappear — a potato, a lettuce, a carrot. At the foot of the street, where the fishermen laid their day's catch out on wooden planks, she hung back watching until a fishmonger was fully occupied in chasing away a group of older boys, and then she walked casually past a pile of yellow perch, neatly extracting two. No one saw her. No one noticed her. No one, it seemed, but Luke.

He lost sight of her as she doubled back along Brock Street, taking care not to retrace her original route. Luke began to wonder just who was looking after whom when it came to the girl and the strange Mrs. Shanahan.

He bought the heel of a loaf of bread and a small wedge of cheese in the market, then ducked into one of the taverns to get a pail of ale. There was a small stoop at the front of his lodging. He would sit there and read the papers while he ate his meal.

The papers he had taken were from three days previously. *The British Whig* carried a full report of the near-riot at the wharf, calling for an official investigation and the laying of charges against those responsible for the melee. The editor of *The Whig* bestowed many compliments on the bravery of the company from Fort Henry in quelling the riot, which he claimed was caused by "Catholic agitators." Luke was distressed at this characterization.

The arrival of so many emigrants was causing enough tension in the town as it was, for it was clear that the disease they carried was no longer confined to the sheds. There had been several cases reported amongst the townsfolk, although the paper insisted that the disease now appearing within the city was a different strain of typhus, and not nearly so virulent as the one that had come across the ocean. In any event, local patients were apparently being looked after at home, it now being considered unwise for anyone to go near the hospitals. Luke was sure that the physicians, not to mention the nursing volunteers, were relieved that this was so. There was no room for any more patients at the hospitals, or in the sheds either.

On the other hand, he had to wonder if these citizens of Kingston had not caught the disease through the visitations of the physicians who attended the sick, then made their way from house to house to see their regular patients. It seemed clear to Luke that the fever spread from person to person somehow, but he had no idea of the actual mechanism. The doctors claimed bad air was the cause. This could certainly be true at the hospitals, where the atmosphere was thick with noxious odours. But the air in the fever sheds was fresh enough — at times the winds blew in off the lake with alarming force and blew away not only the stink, but at times newspapers and pieces of clothing as well — and yet relatives of those already stricken often succumbed themselves days after their kin had begun to recover. Luke didn't like to think what kind of backlash there might be if the good citizens of the town began to die at the same rate as the emigrants.

According to the paper, this could all have been averted if Mayor Kirkpatrick's plan of establishing a quarantine station on Garden Island had been approved by the Colonial Council. The island lay in the St. Lawrence River just south of Kingston and was a centre for shipbuilding and rafting. The plan had been turned down. There was no money for it. *The Whig* reported that Colonial Secretary Earl Grey had written from Britain, "especially when you have to deal with the Irish, it is far better to do too little, than to do too much, and rather then, allow a good deal of suffering to take place, than to take away the motive of exertion."

Luke thought of the ragged, hollow-eyed people who lay dying in the sheds, and wondered how anyone could have given voice to this callous statement. He thought of the emigrants he had seen trudging along the road between Toronto and Guelph. As unfit as they had been, their first question was always whether or not there was work for them. And when the answer was no, only then did they beg or steal.

The newspaper went on to point out that only the poorest of the Irish were arriving in Canada. The fare was cheaper, for one thing. Ships that hauled timber to Britain filled them up with emigrants for the return voyage — a human ballast carried at £3 a head. Furthermore, American port cities were strictly enforcing their passenger laws: a stiff landing tax, heavy fines levied on ships held in quarantine, captains to be held responsible for any of their passengers that became dependent on the public purse. For landowners wishing to clear their farms, for the British government, for the groaning Irish workhouses, Canada was the cheapest and easiest destination.

The Whig took great issue with this as well: "What is to be the end of the barbarous policy now pursued of pouring to the extent of from 80,000 to 100,000 of the famished and diseased population of down-trodden Ireland into this province in one season we cannot tell."

Luke could. In the end, there would be thousands of deaths, both Irish and Canadian.

He was so absorbed in the article that he didn't realize that his activity had drawn a curious little crowd. When he looked up he realized that a small group of urchins had gathered around him.

"Wotcha doin' then, mister?"

"I'm reading the paper."

Several of them blinked in thought, as though this was astounding information to absorb.

"What's it say then?" one boy asked.

He could scarcely repeat Lord Grey's dismissive words to them. He flipped to the front page, where most of the notices were printed, looking for an item that might amuse them. He scanned these and the letters to the editor and was soon rewarded with something lighter. There was a letter from an aggrieved citizen who took objection to the city's bylaw requiring that dogs be tied up and not allowed to roam the streets. The man quite rightly pointed out that Kingston's streets were equally full of hogs, and that council should consider the capture and destruction of these as well.

"Too right," one of the boys said. "One of them near ran me over t'other day."

Another agreed. It seemed that they had all had close encounters with Kingston's porcine population.

In an article on the same page, the Victory Circus from the nearby town of Prescott received an excellent review, with special mention made of Mr. Madigan the Trick Rider and Mr. Gossin, the original American clown. This was greeted with politeness, and it was only after Luke explained what a circus was, and what went on there, that the children looked suitably impressed.

"Do you think we might go see it?" one little boy asked. "I'd like to see the horse rider, I would, especially if he can ride standin' on his head."

Luke wasn't entirely sure that that particular talent was included in Mr. Madigan's repertoire, and, in any event, it was unlikely that any of these children would be able to find the coins it would take to gain them admission.

"It looks like they may have gone on to the next city now," he said, and the boy's face fell.

Several adults had drifted in his direction and sat hunkered down with the children. Among them were Rennie Doyle and her sister, Mary, who pushed past the children to sit on the ground to Luke's right. He ignored them while he scanned the paper looking for suitable news. And then he found a notice that elicited loud guffaws from everyone:

Whereas my wife, Mrs. Bridget McDallogh, is again walked away with herself, and left me with five small children and her poor blind mother, and left nobody else to take care of the house & home and I hear she has taken up with Tim Ghigan, the lame fiddler, this is to give her notice that I will not pay for bite or sup on her account to man or mortal, and that she had better never show the mark of her ten toes near my house again.

P.S. Tim had better keep out of my sight.

Some things, it seemed, were universal.

"Read us more then, Dr. Luke," one of the children called.

There was no more news in the paper that he wished to share with them, so he protested that he was tired. The mosquitoes were also out in full force by that time. "Time for us all to be abed," he said, "but come back another night and I'll read some more."

Grumbling, they rose and wandered away, slapping at the bugs as they went.

Still, Luke couldn't sleep. He stared at the rough plaster of the ceiling above him, listening to the groaning of the house and the muffled voices of his neighbours and the loud snores of the carpenter's helper who rented the room beside him.

He debated getting out of bed and standing at the window as he had done many nights before, but his legs ached at the thought. Finally, he became aware that he was no longer able to ignore his own smell. This was a combination of many things — the sour wine he spooned out during the day, the thin gruel he ladled, the filth he walked through, the miasma that hung in the rafters from so many fetid breaths, the dead bodies he helped to lower into the burial pit. These smells had seeped into his clothing and arose now to creep into his nostrils and choke him. Underneath the smell that was in his clothing was yet another smell, and this one was the worst. It was the smell of his own unwashed body, and he realized that it had been some time since he had done more than sluice down his face or rinse his hands.

He could claim an excuse for this. He worked long and hard in the sheds each day and had little time for personal considerations. He knew his mother would never have accepted such an excuse. She would have insisted that he take a bar of harsh, stinging soap and scrub his face, arms, and feet each night, no matter where he had been or what he had done during the day. She would not have allowed him to sit at the supper table until he had done so. He resolved to find the time somewhere to attend to this, if only because then he might be able to enjoy a night's sleep.

The next morning Luke gathered up his blanket and took it out into the sun to shake it. He was disgusted to find three lice curled in the folds. The emigrants were infested, he knew, but somehow the fact that these tiny creatures had jumped to his own bedding jolted him. He hauled the thin mattress outside and shook it out as well.

That evening, though he was tired beyond belief and longed to simply throw himself down somewhere and rest, he walked along the shore until he found a tiny indentation in the coastline, not enough to call a cove, but well-screened by bushes. He stripped off every article of clothing he had on and submerged himself in the water, hastily scrubbing with the soap and piece of rag he had borrowed from the Sisters. He had taken a handful of old newspapers to dry himself with — he would return them later as they could still be used for cleaning, and he had been unable to locate anything else to use as a towel. At least it was summer and he was unlikely to take a chill if he didn't get himself quite dry.

After a careful look in all directions to make sure that there was no one within eyeshot, he emerged from the water and balled up a fistful of papers to dry off with. They didn't work particularly well in this capacity, but he was able to dry himself enough to don his second set of underclothes.

He took the articles he had discarded and squatted by the shore, scrubbing them against a piece of flat rock. He knew enough not to attempt this with his trousers or jacket — he had seen his mother at the washtub often enough to understand that these would shrink beyond salvaging if he did so, but he wet the rag and carefully sponged them down, hoping that this would be enough to remove the offensive smells they had absorbed. He paid careful attention to the folds and seams, but he found no more evidence of lice. Then he spread them over a nearby bush. He would let them dry a little before he put them on again.

Now that he was clean, he felt much better, and he resolved to find something that he could use as a towel on future occasions. He had used only a handful of the papers he had brought with him. Idly he picked up one of these to read as he waited. It was an issue of *The Toronto Mirror* — a paper that didn't often make its way as far as Kingston — dated August 10, and its editor expressed howls of outrage at an incident that had occurred a few days previously.

Apparently, Toronto's dead were taken from the waterfront, hospital, and sheds to the cemetery at St. Paul's, on the outskirts of the city. At least those who could be identified as Catholic were taken there, and that was apparently most of them. As in Kingston, individual carters had been commissioned for this task.

One of these, according to the newspaper, was a man named Ryan. He had been proceeding toward the cemetery when a lady's hat had been blown into the street by a sudden gust of wind. Ryan's horse had shied and the wagon overturned, spilling the coffin into the street. The ill-constructed box had flown open, revealing, much to the horror of passing pedestrians, that there were in fact two dead bodies crammed inside.

The Mirror howled for a full investigation into Mr. Ryan, Mr. Ryan's horse, Mr. Ryan's *Catholic* associations, and the mechanism whereby two bodies had been surreptitiously crammed into one small coffin. The motivation for this act was, apparently, quite clear — the hospital was granted a per diem by the city for each patient it looked after. Someone was distorting the numbers and, the paper claimed, pocketing the difference. It urged the local police to take a hard look at the tallies.

Luke was intrigued, and wondered if Flea Mullen was involved somehow. He was a carter. He hadn't been carrying the dead that afternoon at Toronto's waterfront, but rather the living, in the form of emigrant women. Luke wondered if he sometimes carried other cargo as well. He thought back to that day. There had been a crowd of emigrants, but it had been early in the season. Only a few hundred had arrived at that point, not the thousands that subsequently came up the river. Perhaps Flea had changed the nature of his enterprise to the more lucrative trade in double-stuffed coffins, although it had been apparent that he hadn't been working for himself. He had made reference to someone named Hans, and had passed a parcel to the constable who had escorted the women to the wagon. What had been going on?

Luke tried to remember more of the details of that afternoon encounter, but he couldn't quite bring it all to mind. He remembered thinking that the whole thing was odd, but hadn't paid much attention beyond that. It hadn't seemed important then, and too much else had happened in the meantime.

In any event, it appeared that the Toronto port officers would now be under scrutiny, as would all of the other carters. Had Flea Mullen decided to escape notice by signing on with Captain Bellwood and disappearing down the lake? But Bellwood had mentioned the mysterious Hans as well, hadn't he? And there really was no evidence that Flea Mullen was involved in anything unethical, just a feeling on Luke's part that something wasn't quite right.

However, it was clear that someone was making a tidy sum of money from the two-body subterfuge, and *The Mirror* was unlikely to stop writing about it until it was determined just who that was:

Two bodies found in one coffin! Mirabile!! — But who put the two bodies there? Answer that, ye men of the quill. Well what has since come to light? Why, just this, nearly 300 patients less in Hospital than Mr. Toby Townsend's daily bulletins have recorded; and Mr. Const. Townsend in his Cab, every morning visited the Hospital and brought to the City Hall, to our bepraised Board of Health, the Hospital returns. Three hundred patients … Not in the Sheds! Where then? In the Shades? Oh no! … Mr. Townsend visited the Hospital. No doubt! Counted heads, but forgot to search for bodies. Three hundred unaccounted for? Where are they?

They "left the Hospital of their own accord." Fortunate mortals! "They were tee-totalers and could not swallow their share of the Wine and Brandy; so they made tracks."

According to *The Mirror*, there were two motives for the over-reporting of numbers — the per diem and the amount of wine and brandy that was allotted to each patient. The question of the per diem was easily answered. Hide the bodies and over-report the numbers. Luke was sure that there must be someone on the Board of Health who was complicit in accepting Townsend's figures at face value, and *The Mirror* certainly insinuated this, not neglecting to cast aspersions on a rival paper while they were at it:

The sapient *Colonist* — the figure-head of the glorious Board of Health not long since stated that 84 deaths per week were equal to an average mortality of one-half percent. Well, well! Eighty-four deaths in one week out of about 500 patients, an average mortality of one-half percent!

About 2,000 patients have been admitted into the Hospital since the commencement of the season; and of this number about 500 are returned as dead: 500 are yet under Brandy and Wine: 300 are in John H. Dunn's House and Stables convalescing — that is coming back to the shades, at the rate of 30 per week! This is a beautiful "one-half percent." About 200 gallons of Wine & Brandy have drunk to the health of the Patients: not forgetting absent friends.

All this is called Medical care of the sick emigrants.

The same jiggery-pokery with numbers would serve the fraudulent diversion of wine and brandy — claim the spirits in the name of patients who were no longer there. Sell the casks to local tavern owners who were willing to ask no questions and return them once they'd been emptied. Or better yet — and suddenly the empty barrels Luke had seen being loaded onto *The Bellweather* began to take on a sinister aspect — switch out full barrels for appropriately marked empty ones. Just exactly what was Flea Mullen mixed up in?

The newspaper noted that emigration agent Anthony Hawke had been appointed as an independent investigator to scrutinize the discrepancy in the books, and that answers to everyone's questions would be forthcoming. No doubt he would discover that Toby Townsend was indeed responsible for the over-reporting of patients in the hospital, as the newspaper claimed, but it remained to be seen whether or not the investigation led to anyone else, or if the "anyone else" included Flea Mullen or Hans. In any event, Luke doubted that a half-glimpsed marking on a barrel constituted evidence of anything.

He put his outer clothing back on — it was dry enough, he judged — and wrapped his still-sodden underclothing in the newspapers he hadn't used. He would have to hang his wet things in his room and let them dry before he could repeat the evening ablutions, but he was determined to do this on a regular basis. He felt like a new man, and was sure that he would be able to drift peacefully off to sleep, in spite of the sultriness of the night.

As he was walking back, Luke passed a luxuriant patch of wild mint. He stooped and picked a generous sprig and took it with him. When he returned to his room, he hung his wet clothes on the pegs that had been nailed into a board on the back of the door and then went back out into the night.

He needed to find a fire and a pot, so that he could boil up a little water and make an infusion of the mint. He was sure that he could borrow a pot from one of the sheds, but he was loathe to walk back down to the lake again. Some of the refreshing feeling he had gained from his swim had already begun to wear off, and much more in the way of physical exertion would dissipate it entirely.

He would have been welcomed by any of the people whose minor ailments he had treated, if he could find them, but they had either retired for the night or had given up on Kingston and moved on entirely. It was such a transient population that familiar faces vanished without a word, whole families melted away as if by magic. In most cases, he had not even learned their names.

However, when he walked around the corner, there sat Mrs. Shanahan with her children, the youngest of them asleep in the yard. Rennie Doyle was there with her mewling baby.

"Where's your sister?" he asked.

"Oh, off down the shore somewhere," she said, with a vague wave in the general direction of the lake. "There's just me tonight."

Mrs. Shanahan seemed pleased to see him as well. "Dr. Luke! Come to check on me thumb? There's no need, you did such a good job you can hardly tell where it was." She held it out. Only a thin white line remained, and he had to look closely to find it.

"I'm pleased to see that," he said, "although I didn't really come tonight for the doctoring. I came to ask a favour."

"Anything you like."

"I want to make an infusion, but I have no fire or pot for boiling water. And I need to find a bottle to put my concoction in afterward, as well."

"You're welcome to use my fire, and my pot, as well. But I don't have a bottle to spare."

And like a pale shadow, the girl, Anna, disappeared. By the time the water in Mrs. Shanahan's pot had begun to boil, she had returned with a dark brown medicine bottle. There was no stopper with it, but Luke could make do with a wadded-up piece of newspaper.

"Perfect," he said and smiled at her. He got nothing but a blank stare in return.

He tore the leaves from the branch of mint and shredded them, doing his best not to bruise them in the process, then he stuffed them down into the medicine bottle and filled it almost to the top with the boiling water.

"Now I just need to wait until it cools a bit so I can carry it home."

"What are going to do with it then?" Mrs. Shanahan asked.

"I'm going to sponge my clothes with it and hope the mint keeps the lice away. I don't know if it will work or not, but at the very least I may smell a little better."

"Lice is bad," Mrs. Shanahan said. "It's the lice that causes the fever."

"Oh, I don't know about that," Luke said, "I just don't like them much."

"It's the lice and the flies and the other funny bugs carries the fever. I know. I seen it happen."

Luke shrugged. "You could be right. The doctors can't seem to tell us what causes it, so your guess is as good as theirs."

"Lice. Lice and flies," Mrs. Shanahan said with a stubborn set to her mouth, "I pick 'em off every night and burn 'em."

She grabbed the child closest to her and began obsessively picking through its hair. "Lice. Lice and bugs," she mumbled as she did it.

Rennie watched her for a moment and then began tentatively examining her own child's head.

Luke left them to it. He cradled the still-warm bottle in the crook of his arm and returned to his room. Once inside, he poured some of the infusion onto his handkerchief and began to sponge his jacket, taking great care to thoroughly wet down the seams and under the collar before he hung it on the remaining peg behind the door. He did the same with his trousers and laid them over the windowsill, where the slight breeze would blow over them. As he had hoped, the scent of the mint wafted into the room. He felt much better than he had, more comfortable, clean and sleepy. He resolved to repeat the evening's exercise as often as possible. His mother was right, he reflected as he drifted off — there is no excuse to be dirty.

Chapter 14

When Luke arrived at the makeshift kitchen the next morning, only Mrs. Thompson was there. Her face was grim as she chopped a handful of wilted carrots.

"Two of the ladies are ill," she said, "and the others are afraid to come here. One of the ministers was supposed to help me this morning, but he's sick as well."

"Is it the fever?" Luke asked.

"They say not, but I don't see what else it could be."

Nor could Luke. It was clear that the efforts to quarantine the emigrants had been a complete failure and that the fever was spreading far beyond the confines of the hospitals. If volunteers were succumbing to the disease, it was unlikely that anyone would be willing to replace them, and this shortfall in helping hands was occurring just at the moment when the need was greatest.

Luke began to understand how a disease such as typhus might spread. With hospitals bursting and resources strained, it would be easy enough to persuade oneself that a slightly feverish-looking man really only had a cold; that a child with a rash was suffering from summer complaint; that the woman moaning on the deck of the ship had anything but typhus. How could you hold them, when you had no place to put them? Better to move them all along in the hope that somewhere farther west could better cope with them. There would be no resolution to this, he knew, until the shipping season ended and the river iced over, but that wouldn't happen for some weeks yet.

He should have left for Montreal a week ago, he realized. Classes were due to start in a few days, and he had yet to register for them, or find a room, or part-time employment, or complete any of the arrangements that he needed to have in place for the coming year. But how could he leave Kingston, with the sheds so full and so few to help?

He and Mrs. Thompson served up the morning's meal, which was becoming less of a stew and more of a soup as donations of food fell off. He then went on to the sheds and was saddened but not surprised when he discovered that John Porter had died in the night. The man had struggled through severe delirium and racking pain, the rash and the headache, fighting ferociously to ward off what had seemed to be imminent death. His fever had abated, and he had had a few days of lucidity, but then he had begun to cough, hacking up gobs of greenish pus that quickly became tinged with red.

Sister Bourbonnière had established a routine for dealing with the dead and insisted on the proper keeping of records. After a trial period, when he had evidently shown a clerkship consistent with her standards, she was willing, at times, to delegate this task to Luke.

He had little expectation that he would find much of anything on the dead man's person. No doubt he had passed whatever monies and belongings he possessed to Anna for safekeeping. Nevertheless, he retrieved the big leather-bound ledger the Sister used to record information. Luke made a note of the name, then looked under the bed and the pillow, and thoroughly searched through the bedding, Sometimes patients hid their things, when they had no one to take them. As he expected, there was nothing.

Then came the more odious part of the task, when he must fish through the man's pockets and clothing. He could find nothing except for a scrap of fabric tucked between Porter's vest and his shirt. Luke nearly left it where it was. It could have no value. But in the name of thoroughness, he drew it out. It was nothing but a tiny scrap of green ribbon.

Luke stared at it in puzzlement for a moment, not sure of its import. Somewhere in the back of his mind there was a tiny spark of memory, something he had heard about a green ribbon, but he couldn't coax the details to the front of his mind. He tucked the ribbon into his pocket. John Porter had no possessions on him, or any pockets even. That was all there was.

He and one of the local priests moved the body to the dead house behind the shed. John Porter would join

the tiers of bodies that now lay in the pits, the bottom-
most settling into corruption to make a foundation for
the newly arrived.

In the meantime, Porter's bunk was needed, and
there was no delay in filling it — by the time he returned
to the shed, one of the sicker patients had already been
moved from the floor to the bed.

Throughout the rest of the day, Luke wondered
how best to tell Anna Porter, although for all he knew
she had already slipped unnoticed into the shed and
discovered that her father had died. She had seemed
quite prepared for this eventuality. "He's dead," she
had stated, even though at that moment it had seemed
that John Porter would successfully fight off the disease. The sisters, Rennie and Mary, said that she was a
merrow, a sea creature who could predict the passing
of souls, but this was nonsense. She had been trying
to ward off death, he was sure, in the same way that
some people claimed never to be lucky, in the hopes
that luck would more easily come their way by virtue
of their denial.

She was such an odd little girl. She seemed perfectly
happy staying with Mrs. Shanahan, but he knew that
he should inquire as to whether there were relatives
somewhere in Canada who might take her in. After
all, Mrs. Shanahan, besides being quite mad, was not
kin to the Porters. It sat uneasily on Luke's conscience
to leave a child in the care of a madwoman when there
might be someone better-suited to look after her. Her
father had mentioned two other children, he recalled
— a boy who had been quarantined in Montreal and a

sister who had gone looking for baggage. Perhaps they might yet be found.

After he could carry no more water, empty no more slops, and bury no more bodies, Luke reluctantly dragged himself back to Stuartsville. He discovered Mrs. Shanahan pacing up and down her tiny yard.

"I can't keep her," she said when she saw Luke. "She's eight. There can't be eight!"

For a moment he thought that she was referring to Anna, who, for all Luke knew could well be eight years old, but then he realized that the bundle in Mrs. Shanahan's arms was emitting a low whine. It could only be Deirdre Doyle.

"She's eight. That's not right." She held the bundle out to him. "You'll have to go find Rennie and give her back."

"But where is Rennie?"

"Gone. She said she'd be back, but now there's the wrong number."

"Gone? Where?"

"She went with Mullen," Anna said. "She said she'd be back tonight."

"With Mullen? Which Mullen?" Luke's first thought was of Flea, but he couldn't imagine a girl like Rennie Doyle taking up with a man like Flea Mullen.

Mrs. Shanahan was holding the baby at arm's length now, as if it were something that might contaminate her if she held it closer. Luke took the crying bundle from her and turned to Anna. "Does she drink?"

When Anna nodded, he reached into his pocket. "Can you run to the market and see whether or not there's anyone there with milk? Goat would be best, but cow's milk would do as well." He handed her the coins. "And buy it, don't just take it, do you hear me?"

Anna disappeared and Luke jostled the baby, but it did little to mollify her. Mrs. Shanahan had, however, calmed down, now that she was no longer holding the child. She hunkered down by her fire and moved the pot over the flame.

The evening had taken off in a strange direction, Luke thought. He had expected to be comforting a little girl who had lost her father, not a baby, and certainly not Mrs. Shanahan.

"When exactly did Rennie leave?" he asked.

Mrs. Shanahan shrugged. "This morning. She said Pierce Mullen was waiting for her down by the wharf. She always did have a soft spot for Pierce. I don't know why she married Connor Doyle in the first place, when it was Pierce she really wanted. Silly girl."

Pierce Mullen? In Kingston? He must have joined the regular crew of *The Bellweather*, which continued its ferrying of emigrants from Kingston to points west. Unless he had returned on his own in order to check on his brother, Dermot, who still lay in the grip of fever in one of the sheds.

He hadn't known that Rennie and the Mullens were acquainted, although he shouldn't have been surprised. Mrs. Shanahan seemed to know an enormous number of the emigrants, and Father Higgins, when explaining why he could not carry on as planned to Wellington, had stated that "half his parish" was here.

"You knew Rennie from before?" he asked.

"Oh yes, I knew them all. Rennie, the Mullens, the Porters. Old arguments, it's all old arguments now, isn't it? As if any of it matters anymore."

"But why didn't Rennie leave the baby with her sister?"

Mrs. Shanahan shrugged and subsided into a confused mumble as she poked a wooden spoon into the pot.

Luke could pick out only a few of her words here and there. "Can't have eight … seven gets to heaven … make it right again." Occasionally she would cross herself and mutter what Luke assumed was a prayer, although it was in a language that he didn't understand.

Eventually, Anna returned with a pail of milk and a little tin cup. Luke poured a little out and held the cup up to the baby's mouth. She tried to bat it away.

"Do you have any bread?" he asked, and Mrs. Shanahan produced a heel that was only a little bluish at one end. He tore off a chunk and soaked it in the milk, then held it up to Deirdre's mouth. She sucked at it eagerly and gummed the softened bread. Then he tried the cup again and she was able to take a sip, although a lot of it ran back out of the sides of her mouth. It appeared that the milk-soaked bread might prove the best solution.

Eventually she took enough to satisfy her and she dropped off into a fitful sleep.

"What do you want me to do with her?" he asked.

"I can't have eight," Mrs. Shanahan said firmly. "Eight is the wrong number."

Luke thought that unless he could find Mary, he would have to take the baby to the Sisters — they had had orphans under their care prior to their breaking cloister to take up their work with the emigrants — but that would mean taking the baby into the heart of the fever, and the Sisters already had enough to do without having to deal with a fussy infant. He would have to find Mary.

He laid the sleeping baby down beside one of the smaller children, who began idly swatting the flies away from her. The child could wait for the moment.

"Do you want to take a walk with me, Anna?" he said.

"I already know. Me Da's dead."

So the little ghost had slipped into the shed unseen. Luke was just as happy about this. She would have had time to come to terms with what had happened. He hated the idea of being the one to impart such awful news.

"Do you know where your family was headed, Anna? Did you ever hear someone mention a place?" They might have been on their way to join a relative somewhere, someone perhaps who had sent them money to help them get here.

Anna nodded. "Canada. Where the potatoes fall down from the sky."

No doubt she was too young to have been privy to the family's plans, and had too sketchy a notion of geography, Luke thought. Even if she had heard some place name, it wouldn't have meant anything to her. But then she went on. "Uncle George wrote us a letter and told us about the potatoes."

"Uncle George? You have an Uncle George who was here already? Do you know where?"

She nodded. "In Canada."

"Do you know what happened to the letter?"

She nodded again. "It's in the trunk." She disappeared into the shack and dragged out a small, battered, leather-covered trunk.

Mrs. Shanahan watched her with suspicion. "What are you going to do with that?" she asked.

"I'm just going to show him." She undid the stiff leather straps and opened it. There was not much inside — a Bible, a couple of pots, an old shawl — and under this a thin sheaf of letters tied up with string. Anna picked up the letters and handed them to Luke.

Two of them were from a George Harliss — "Uncle George," apparently. Luke looked at the outside of these carefully, but the postmark was blurred with damp and difficult to make out. Beverly? Bexley? Bewdley? He hadn't heard of any of those places. The ink of the handwritten cancellation dates was more legible, though, and indicated dates from two and three years previously.

He scanned the body of the letters, looking for any information that might prove helpful. They were difficult to read, having been cross-written in a close hand, the sheets of paper covered with writing in one direction, then turned sideways, so that extra lines of text could be added.

It appeared that George Harliss had emigrated to Canada West and secured some land that he intended to farm, although nowhere in the letters did he specify exactly where. He did, however, mention that he disembarked from a steamer at Cobourg. Most of his missives were inquiries concerning various members of the family and it was clear that he was expecting the John Porter family to join him. This was evidently an emigration that had been planned long before the current crisis in Ireland. A David was mentioned, but it didn't appear from the context that he was intending to emigrate with John.

In the second letter the Porters received, dated July 16, 1846, Harliss painted a rosy picture of farming in Canada, promising that riches awaited them all:

This is truly a land of wheat — field after field of golden grain — and of fine orchards, handsome herds of cattle, prosperous towns built around busy mills, with every farmer in the land clamouring for help at harvest. No one works for another for long. As soon as a few pounds are in hand, any labourer can find his own land on easy terms.

Last fall I secured a lot of one hundred acres of the finest land and I am in the process of putting up a cabin. Timber abounds and has provided the lumber for my little abode, although a great deal of this must be cleared before I can begin to plough. They say that once sown, the wheat springs up out of the ground as if by magic, and selling this provides the money needed to stock the farm. In the meantime, an acre or so put in potatoes and turnips are provision enough to see me through the winter.

Once you are here, our combined labour will very shortly make this a model farm, and we can begin to acquire cattle, sheep, etc. in very short order. This is truly a land of plenty. One scarcely needs but a clearing and a good livelihood is assured.

Letters like this had lured many an emigrant to Canada, Luke knew, emphasizing the fertility of the land and minimizing the backbreaking labour of clearing it. After at least a year on his land, Harliss had not yet finished a dwelling, and had evidently chopped out only a small section of land — enough for potatoes and turnips, subsistence crops — and was awaiting the arrival of the Porter family to clear enough land for wheat. Without the help of unpaid family labour, Luke thought it unlikely that Harliss would be able to make a go of it. And if he was struggling that hard, he would scarcely be in a position to take on the responsibility of a young orphaned niece.

"May I look at the Bible?" Luke asked. The girl nodded and he picked it out of the bottom of the trunk. There were no notes in it, no listing of births or deaths or marriages, no information that would help him find her relatives. But then, in the back of it, he found three more letters. They were all addressed to different people in Banesalley, County Kerry, Ireland — a Patrick Shaughnessy, a Declan O'Toole, and Mrs. S. Grogan.

"Are these people relatives of yours?" he asked, and read out the names.

"No," Anna said. "They're just pieces of paper that someone gave us. In case we met up with any of them."

This sounded odd to Luke, but Anna continued to regard him with her pale, expressionless eyes, no flicker of emotion behind them. He supposed the Porters might have been asked to look for people, in much the same way that he himself had been asked to look for Charley Gallagher. The letters must have been given as a means of identification.

"What about the rest of your family, Anna? What's happened to them?"

The little girl was very matter of fact as she related her family's tragedies. "George and Grace got sick and they made them get off the boat. They're dead. Then Jack got sick. He's dead too. Maggie went looking for the other trunk. Mam and Da and I went one way and Maggie went the other, to try to find it. But when we got here, me Mam died. And now me Da's dead too."

There were two routes that led to Kingston — up the Ottawa River to Bytown and then south again along the Rideau Canal, or up the St. Lawrence, working past the rapids. Maggie was obviously old enough to travel by herself, and had probably been given instructions to meet her father and sister at their ultimate destination, somewhere farther to the west. John Porter hadn't anticipated falling ill and being hospitalized at Kingston, and Maggie would have been unaware that the rest of her family had been held up. She would have continued on her journey, hopeful that they would all meet up as arranged.

If Maggie was old enough to travel alone, she would be old enough to take responsibility for her younger sister, and, Luke figured, the best place to look for her would be wherever George Harliss was. He looked at the smeared postmark again, but it was no more legible on the second perusal.

"Put your uncle's letters away safely," he said. "I may need to look at them again, but in the meantime I'll write a letter to him to see if he knows where your sister is."

It was Mrs. Shanahan who replied. "You can't take Anna," she wailed. "Then there would only be six."

"There will still be seven if Rennie Doyle doesn't come back, and I can't find Mary," Luke pointed out. "I don't suppose you could look after the baby for a little while until we sort it out? It will be seven one way or the other, I promise."

Mrs. Shanahan blinked a few times while she digested this proposal. "I suppose," she said. "But only for a little while. You tell Rennie Doyle to come back."

"I don't want to live with Uncle George," Anna said. "I don't even know him."

"I'm only writing to him to see if he knows where Maggie is," Luke said. "You'd live with Maggie, wouldn't you?"

She considered this for a moment. "But Maggie's dead."

She said this with the same lack of emotion she had shown when she stated that her father was dead.

It unnerved Luke, the more so because her statement had been accurate.

"Maybe, if I can find Maggie, I could bring her here," he said.

"But then there would be eight again," Mrs. Shanahan said. "There can't be eight."

"Would that be better, if she came here?" Luke asked, ignoring Mrs. Shanahan's protests.

"But then there'd be eight!" Mrs. Shanahan's wails sounded like some strange choral commentary, Luke thought, almost like an exhorter at a Methodist camp meeting.

Anna fixed him with her unblinking, unnerving stare: "Maggie's dead."

"We don't know that for sure," Luke said. "Maybe she found the trunk and went to your Uncle George's. Or maybe she's somewhere else, but I'll try to find her, all right?"

"But me Da knocked down Mrs. Shanahan's house."

This made no sense to Luke, but when he pressed Anna for more details, she refused to answer.

Luke was just about to enter his lodging and go to his room, when he was hailed by Rennie Doyle's sister, Mary.

"Have you seen Rennie?" she asked.

"Apparently she's gone off with one of the Mullens," he said.

Mary blushed a little. "Pierce is here? If I'd known that, I'd have —" She bit her lip to stop herself from saying whatever she had intended.

"The baby is with Mrs. Shanahan. You'd best retrieve her, because the good lady is quite upset about it."

"Thanks," Mary said and dashed around the corner before he could ask where she herself had been. It was none of his business, he supposed. And if Mary retrieved the baby, at least there was one less defenceless child in the hands of an absolute lunatic.

Chapter 15

Luke was allowed no lamp or candle in his room at the boarding house, but he rose early the next morning and by the wan light of first dawn took out his pen. He would write to "Uncle" George Harliss, in spite of the fact that he couldn't make out the origin of his letters. He would simply write to all three of the places he thought it might be. Briefly, he wondered if he should wait and consult his father. Thaddeus seemed to know every small village in Canada West, and might make a shrewder guess as to which one was correct.

That would delay the sending of the letter, though. Better to write all three and hope one of them hit the mark. As he took out the stationery box he had been given, he wondered why he was going to such trouble for one child when the streets of Kingston were full of orphans and the newspapers full of notices posted by frantic parents looking for lost children. One thing at a time, he decided. He couldn't help them all, but it was within his power to help one of them, so he would do his best.

Luke wrote standing up, the wall serving as a desk, the windowsill as a ledge for his inkpot: "Dear Mr. Harliss," he began. What now? How to explain this appalling situation in terms that were less than appalling? He couldn't: "I can only hope that this letter has reached the correct hands. I am sorry to inform you that your relative, John Porter, has succumbed to the malignant fever that is currently devastating the emigrant population."

Too stark, Luke thought, but changing it now would waste an entire sheet of paper. Besides, how does one break such bad news gently? He continued:

Mrs. Porter and two of the children have died as well. A son named Jack was detained at one of the ports and his fate is unknown. However, a daughter named Margaret travelled ahead of the family and I do not know what has happened to her.

One of the smaller children, Anna, is here in Kingston. She is being looked after at present, but with her father dead and her remaining family unaccounted for, her future is uncertain. I am writing in the hope that you are in a position to retrieve her, and to provide her with a home.

If I have indeed reached the correct address, please respond to

Here Luke hesitated. He had not yet made up his mind what he was going to do, and so had no notion of where he might be by the time Harliss responded. With no fixed address, the letter might well go astray. And then he had an idea. He wrote: "Luke Lewis, c/o Thaddeus Lewis, Wellington P.O, Canada West."

His father would know where to find him.

He copied the letter twice and addressed it three times: *George Harliss c/o Bewdley P.O., Beverley P.O., Bexley P.O.*

Surely one of the arrows would find its target.

It was nearly noon by the time Luke had helped the carters load and bury the eight souls who had died during the night. It would be a few hours yet before he would be needed at the brewery wharf to help with the newest arrivals, so he went in search of Father Higgins, who he was told was with a dying man in the fever shed at the foot of Emily Street.

The priest was at the far end of one row, his cross held before him while he murmured his incantation in a language that Luke thought must be Latin. He had only just been in time, apparently, for a few minutes later Higgins left the man's side. Luke located a stretcher and walked with it down the aisle.

When Higgins saw Luke, he waved away the other priest who had stepped forward to help in the removal of the body. "We'll do this," he said.

As soon as they slid the body onto the stretcher and manoeuvred it into the aisle, the priest snatched the blanket that had covered the bed. A quick shake to dislodge the lice, and the cot would be ready for its next occupant.

Wordlessly, they deposited the corpse beside the shed — the first one there, but likely a harbinger of what the rest of the day would bring.

"Are you on your way to the wharf?" Higgins asked. "There's another two waiting for me there. I'll walk with you, if you don't mind."

Luke was only too glad to oblige, not only because he had questions that he hoped the priest might answer, but also because he enjoyed the man's company so much.

"You knew John Porter, you said one time."

"I did," Higgins replied.

"Do you know his daughter? The odd-looking one with the scaly skin."

"Anna? Everybody in Banesalley knows Anna. Or everyone who *was* in Banesalley, I should say, since I expect the entire village is either dead, scattered, or over here by now."

"Someone told me she's a merrow."

Higgins snorted. "Ah yes, Anna Porter is a merrow. And Florence Mullen is a cluricaune. And the fairy world is responsible for all the evils in the world."

"A cluri-*what?*"

"A cluricaune. A wizened little dwarf who causes mischief. And come to think on it, that's not a bad description of Flea Mullen."

"Do you know Bridie Shanahan?"

"Of course."

"She's taken Anna Porter in."

"Really?" Higgins looked puzzled at this.

"Mrs. Shanahan got quite upset when I offered to try to find what's left of Anna's family. She said there had to be seven, but I don't know what that means."

"The Shanahans had seven girls, I know that," Higgins said. "I don't know what's happened to them."

"And she said poor Charley Gallagher was shot down, but there was no point in anybody being sorry about it because it wouldn't bring him back. And Anna said that her father pulled Mrs. Shanahan's house down. What happened?"

The priest stopped walking and turned to Luke. "What do you want to know about that for? These are old quarrels that happened an entire ocean away. Bridie Shanahan is right, being sorry won't bring anybody back, least of all the thousands of people who have died of poverty and starvation and a government that doesn't give two figs whether they live or die. We have a great deal more to worry about than what happened to Bridie Shanahan's cabin."

"But why would someone tear it down?"

Higgins started walking again, his pace a little quicker than before. "The landlord decided to clear them out. Have you ever witnessed an eviction?"

"Of course not," Luke said. "It doesn't happen a lot here." Although he did spare a thought for the man in the timber trade who had now lost his warehouse to Archibald McFaul. That was different, though. Presumably the man still had somewhere to house his family.

"A landlord can demand his rent at any time," Higgins said. "Since most of his tenants are in arrears all the time anyway, if he wants to be rid of them, all he has to do is post a notice stating that they have to be paid up by a certain date. When they can't pay, he orders them out."

"So when the rent isn't paid by the date posted ..." Luke prompted.

"A notice of eviction is served, and on the appointed day the bailiff and the estate agent and a crew of destructives show up."

"What are destructives?"

"Men who are hired to destroy the cabins. It's not hard work. In fact, it's pathetically easy to tear down an Irish cabin — they're so flimsy to begin with. All you have to do is tie a rope around the roof beam and run it out through the door. A few quick chops, a pull on the rope, and the roof comes crashing down. The rest can be easily dismantled with a few crowbars. That way the evicted tenants can't just creep back into the cabin and squat there."

"But where do they go?" Luke had a sickening suspicion that he knew the answer.

"Out on the road. Up in the hills. To the work-houses. They don't really have anywhere to go."

"And on the day the Shanahans were turned out?"

"Why do you want to know all this?" Higgins again demanded.

"I don't know," Luke said with a shrug. "I'm just curious. Why did Anna say it was her father who pulled down the Shanahans' house?"

"Because he did, although he wasn't the only one." Higgins exhaled in one large exasperated puff of air. "There had been a large number of evictions on that particular estate already. The tenants were being well and truly cleared out, and every single time, there were the Porters, standing in line ready to help clear them. Mind you, if it hadn't been them, it would have been someone else."

"But there was trouble this time?" Luke asked.

"Yes, and the bailiff must have been expecting it, because he armed some of the destructives with guns — three hunting rifles so old they looked like they'd fall apart if anyone tried to fire them — but a gun is a gun and threatening nonetheless, I suppose. John Porter had just fastened the rope around the roof beam when a mob of men arrived to protest. Some rocks were thrown, some shots were fired, and at the end of it a man lay dead."

"Charley Gallagher," Luke said.

"Yes, Charley Gallagher."

"And everybody thinks one of the Porters fired the shot?"

Higgins shrugged. "All I know is that David Porter disappeared the next day."

"Where do you think he went?" Luke asked.

"It would be easy enough to disappear, if you had a head start. Ireland's roads are clogged with people looking for food and shelter. He wouldn't have to go far before he could find a place where no one knew him from Adam."

They had reached the brewery. The rest of Luke's questions would have to wait, he realized, for two steamboats were approaching the wharf, each low in the water from the number of emigrants it carried. Wagons were already arriving to carry the sick away. It would be just another day of carting bodies, Luke thought, from the wharf to the shed to the pit.

Just before they parted company, though, Luke turned to the priest. "One more question, that's all," he said. "Were the Mullens there?"

But Higgins strode off without answering.

Chapter 16

September 16, 1847

Dear Pa, Ma and Everybody in Wellington,

I must make this a short letter as it's quite late and the light is fading, but I thought I should let you know that I have decided to delay my departure for Montreal. I have already missed the beginning of the academic year, and there is no point in going there to do nothing when my assistance is so desperately needed here.

Emigrants continue to arrive in droves every day, although I am told that their numbers should soon start to dwindle as we approach the end of the shipping season. In the meantime, many of the volunteers have contracted the disease and others are now afraid to take their places. Sister Bourbonnière has requested additional help from her Mother House in Montreal, but she is not optimistic that they will be able to spare anyone.

Under the circumstances, I feel I ought to stay. I am hoping that I will be able to register for my courses after Christmas. Otherwise I will wait until next year.

I hope you are all well, and I would welcome a visit should you find an excuse to come to Kingston.

Your loving son, Luke

The oppressive summer heat had finally broken. Although the days were still warm, each evening brought a freshening breeze that blew the mosquitoes away and washed the air clean of the smoke and haze that had hung over the city for weeks.

Luke settled down on the front stoop with a bundle of newspapers and, as had been the case for all of his readings, people soon began to drift over. He had browsed through the papers before he took them, hoping for articles that had nothing to do with the current situation. These people did not need to hear how lightly the British government regarded their plight.

He had wondered if they might be interested in news about the war between Mexico and the United States. The articles were full of exotic-sounding names like Puebla and Veracruz and Chapultepec, but the latest intelligence — thanks to the prompt reporting made possible by the telegraph — was that the war was not going well for the Mexican general Santa Anna, and that American troops now occupied Mexico City. Luke thought of his father's concerns that the U.S. Army might now turn its attention to the northern border in its quest for continental domination. These poor souls didn't need to hear that there might be a war in their future.

Mary and Rennie were amongst the first to arrive for the reading. Luke was relieved to see that Rennie had returned from wherever she had gone with Pierce Mullen, and he hoped that little Deirdre wouldn't disrupt the entertainment with her crying. But her low whimper was only just audible as she lay sleeping in Rennie's arms. Mary plunked herself down on the stoop beside Luke, sitting far too close for his comfort. He shifted himself away from her by making pretence of leafing through the papers and not finding quite enough room to hold them open.

Only a few familiar faces were in the crowd, but here and there he recognized someone who had asked for help with a sunburn or a broken toe or a cough. Mrs. Shanahan arrived with her little crowd, but Luke noticed that no one was willing to sit very close to Anna. Evidently these people really believed that she was a creature from another world.

In the paper, there were several notices of relatives looking for lost family. It wasn't exactly the light reading he had found for them before, but he knew they would be of interest; so, in light of his resolve to do what he could for at least one of Kingston's orphans, he read these out in the hope that a connection might be made somewhere.

"Searching for William Taylor, 14, Nathaniel Taylor, 12, and George Taylor, 11, left behind at Bytown July 5. Any information appreciated."

No one seemed to have heard of the Taylors, but they murmured their sympathies. "Left two in Bytown myself," one of the men said.

"Looking for information regarding the whereabouts of Amelia Kelly, 36," read another one. "Last seen at Montreal, July 14."

"I knew an Amelia Kelly," one woman said. "I wonder if it's the same one." She shrugged. "I haven't seen her since I left Cork, though."

Luke wondered if he could use this interest in missing relatives for his own ends. Turning a page of the newspaper, he said, as if reading, "Searching for Charley Gallagher, expected aboard the ship *Syria*, late May. Any information gratefully received."

Only a few people reacted, but this was not surprising, Luke supposed, as the concentration of people from Banesalley must have been diluted by death or exodus by now. One or two shifted uneasily, but no one commented until Mrs. Shanahan said, "Charley Gallagher was shot down dead. You won't be finding him."

"That's true enough," one of the other women muttered.

"What happened to him?" Luke asked, but he was met with silence and averted eyes. There would

be no more information forthcoming about Charley
Gallagher, he could see. Not this evening at any rate.

He picked up a different newspaper and found an
item that seemed to drive any thoughts of shootings
out of their heads:

Eight Hundred Thousand Acres of Land in the
Huron Tract

Notice to Old Settlers, Emigrants and Others
      The Canada Company have thrown open
all their lands in the Huron Tract for disposal,
by way of lease for 10 years — no money being
required down. The rent payable on the 1st
February each year is not much more than the
interest upon the price of the Land — the right
to purchase Freehold at any time within the ten
years at a fixed price named in leases, secured
to the Settler, who would save all further payments of rent.
      The Huron District is known to be one of
the most healthy and fertile Tracts of Land in
Canada. Land is in blocks, therefore affording
facility for the settlement of families and their
friends.

"Now, would you have to rent the whole thing?"
one man asked. "Could ye not take maybe an acre
or so?"

Luke explained that 800,000, a number that was so large that it seemed to mean nothing to his assembled listeners, was the total amount of land that was available, and that it was usually leased or sold in blocks of a hundred acres.

"A hundred acres? Whatever would a man do with a hundred acres?"

"Well," said Luke, "I know it seems like a lot, but you would need at least that much if you were going to grow something like wheat, which is the best crop in those parts. You can make money growing wheat." *Or you could*, he mentally corrected himself, *before Britain destroyed Canada's markets*. Still, surely someone, somewhere, would buy Canadian wheat.

"Where is this Huron Tract, exactly?" Mrs. Shanahan wanted to know.

"Way to the west of here."

"And would there be a good cabin there, do you think?"

"No, there wouldn't be anything there. You'd have to build something." Luke grappled with how to explain the realities of Canadian homesteading to a group of people who had always hardscrabbled on a few rocky acres of land.

"You couldn't just move onto the land tomorrow," he said, as patiently as he could. "You would need to gather together some things to take with you. Like axes and shovels and tools. You have to cut down the trees first, you see. Then you take some of the logs and make a cabin. And you'd have to clear a field before you could plant anything."

He could see that this was enough to discourage many of them.

"How would we ever get those things?" said the man who wouldn't know what to do with a hundred acres.

"You'd probably need to work somewhere for a time, until you could afford to buy the things."

"Ah, well," said the man, "the land would probably be all gone by then, wouldn't it?"

"No, it wouldn't," Luke said. "There's so much of it, you see. The Canada Company has been offering land for a number of years, and it's still not even close to be being filled up. There's plenty for everyone."

This caused a cascade of questions: Was the land really fertile, or just a jumble of mountainous rock? What did 'secured to the settler' mean? Was it really true that the Canada Company would lease to the Irish as well as to anyone else? Had Luke ever been there?

It caused a great stir when he said he had. "That's where I came from. I was farming there with my brother. The land is as good as they say."

"Why'd you leave, then?"

"Oh, don't be silly," said Mrs. Shanahan. "Why would a doctor stick around somewhere just to grow a few potatoes?"

The concept of taking land on the Huron Tract was beyond most of the emigrants, he realized, and perhaps that was just as well, as they seemed so ill-equipped for the task. Still, there were four men who approached with more questions after the crowd had dispersed, and who asked for his assistance in drafting a letter of application to the Canada Company. These men had been amongst the early arrivals that spring, and wore the pale countenance of the convalescent fever patient. They were still weak and a little shaky, but having survived, they seemed determined to start planning a future.

"If we all lumped in together, do ye think we could make a go of it?" they asked.

"You would certainly have a better chance of success," Luke said. "If you applied for four lots that were together, you could all work on each in turn. You'd get a crop in a lot faster that way."

The men held a mumbled conference, then repeated their request for help.

"I'll send a letter off tomorrow," Luke promised, and he noted that, as they walked away, the men stood a little straighter and stepped a little more briskly.

Chapter 17

Careful observation had made Thaddeus Lewis an expert at reading the signals that warned of one of his wife's sudden fevers. Storms were always likely with the approach of the autumnal equinox, but even if he had not known this from experience, he would have been able to tell that bad weather was on its way by Betsy's sudden stillness. He found her in the hotel kitchen, dish towel in hand, staring out the window at nothing.

He wasn't at all surprised later that day when he returned to their little house behind the Temperance Hotel and found her lying on the kitchen bed. He had expected it, for this was usual when the ague took her. She would huddle under a quilt, shaking with cold or drenched with fever until the stormy weather had passed and her limbs had stopped aching. After that an hour or two of deep sleep would restore a semblance of health, and she would soon be up again, not exactly bustling, but certainly able to brew her own tea and keep Sophie company in the hotel kitchen.

But as Thaddeus drew closer to the bed, he realized that this time something was different. She had not pulled the quilt up around her ears, nor were her eyes closed against the light. Her mouth drooped at one corner and her right eye was half-closed. Her left eye fluttered when she saw Thaddeus and her mouth moved as she tried to speak, but she could muster no words for him.

He ran back to the hotel and asked Francis to fetch the doctor.

It was the second apoplectic fit they had been warned to expect. The first had pulled Thaddeus off his ministerial circuits once and for all and sent them scurrying to family in Wellington, where a more settled life had given he and Betsy three reasonably good years. But all the time, the shadow of another sudden stroke had loomed over them.

Dr. Keough, when he arrived, could only shake his head at Thaddeus and tell him to prepare for worse to come. "She might recover somewhat, like she did before," he said, "although it's unlikely that she'll ever be as well again." He pursed his lips in worry. "I have to tell you, though, that I don't like what I'm seeing. Her pulse is irregular, and she's having trouble swallowing. We may be seeing an event that is still in progress, and I'm afraid that the prognosis is not good."

"Is there anything we can do?"

"Just keep her as comfortable as possible," Dr. Keough said. "The only other thing you can do is pray."

He would pray as he had never prayed before, Thaddeus thought, but not before he did the one thing that he knew might bring Betsy great comfort. As soon as Sophie had bustled in with extra pillows and Francis had arrived with a bowl of tepid water to sponge away the drool that collected at the corner of Betsy's mouth, Thaddeus found a sheet of paper and some ink and sat at the kitchen table to write a letter.

Chapter 18

Steamers were still depositing droves of emigrants every day, but Luke thought he could detect, just slightly, a lessening of the numbers aboard each boat.

Mrs. Thompson confirmed this as Luke helped her serve up the morning's pottage. "Another three weeks and we should start to see the end of it," she said. "Soon the autumn storms will make it too dangerous to risk an Atlantic crossing, and the captains have to time their voyages to arrive in Canada before the St. Lawrence ices over. Whoever is coming this year has left Ireland by now."

"What will happen to the patients in the sheds?" Luke asked. "They'll have to be moved somewhere inside before long." Even the patients who had apparently recovered from typhus were weak and listless and would require a period of convalescence before they could be sent off on their own.

"I don't know," Mrs. Thompson said. "There's some talk of trying to winterize the sheds. And then, of course, something will have to be done for the ones living outside. They can't survive a winter in the open."

It appeared that Kingston's crisis would not end with the close of the shipping season. It was no wonder that tempers were becoming frayed in the town, Luke thought, as the disease spread and the need grew.

Luke knew that he had used his last sheet of paper to write to his father, so after his day's work he walked down Store Street where he knew there was a stationer's shop. He was challenged at the corner of Montreal Street by a man with a constable's badge.

"Where do you think you're going?"

"I'm going about my business," Luke replied. "What business is it of yours?"

"Beg your pardon, sir," the man replied. "We've been told to keep the emigrants out of the city and down by the shore, so the fever doesn't spread any more than it has already."

Luke wanted to point out that it was far too late for this sort of precautionary measure and that the fever had already spread beyond anyone's control, but he didn't want to be questioned too closely. If this man knew that he cared for emigrants every day, would he, too, be denied entry to Kingston's centre? He tipped his hat to the man and walked on.

He completed his task at the stationer's, risking the wrath of the merchant by asking to borrow ink and a pen. After he completed the letter of application

to the Canada Company on behalf of the four wan
Irishmen, he walked back toward Hôtel Dieu. He
would borrow a piece of sacking from the nuns and
walk down the shore until he found a secluded spot
for bathing.

He was challenged again by a constable as he
walked west along Brock Street. He wondered how
any of these temporary watch guards would be able to
tell if someone was an emigrant, or was anyone who
had an Irish accent being told to turn back and huddle
by the shore? If so, Mayor Kirkpatrick himself might
have a hard time entering his own city.

The virulent spread of the disease became all too
manifest, however, when he entered the hospital. Sister
Bourbonnière stood near the front door, steadying herself against the wall, her pale face covered in a sheen
of sweat.

"You need to lie down," Luke said.

She shook her head. "I 'ave too much work."

"Is it the fever?"

"I don't know. It doesn't matter. There is no place to
lie down even if I could do so. The beds are all in use."

"But where have you been sleeping?"

"We sleep on the floor. In the passageway. But
we are too much in the way during the day." She
straightened herself up, took a deep breath, and
stumbled down the hall, determined to complete her
day's work.

He followed her to the tiny pharmacy closet. "If
you won't go and get some rest, is there anything else I
can do to help you?" he asked.

She turned. "You are already a great 'elp, Luke. But yes, there is one more thing you can do. You can pray for me."

And then, with a little surprised cry, she said, "Oh, I almost forgot." She reached into the folds of her habit. "This came for you today." She handed him a letter.

He recognized his father's sloping copperplate handwriting. He hadn't expected a reply so soon. He broke the seal and folded out the page, expecting to see words of reproach that he was not on his way to Montreal, or words of approbation that he was selflessly remaining in Kingston, he wasn't sure which. The words he read were completely unexpected.

September 22

My dearest Luke,

Your mother has quite suddenly suffered another apoplexy and the doctor has told us that her fate is now in God's hands.

I know that you were very worried about her prior to leaving Wellington this summer, but please rest assured that we had been warned to expect this, and that nothing could have been done to prevent it. I do know that seeing you again afforded her great delight and brought her an enormous amount of joy.

We can do little at this time but pray and wait, but if it is possible for you to come to

Wellington, I believe that your presence would bring her much comfort, as it would me.

Please come.

Your loving father

He folded the paper again carefully, as if he knew that this missive was one that would be tucked away somewhere, saved for a future generation to find and weep over a little.

Luke was aware that Sister Bourbonnière was watching him with concern.

"I'm afraid I have to leave you," he said.

"It was bad news then? I'm sorry, Luke."

"It's my mother. She's …" He choked a little on the words. "She's dying."

The nun touched his arm. "You must go to her. And I will pray for her and for you, too."

He stumbled down the hall toward the door, nearly colliding with Father Higgins. "Sorry," he mumbled, "wasn't watching."

"Are you all right, Luke?"

"I … I'm fine," he stuttered. "Excuse me."

All he wanted was to be alone somewhere so he could re-read the letter and absorb its contents in private.

"If there is anything I can do …"

Luke shook his head and brushed past the priest. He left the building and began walking away from the city. When he neared the brewery, he veered north in order to avoid the emigrant sheds. There was a path that seemed to continue west. If he kept to this route, he judged, he would eventually find himself at Portsmouth Village. But he had no wish to reach the settlement. He had no wish to talk to anyone. He turned south again, and soon reached the lake, where the land ended abruptly in a jagged limestone shelf.

He sat down on the edge and opened the sheet of paper, one small boyish part of him hoping that he had misinterpreted his father's words; but there was no mistaking the message it held. His father must have written many of these letters in his time, Luke reflected. He put the shocking news right at the beginning, so that the recipient would not have to work to discover what information was so urgent. Then the assurance that nothing the reader could have done would have made the slightest difference. There was no guilt to be assigned, no recriminations to be made. Everything was God's will, and God's will would be done.

What was surprising, he found, was the tail end of the letter — Thaddeus's admission of his own need for comfort and the brief, almost plaintive "please come." This was the first time that Thaddeus had ever needed Luke, and not the other way around. Another indication of the passing banner of the generations? It made him feel sad and old and weighed down with the responsibilities that would soon, apparently, be his. He wanted to turn time on its head. He was the youngest, the baby. He had been saddled with fewer expectations than his older brothers and sisters. He wanted it to stay that way. He wanted always to be able to run home to his mother.

His chest felt tight and his breath choked in his throat. He was hot. He threw off his jacket, then the rest of his clothes. He climbed down to the edge of the lake and slid into the water. Although the evening air was cool and the breeze had a bite, the water still retained some of the warmth it had soaked up from the afternoon sun.

The silky water soothed him, and finally let him start to organize his chaotic thoughts. In spite of his father's words, he regretted that he had not stayed in Wellington, that he hadn't spent the last few weeks tending, not to fevered emigrants, but to his own mother. And in the same moment, he knew, as his father had assured him, how futile that would have been. There had been no way to predict Betsy's last stroke, except to say that it was on its way. It could have happened anytime — before he'd arrived in Wellington, or three months from now when he might have been sitting in a classroom in Montreal, or even tomorrow, instead of yesterday. There would have been no point in merely sitting by her side, waiting for it to happen, and it would have done neither of them any good.

Besides, he had not been with her these five years past, had he? He had gone blithely off west with his brothers, in search of an adventure that had proved elusive. How hard it must have been for her when he left. She must have wondered if she would ever see him again. Yet again, what had been the alternative? Stay at home with her, working for poor wages at the livery stable, or at the blacksmith's, or at some other menial job? Or follow his father into the unappealing professions of teaching or the ministry, merely so that he could be by her side? This was never the way of young men, to tie themselves to hearth and home. And she would not have wanted it for him.

He felt a sudden surge of pity for the emigrants who had washed up in Canada, shedding family members along the way. Their sense of loss was no less than his own, he realized. They had their faith, he supposed, to help them, and their rituals seemed to somehow ease their pain. Like his father, they could turn to a belief in a better place, an eternity after death where all suffering was abolished. Luke had no such belief to cling to.

He flipped over on his stomach and opened his eyes to stare at the rocky lake bottom beneath him. There were a few weeds growing here and there, but otherwise it was a sterile place.

He wished he could see something there, some sign that would lead him to the certainty of the ultimate reunion of loved ones. That was the core of his pain, he realized, for he couldn't bring himself to believe that someday he would see his mother again. She would be gone, and he would be lonelier and more vulnerable without her.

His feet found bottom and he stood, maintaining his balance with a gentle sweep of his arms until the cold of the water began to creep into his joints. He waded toward shore, but suddenly, when the water level was only knee-deep, he doubled over and vomited. He made no attempt to move away from the mess, but merely stood and watched as the current gently pulled the sick out into the open lake. And then he began to cry, the tears rolling down his face in silent streams. He staggered to where he had left his clothes, but made no attempt to dress himself. He sank down beside them and let the tears spill to the rocks.

Immersed in his sorrow, he hadn't heard anyone approach. Suddenly, someone sat down beside him, reached out black-clad arms and enfolded him in an embrace.

"It's all right, boy, let it out." It was Father Higgins, who must have followed him along the shore. "It's all right, let it all out."

Luke was unprepared for his reaction to this embrace and the intimate circumstances of the encounter. For a moment, he closed his eyes and let himself be seduced by the feeling of warmth and comfort and then, unexpectedly and shockingly, he felt a surge of emotion and a stirring of passion. He pulled away. Blushing and embarrassed, he rushed back into the water, and when it grew waist-deep he plunged headfirst into it, swimming furiously away from the shore.

"Luke! Come back," he heard Higgins calling, but he had no intention of heeding. He flipped over onto his back, treading water as he watched the priest.

"Come back! What's the matter?"

In answer, Luke flipped over onto his stomach again and dove for the bottom, holding himself under the water until his lungs were bursting. When he surfaced with a great gasping intake of air, he saw that the priest was gone.

Chapter 19

His father looked as if he had aged ten years since Luke had seen him last. To be sure, it had been a shock when he had first arrived in Wellington and discovered that the parent of his memory had acquired grey hairs and a cautious gait, but Thaddeus had still looked like a man in the latter stages of his prime. Now the stress of his wife's latest and presumably last illness had accelerated the signs of aging: his hair was almost completely grey and his once upright posture was now slightly stooped.

It was Luke's brother-in-law, Francis Renwell, who led him down the hall to his mother's room. Betsy had been moved from the small cabin at the rear of Temperance House into a bedroom on the ground floor of the hotel, to make it easier for everyone involved in caring for her. She was propped up on a mound of snow-white feather pillows, a crazy quilt tucked lovingly around her feet. Martha was sponging her grandmother's face with a soft cloth when Luke entered. She gave him a wan smile in greeting.

"You see, Grandma, Uncle Luke is here," she said to the motionless form in the bed. "I told you he would come. Now you'll feel better, won't you?"

His mother looked tiny lying there, Luke thought, the round flesh of her cheeks sunken, heavy circles under her eyes.

"Hi, Ma." Luke sat down on the side of the bed and took his mother's unaffected left hand, stroking it gently. "I hear you've been ill."

She attempted a smile, but the asymmetry of her face turned it into a grimace. Then her good eye looked past him to Thaddeus, who had come into the room behind him. There they stayed, Martha gently crooning to her, Luke sitting on the bed, Thaddeus standing with his hand on his son's shoulder, until, just as the sun was setting, Betsy gave a huge shuddering gasp. Luke held his own breath, willing her to inhale and begin breathing again, but when it became clear that this would not happen, he and Thaddeus each took a corner of the quilt and drew it up over her.

After that, there was nothing more to do than to get out of the way while Sophie, with the help of two of the neighbourhood ladies, attended to the body. Thaddeus walked around the hotel to the front verandah, where he found his favourite rocking chair. Luke followed him. There was a wooden chair beside the rocker, but somehow he felt awkward about taking it. Instead, he sat down on the top step of the wide stairs that led to the front door.

"Although we feel her loss severely, yet we are comforted in that she departed this life in the triumphs of faith, having her last enemy under her feet. Glory be to God, we do not mourn as those that have no hope." Thaddeus mumbled this as he rocked. Luke knew that this was a speech his father had given before, a quotation perhaps, or something he had pronounced at a sermon or service. Saying it aloud was patently an attempt to convince himself of the truth of the statement. It was also an invitation to talk.

"I can't believe she's gone," Luke said, fixing his attention not on Thaddeus but on a labourer who was pushing a wheelbarrow down the street.

"She's gone to a better place." His father's voice sounded cracked and rusty, as if it hadn't been used in a long, long time. "She departed this life in the triumphs of faith."

"I know that," Luke replied, "but somehow that doesn't make me feel any better right now. I guess all we can do is hope to join her some day."

The old man's eyes turned to his son. "I keep telling myself that. All my life I've urged others to rejoice in God and look forward to the day when we join our loved ones in His embrace. But this death is hard for me to bear."

Luke was stunned. He had expected his father to find perfect solace in the faith he had embraced so long ago, and to urge others to do the same. Thaddeus's belief had sustained him for so long — or so it had always seemed to Luke. He hadn't realized how much effort it took to believe, and how easily the faith could fall away when challenged. He let the silence grow while he tried to frame his next words.

"I have seen far too much of death in these last weeks. I have seen what little flesh remained on starving bodies seep away in filth. Each one of them believed they were going to a better place, even with their last breaths. It could well be that they are right, and the sorrows of this earth are left behind. But that was no consolation for me. All I've wanted to do is face death down, tell it to be gone. And yet, I've also learned that death can sometimes be a friend as well. I think maybe it was for Ma."

Lewis merely nodded, but his eyes narrowed as the words struck home.

They sat in silence for what seemed a long time, until finally thirst drove Luke to stand and go to the kitchen. To his surprise, his father followed him.

Francis and Sophie were at the kitchen table, engaged in what appeared to be a deep discussion. They hastily broke it off, but Thaddeus re-initiated it. "There's no need to try to spare my feelings," he said. "Nothing can do that, so spit it out."

"It's about the visitation," Francis said, "and the funeral."

Most families buried their dead from home, but Betsy's home had been the tiny cabin behind the hotel, completely inadequate for the numbers of people who would be likely to pay their respects.

"We could use the hotel itself," Francis went on, "except that we have paying guests at the moment. I don't see how we can expect them to share any of the public rooms with a ..." He reddened as he searched for a more appropriate word than *corpse*.

"With Betsy," Thaddeus said. "Yes, I see." He considered for a moment, and then he said, "I think the Methodist Meeting House is the obvious choice, although it would be unusual. Let me ask the Elders what they think."

"Of course," Francis said, "that would be more than appropriate. But let me do the asking."

Thaddeus nodded. "Let me know if there is any objection. I'll be with Betsy."

Francis waited until his footsteps could no longer be heard. "Well, that was awkward," he said, and Sophie poked his arm. "It still is," she said, gesturing toward Luke.

"It's all right," Luke said. "Someone has to make the arrangements. Pa and I both thank you for doing it, Francis." He wondered what they would say if he told them that he had spent the last weeks doing little more than making burial arrangements, if one could refer to piling bodies in a pit as an arrangement. Suddenly all the corpses he had looked upon rose up in his mind and became one with his mother's lifeless body. He felt physically ill.

"I'll be back," was all he managed to get out before he rushed out the back door and ran to the side of his mother's cabin, where a tall stand of hollyhocks hid him from view. He bent over, his hands on his knees while his heart raced and his head spun, a kaleidoscope of images cascading through his mind — putrefying flesh, skeletal limbs, blood and pus and phlegm, and the drooping lid of his mother's eye, and the awful thing, the shameful thing that he had not allowed himself to think about. He dropped to his knees and let his head fall forward into the earthy, loamy smell of the hollyhock roots. His hands dug into the soil, looking for purchase to stop the terrible spinning.

"Are you all right?" It was Martha. "I was sick. Only not here."

The sound of her voice steadied him. He had forgotten about Martha. She was only a little girl, after all. How would she cope with this? He needed to pull himself together, if only for her.

"Are you all right now?" It was an inane question for him to ask. Of course she wasn't. How could she be? Although Betsy was her grandmother, she had been raised by her. In all but name, she was Martha's mother too.

"No. I don't like this."

"Nor do I."

She sat down matter-of-factly beside him, as though it was perfectly normal for people to sit in the middle of a patch of hollyhocks. Luke's heart slowed, his breathing evened out and became easier, his hands stopped shaking.

"Do you want to go for a walk?" she asked.

"Maybe."

"Along the shore? That's the best place when you're sad."

They walked without speaking, away from the wharves at the centre of the village and along the narrow, rocky beach that stretched away to the horizon until it wound around a distant spit of land.

Martha had been a baby when Luke left. Now he wasn't sure what to say to the girl she had grown up to be, but it seemed that words were unnecessary. They lifted their faces to the lake breeze and let their steps fall into synchrony. Luke felt the shadows that had overwhelmed him retreating. They would rise again, he knew, but for now he found comfort in the presence of this niece he didn't know.

They walked until they reached what was left of a large tree that had fallen over into the water, the anchoring soil stripped away from its roots by the incessant action of the waves. They would have to wade if they wanted to get past it. Instead, Martha scrambled up to sit on its trunk. Luke stooped and picked up a flat smooth stone and pitched it into the lake with a sideways motion. It skipped along the surface of the water twice before it dropped to the bottom.

"I can skip it more times than that," Martha scoffed.

"Prove it."

She jumped down and took a few moments to consider her choice of stone, then took careful aim before she let it fly.

"One, two, three," Luke counted. Then there was another short hop and the stone sank.

"That was four," Martha said.

"No it wasn't, it was only three."

"There was a little one at the end."

"No there wasn't."

"It was real quick, but there was a double skip at the end." Suddenly she bent over and grabbed a handful

of stones and started throwing them into the water as
fast as she could, the splash from each obliterating the
ripple from the one before.

Just as suddenly she stopped and turned to Luke.
"This is where we found the whale. Grandpa says it
was a drowned man, but I don't think so. I'm pretty
sure it was a whale, only not as big as the one that
swallowed Jonah."

"No, that would have to be really big." Luke had
to think for a moment before he understood what she
was talking about — and then he remembered the
strange disguised corpse the children had discovered
on this shore. The grisly find had obviously made a
great impression on Martha. She'd told him about it
when he'd first arrived in Wellington, announcing it at
the dinner table as a topic of great interest. He didn't
understand, however, why she was bringing it up now,
unless, somehow, she had connected the bloated corpse
with her grandmother.

"Do you understand what's going to happen now?"
he ventured, hoping that his assumption was correct.

"Everybody has to come and see Grandma and
then we have a service and then we put her in the
ground." As a child who had been raised by a preacher,
she was obviously well-acquainted with burial rites.

"Are you afraid to look at her?"

Martha nodded. "Will she look like the drowned
man?"

Familiar with the rites, but not with the practicali-
ties. Luke was relieved that this would be so easy a fear
to soothe. "No. The man you found had been in the

water for a long time. That's why he looked the way he did, all swollen and discoloured. Your Grandma will look like your Grandma."

And then his previous conversations about the drowned man came back to him in their entirety: Speculation as to why a man had been dressed as a woman. Dr. Keough's gruesome clinical description of the corpse. The fact that there had been no way to discover the man's identity. Nothing at all in the monster's feminine pockets, Keough had said, other than a scrap of green ribbon.

He had almost forgotten about the scrap of green ribbon he had found in John Porter's clothing. What had he done with it? He had been paying so little attention to it that now he couldn't remember.

Were the ribbons connected? It seemed unlikely. There had been conjecture, he now recalled, that the drowned man had been an emigrant who had somehow fallen overboard, but there was no proof of this. He could equally well have fallen from a fishing boat, or off a dock, or had gone under while swimming in the lake. Except that fishermen and sailors and swimmers rarely clad themselves in skirts to perform these activities. The dress had been a disguise, obviously, but what had the man been hiding from? Luke wasn't even sure that it mattered. Except that it seemed so odd. And it gave him something to think about besides all the things that he didn't want to think about.

"We should go back. I'll need to help Sophie," Martha said.

"All right."

Again they walked along in silence, but when they arrived back at the hotel, Martha turned to him. "Thank you, Uncle Luke. Grandpa says I talk all the time, but I don't really. Sometimes it's nice when nobody says anything."

"I know what you mean. I liked it too."

And with that, she ran through the back door to the kitchen.

Luke walked to the front of the hotel where his father was once again sitting in the rocking chair. He took a seat nearby. Thaddeus nodded, but said no word of greeting. It seemed that silence was a prized commodity in the Lewis family at the moment.

He briefly wondered what Martha's life would be like from now on; then he realized that, except for the fact that she no longer had her grandmother, nothing much would change for her. She still had her grandfather, her father, Sophie — people who cared about her, who would look after her.

The Irish children who had lost parents had also, in many cases, lost the rest of their families and their communities and even their country. His own loss, he knew, was small beside it, and yet he felt nearly as alone.

The Wellington elders not only agreed to the unusual use of their meeting house, but the ladies of the congregation offered to set up tables so that tea and refreshments might be served to those who took the time to pay their respects. Each of them promised to bring something — a tray of sandwiches, a plate of cakes, some pickle. The arrangements were made easier by the fact that there would be only one day of visitation, the church being needed the following day for meeting.

Luke barely slept the night before his mother's funeral, the solitude of the small hours a dark chasm his mind fell into. He clung to memories of his mother as he tried to will himself to sleep: Betsy scrubbing his face and hands as he went off to the first day of school. Betsy chasing his brothers away from an old tin drum he had found. Betsy hugging him, smiling at him ... always smiling. But that image quickly dissolved into Betsy's last lopsided smile, and he was overwhelmed with a sense of loss. He shoved this last memory away, but other, darker thoughts crept in, and all hope of sleep vanished.

He replayed the scene at the shore a million times in his head, and he was still unsure about what had taken place. Had Higgins been aware of Luke's odd and inappropriate response to a gesture of comfort, or had Luke pulled away from the embrace before it had become apparent?

If he had noticed, would the priest have dismissed it as a strange reaction to grief? People did bizarre things when they were upset. He had heard of one woman in Goderich who had cut up all her dresses when her husband died, and a man near Guelph who burned down his barn the night his wife passed on. Higgins was a priest, a Catholic priest, above all temptations of the flesh. Except that Luke knew that "flesh" was meant to refer to women, not to other men.

As the child of a preacher, he had been required to memorize long passages of the Bible, and bidden to repeat them regularly. He had not understood many of them at the time, his learning rote and automatic. Now, an inventory of the abominations of Sodom came back to him and Paul's epistle to the Romans haunted him.

Thou shalt not lie with mankind, as with womankind: it is abomination, a sin that, according to Leviticus, was as great as lying with beasts or uncovering the nakedness of one's sister.

And likewise also the men, leaving the natural use of the woman, burned in their lust one toward another, turning God's truth into lies along with backbiters, boasters, inventors of evil things, covenant-breakers, fornicators, murderers, the malicious, the envious, and whisperers.

He was grateful that his mother would never know what he was. He could not have stood it if her constant smile had turned to contempt.

Frantically, he sought some other topic he could dwell on, and his mind turned to Anna Porter and her missing relatives, and the mysterious events that seemed to surround Mrs. Shanahan's eviction. Higgins had answered any question he had been asked, but Luke was sure that there were things that had gone unsaid. This brought him back to the priest again, and the incident at the shore, and then to his mother's death. Round and round he went until he at last fell into a fitful, exhausted sleep.

He awakened at first light to a gnawing apprehension that he couldn't quite identify, until he remembered what day it was. He forced himself to lie in bed until he heard the rest of the household stirring. He would wait until breakfast was underway, and hope that the morning bustle in the kitchen would chase away the night's shadows.

As he shrugged himself into his clothes, he realized that one elbow of his jacket was stained. He sniffed at it. Despite his best efforts with his minty infusion, it still carried a whiff of the fever sheds and their attendant smells. He would have to sponge it off and perhaps ask Sophie what he should do to deodorize it.

She whisked it away from him as soon as he mentioned his difficulty. The stain was efficiently sponged away, and then she began sprinkling the jacket with rose water, dabbing most of it, he noticed, on the inside.

"That way if it takes a little time to dry, no one will notice the damp spots," she said. She shoved her cloth down inside the pockets as well. When she did this to the right hand pocket, her cloth drew out a small scrap of green ribbon.

"What's this?" she asked, smiling at him. "A favour from your best girl?"

"N-n-o, it isn't," he stammered and took it from her. "It's something else entirely." He hadn't thrown it away after all. He must have absent-mindedly tucked it away in his pocket.

"There you go," Sophie said, giving the jacket one final shake. "You should be presentable enough now."

Luke was grateful for her help, but a little intimidated by her efficiency. He thanked her and scuttled out to the verandah where Thaddeus was waiting.

It was still far too early to leave for the meeting house, so he sat in the chair beside his father. Wordless minutes passed. Luke would have appreciated some words, to take his mind away not only from the ceremonial ordeal that lay ahead of him but from his other worries as well.

He was about to offer a chance remark about the weather, just to break the silence, when his father suddenly sniffed and said, "What's that smell? Is that you?"

"My jacket was a little ripe," Luke said. "Sophie sponged it down with rose water."

"Hmmph," Thaddeus said. "You smell like a brothel."

Luke was taken completely aback, not at his father's apparent objection to the flowery scent he was giving off, but at his reference to a brothel.

"How do you know what a brothel smells like?" It was the first response that jumped into his mind, and he gave it before he considered what he was saying.

But Thaddeus seemed not at all upset. "I was a soldier, you know, in Mr. Madison's war. Later, I attempted, on occasion, to confront the devil in his own den. I had some success in persuading some of the women to repent of their ways, at least temporarily. I had less success with their customers."

Somehow Luke could well imagine his upright and righteous father striding into a bawdy house and demanding that everyone clear out to attend the local camp meeting. He nearly laughed at the mental image, but his father's next words killed his mirth.

"If you are ever tempted, my boy, take it to the Lord and ask for his help. Men are tormented by demons, but demons can be wrestled down."

Luke felt his face growing hot and was sure that he must be turning bright red. He wondered if this was a jab designed to prod at the demon that he had spent most of the night wrestling. But how could his father know? He himself scarcely knew what it was, just that it felt shameful and wrong. And from the little that he did know, he was sure that the Lord would have no patience with this particular temptation.

The conversation came to an end as the rest of the family emerged from the hotel. Mrs. Donovan, who lived across the road, was coming in to serve dinner to the Temperance House guests, helped by her son Michael, a favour proffered so that Sophie could attend the funeral.

They walked down the street toward the Methodist Meeting House in a chill, mizzling rain. Their black clothing and fluttering crepe arm bands made Luke think of a flock of earthbound crows. The only relief to the eye was the band of purple grosgrain that trimmed the hem of Martha's Sunday dress. It should have been removed, he guessed, but had been overlooked in the rush of everything else that had needed doing.

When they reached the church, they took their places by Betsy's casket, a plain enough pine box, but at least it had been sanded smooth and the edges beveled, unlike the rough planking that he had handled in Kingston.

Within a few minutes people began filing past them to express their condolences. Although not active in church affairs, Betsy had been well-liked, and Thaddeus was held in high regard in the community, partly due to his station as a former minister, and partly because he had been instrumental in uncovering a case of fraud and murder two years previously — and for catching the murderer, Simms, of course. He spoke politely to everyone who passed, but Luke guessed that his father would be anxious to see this day at an end. He had weeks and months of mourning ahead of him, but that would be a private affair that he would not have to share with strangers.

Luke recognized very few of the people who spoke to him and he had to force himself to concentrate in order to make appropriate responses to the words of condolence that were on everyone's lips. The only ones he recognized with any certainty were Dr. Keough and his father's employer, Archibald McFaul. When McFaul shook his hand and said how sorry he was, the Irish lilt in his voice sent Luke's mind spinning toward the question of the green ribbons and what they meant. He wondered if McFaul might know. He resolved to question the man, but in the meantime there were sympathies to acknowledge and cakes to consume before the funeral party wound its way down the street for the graveside service.

He was grateful for the distraction of the puzzle as they all gathered in the graveyard. If he could keep his mind working on the connection between the ribbon found with the body at Wellington and the one in John Porter's vest, he could ignore the fact that it was his mother's body that was being lowered into the ground.

Green ribbons weren't so common that they just popped up everywhere. The only other connection between the two men that he could think of was that both of them might have been Irish.

The Wellington corpse had drowned, that much was certain. John Porter had been sick and he died. There was no similarity there.

Suddenly, Luke felt a small hand slip into his. Martha had stayed close to her father throughout the visitation and stood beside him for the service. Francis held one of her hands firmly in his own, but she must have needed extra assurance, and looked to Luke for it. He was surprised. They had had little connection beyond their walk by the shore. It would have been more natural for her to seek out her grandfather.

And then he realized that they all had moved away from Thaddeus, giving him a respectful circle of solitude as he said goodbye to his beloved Betsy. Luke squeezed Martha's hand as they murmured in prayer, and then, as the final words were spoken, the rain started to fall harder and they all went scurrying for cover.

Chapter 20

A few days later, Luke found Archibald McFaul in the small office he maintained at the back of his store.

McFaul looked up, smiling, when Luke knocked. The door was open, but he didn't want to barge in and interrupt the man, who was, after all, Wellington's leading citizen.

"Hello, Luke," McFaul said. "How nice to see you again." Luke marvelled at McFaul's ability to remember names. They had met only twice, but there was no hesitation in the greeting.

"I'm hoping you might be able to explain something to me," Luke said, as he dug the small scrap of ribbon out of his pocket and held it out. "Do you know what this means? I found it on a dead body."

He knew there was some significance to the ribbon by the look on McFaul's face.

"Whose dead body?"

"A fever victim in Kingston. According to Dr. Keough, a similar piece was found with the drowned man on the beach here."

McFaul sighed. "Captain Starlight. I had hoped never to see anything like this in Canada."

"Who is Captain Starlight?" Luke asked. It was such a bizarre and romantic-sounding name, he imagined someone with a plumed hat and a sword, engaging in dazzling swordplay or serenading a young woman from beneath her balcony.

"It's not a *he*, it's a *them*. Captain Starlight is one of the names used by vigilante groups bent on exacting retribution. These groups use many names — White Boys, Ribbonmen, Captain Rock. Captain Starlight was the name used in the district I came from."

"Retribution for what?" Luke wanted to know.

"For all the injustice in Ireland — eviction, miscarriage of justice, hunger." McFaul's eyes narrowed as his mind was cast back into his past. Luke waited respectfully while the silence stretched out, but then McFaul heaved another sigh and began to speak. "You have no idea what it's like to be a pauper in Ireland. You can work your whole life and do nothing more than provide your family with the barest living. And at any moment, and on the flimsiest of excuses, the landlord can take away even that, and you can find yourself huddled on a rocky mountaintop, your starving children crying around your feet."

He seemed to speak from so far away that Luke wondered if he was recounting an experience from his own past. Perhaps this explained the man's generosity, his unfailing courtesy toward everyone.

"And so when something bad happens, there's a backlash?"

"Only as a final straw sort of thing. If a landlord was evicting wholesale, or if some crime was committed and the culprit was unfairly let off. The law was never a friend to an Irish Catholic. The law was made to protect the landowners. So, yes, sometimes people would manufacture their own justice."

"What would the vigilantes do?"

"Sometimes it was just destruction of property, smashing windows and so forth," McFaul said. "Sometimes it would be more serious — setting fires or killing livestock — and in some cases it was quite extreme. I know of more than one instance where someone was gunned down."

Luke was beginning to understand. "And something would be left with the victim? Like a green ribbon?"

"Yes. It's a marker, a token. So that everyone will know it was community vengeance and not an ordinary crime perpetrated by an individual."

"But why use it here? None of us know what it means."

"I did," McFaul pointed out. "As would any relatives of the victim. Not to mention the person who was wronged to begin with. It's a signal that justice has been done."

Two green ribbons on two different dead bodies seemed less and less of a coincidence. And there was certainly justice to mete out, if what Father Higgins had said was true. Charley Gallagher had been shot down, and everyone thought it was David Porter who was responsible.

"How far does the retribution go?" Luke asked. "Would Captain Starlight go after only the person responsible for the crime, or would other family members be held to account for it as well?"

"Normally it would end with the culprit," McFaul said, "the person who had done harm in the first place, but that, of course, would depend on what had happened. If the sense of outrage was deep, or of long standing, there could be quite a spate of reprisals. Sometimes these feuds go on for generations, once they get started."

The Porters had not been well-liked, that much was clear, Luke thought. And John Porter had certainly been alarmed when he saw Pierce Mullen standing in the fever shed that day. John Porter had not fired the shot that killed Charley Gallagher. But he had been there.

"You would think, wouldn't you," McFaul mused, "that Ireland has enough grief without carrying its feuds across the ocean."

"I don't know for sure that the man in Kingston was a victim of anything but fever," Luke said. "He was over the worst of it, but all too often complications set in and the patient dies anyway. The man was left with a severe lung complaint, and there's every reason to believe that he died of it."

"Then why would someone leave a ribbon?"

"I don't know," Luke said. "I think I'll need to go back to Kingston to find that out. There are a couple of people who may be able to shed some light on this, if I can get them to talk to me."

"Have you ever noticed how the Irish can talk and talk and talk and still not answer a question? I'm not sure you'll ever discover what it's all about. It's the sort of thing that everyone knows and nobody talks about. And mark my words, the roots of this story are in Ireland, not Kingston."

"Well," Luke said, "I'm not prepared to go quite that far."

"I'm surprised you're prepared to go any distance at all. It seems an odd thing to bother with, given your current troubles."

Just for a moment, Luke wasn't sure what McFaul meant by this, but then he realized that the reference was to the passing of his mother. He forced himself to calm down, hiding his shaky hands behind his back.

"I'm not sure why myself," he said, in answer to McFaul's comment, "except that a puzzle seems like a good way to keep myself occupied at the moment."

"My goodness, you really are a Lewis, aren't you? There's nothing your father likes better than a puzzle. In fact, it might not be such a bad idea to enlist his help with this one. I suspect a change of scenery would do him some good at this juncture. You could take him to Kingston with you."

"My father? Why?"

"For heaven's sake, young man, you've got one of the most intelligent men in Upper Canada at your disposal and he's not doing anything right now but sitting on a verandah. I'm sure he would feel much happier if he were on the road to somewhere."

"He's in mourning," Luke protested. But he liked the idea. His father could be a buffer if he had to talk to Father Higgins again.

"He'll be in mourning for the rest of his life. That doesn't mean he should spend it staring blankly at the main street of Wellington."

"But —"

"Not to worry," McFaul said with a wave of his hand, "I can manage without him for a time. Just promise me that you'll bring him back at some point. And when that happens, you can tell me the whole story."

Chapter 21

As summer came to its stormy end, Canada was shocked by the death of Toronto's Bishop Michael Power. All of the newspapers that found their way to the Temperance Hotel shouted the news in black headlines on their front pages, followed by eulogies that lauded him as a hero for his efforts to help emigrant victims of the typhus epidemic:

> The loss to the Diocese of Toronto, which Dr. Power distinguished by the value of his sacred offices and the virtues of his life, is at this moment heavy and severe. It is said that neither night nor day witnessed his absence from the depositaries of disease, until at length kneeling over the bed of infection, and listening to the sorrows of some poor penitent, he inhaled the miasma of death. Grief

of such a loss is natural. The associates of his youth, who well remember him, deeply lament in this community the privation even Canada has sustained.

Thaddeus had not known Bishop Power, but he had certainly known *of* him — he was one of those who sat on the province's first school board, to oversee the educational system that Egerton Ryerson had put in place. It had been Catholic Bishop Power who had persuaded the staunchly Protestant Toronto Council, overrepresented by members of the Orange Lodge, to reluctantly vote funds to help the emigrants.

It didn't surprise him that Power had spearheaded a collection of volunteers, Catholic and Protestant alike, to nurse those struck down by typhus. The same had happened in Kingston, Luke had told him, the Catholic Bishop Phelan and the Protestant Mayor Kirkpatrick coordinating the efforts of the Sisters of Hôtel Dieu with those of The Female Benevolent Society, the local Catholic priests with the local Protestant ministers. It was no surprise, either, that some of these volunteers would contract the disease they worked so hard to contain. The Sisters of Hôtel Dieu were all ill, apparently, as were a number of the Benevolent Ladies. One priest had died, Luke said, and one nun was critically ill.

What stunned Thaddeus were the sheer numbers of emigrants reported in related articles. It was claimed — and he had no reason to doubt it — that over thirty thousand emigrants had arrived at the wharves in Toronto in the previous four months — ten thousand more people than were in the entire city. It was the same story in Kingston, Montreal, Prescott, and Bytown. Every port the steamers had reached had designated hospitals, built sheds, and tried their best to care for the sick and starving; but in the face of the multitudes that had arrived, their efforts would have as much effect as trying to paint the wind.

He was trying to absorb what it all meant when Luke returned from his errand and took a chair beside him. He could tell that his son was waiting to see whether or not his father would engage in conversation. Since the funeral, Thaddeus had spent his days on the verandah, rocking gently while the world went by him unremarked. He knew that his family was worried about him. He should have explained to them that he wanted a little time to catalogue his memories and mull over his grief, but for the first time in his life he had not been able to find the words. Instead, he had ignored them all and continued to rock in silence whenever any of them approached.

Enough, he had thought to himself that morning. *Betsy wouldn't want this.* And for the first time since he had found his wife lying helpless on the bed, he had gone to the guest parlour and taken a newspaper out to the verandah with him.

"I'm listening," Thaddeus said to his son, who was sitting patiently beside him. "I know I haven't been the last few days, but I am now." He expected to hear that he needed to pull himself together, or words to that effect, so he was surprised when Luke presented him with such a strange story.

"I have a conundrum," Luke began, and repeated what McFaul had told him about the green ribbons.

"And you think this Irishman was murdered?"

"I don't know," Luke admitted. "I don't know what to think, but there seems to be something very odd going on." He detailed all of the events that had struck him as peculiar — the wagonload of women being driven down a Toronto street, the empty whiskey barrels loaded onto *The Bellweather*, the Porters and their role in the death of Charley Gallagher. He included his concern that Bridie Shanahan was less than an ideal guardian for Anna Porter. "I wouldn't have given the whole matter a second thought if I hadn't read that business about the coffin in Toronto spilling two bodies into the street — that and my promise to Henry Gallagher that I'd try to find his brother."

Thaddeus set up a gentle rocking while he digested the story. Luke stayed very quiet while he waited, realizing that this was not the Thaddeus gone away to some place where his grief was paramount. This was the Thaddeus that McFaul claimed was "one of the most intelligent men in Upper Canada," and he was using his intelligence to make sense of the senseless.

Finally, after a few moments, he spoke. "You have three conundrums, not one. They may all be related. They may not. First of all, the little girl needs to find a relative. None of the rest of it is contingent on that, is it?"

"No, it isn't. And by the way, I've sent some letters off. If there's a reply, it will come here."

"There was an older sister, but you don't know what happened to her, is that correct?"

"Yes. She went ahead to collect a missing trunk."

"There must be some record of how far she got. The emigrant agents are supposed to keep track. Certainly, had she been quarantined in some other port, that would have been recorded, wouldn't it?"

Luke thought of the careful records Sister Bourbonnière kept, records that he himself had maintained. He wasn't sure that everyone would have been as careful as the nun.

"I suppose," he said, "but apparently some of the records are a real mess. I was told that when I asked about Charley Gallagher in Toronto. That was early in the season, but even then I was told that they were unreliable."

"Perhaps. But they're still worth checking."

"So, what's the second conundrum?"

"The ribbons. Who left them with the bodies? We have an indication of why, but we have no way to ascertain if the two deaths are related in any way, or if they truly indicate any sort of foul play. Whether or not you pursue that issue depends on whether or not you believe there was murder done."

"*Murder* is a strong word."

"It is. I'm just trying to point out what you may be getting yourself into."

"Fair enough. And the third?"

"Everything else, which I'm not sure actually has

anything to do with the first two puzzles. You may have a moral obligation to make the authorities in Toronto aware of what you saw — not that they're likely to do anything about it, in my experience. But I don't understand what your interest is otherwise."

"Only that I saw the same wagon driver in both Toronto and Kingston. And I suspect that he was present when Charley Gallagher was shot."

Thaddeus nodded. "It does seem like too much of a coincidence, doesn't it? And yet," he said, as if to himself, "coincidences twice as strange occur every day and go entirely unremarked."

"What do you think I should do?" Luke asked.

"That's not for me to say. It depends on how much of this you feel responsible for. And how much time you're willing to spend sorting it out. By all accounts, you've done real service in Kingston, and I admire you for that, but there comes a point when you have to consider your future. Have you decided when you're going on to Montreal?"

"I don't know," Luke said. "I may have to wait until next year. I'm not sure what I'm going to do."

Thaddeus looked closely at his son, who seemed determined to avoid his eye. Something else was amiss that the boy wasn't telling him about, but he didn't know Luke well enough to guess what it was. He had been gone too long, and had grown up while he was away. But Thaddeus realized that he had probably never known this son well enough to gauge what he was thinking. It had been Betsy who had raised him, with Thaddeus only a bystander.

"So, what do you want to do?" he asked.

"I don't know," Luke said. "I've made a lot of promises. I promised a man I'd try to find his brother. I found out what happened to him, but I still don't know why it happened. I promised an orphan I'd try to find her sister. I even promised a lady I'd try to find her a new pair of boots."

"I've made a lot of promises in my time," Thaddeus said. "I broke most of them, except the one that really mattered." He began rocking his chair again, looking off into the distance as he spoke. "I don't know if you remember your mother when she wasn't sick. You're the youngest, so I expect you don't. The first time I ever saw her she was picking wildflowers with my sister Susannah. I was just home from the war then and my heart was sick. I'd seen nothing but blood and dirt and lice and hate, and I wanted to forget it all. I tried to do it with drink. I was drunk for days on end, but it wasn't enough to make me forget. But when I saw your mother it was as if a flower-scented spring rain had blown into my head and swept all the horror away. I resolved then that I would do anything if only she would notice me. She didn't for the longest time."

"What changed her mind?"

"I had to become a better man. I may have overdone it somewhat. I wish I could take back those years I left her alone. Perhaps it would have been better if I had just stayed with her, and not taken it into my head to go off preaching. But I'd made a promise, you see."

"I don't understand."

"I was called back into service," Thaddeus said, "but I was so broken-down and sick that I was declared unfit. I was told I would be sent to England, to the Chelsea Pensioners' Hospital, where I would receive treatment. But the chances that I would ever be able to return to Canada would be remote. I promised God that if he let me stay and be with Betsy, I'd devote the rest of my life to him." He turned to look at Luke. "A few weeks later, the war ended and I was discharged with no more mention of me going to England. Your mother agreed to marry me. To my mind, the bargain had been struck."

"That's the most romantic story I've ever heard," Luke said with a laugh.

"Yes, it is, isn't it?" Thaddeus agreed. "Good enough for a novel. But I think the true moral of my story is that my promise was made as much to myself as it was to God. And that's why I was able to keep it."

"A lot of these promises I've made have nothing to do with me, do they?" Luke said.

"No, they don't. Don't take me the wrong way," Thaddeus hurried to add, "when a moral man gives his word, he keeps it, but I don't think that's necessarily the case here, do you?"

"No, it isn't," Luke said. "I just said I'd do my best."

"And so ..." Thaddeus waited while Luke thought this over.

"I did promise someone a new pair of boots. That's a promise that's easy enough to keep."

"Fair enough," Thaddeus said.

"I said I'd try to find the long-lost sister and I've already taken steps to try to do that. And I've certainly found out what happened to Charley Gallagher, although it wasn't the answer his brother was looking for."

"And the rest of it?"

"I haven't made any promises to myself or to God either," Luke said. "And maybe that's the problem. I'm no longer sure what bargain I want to strike."

There was an innuendo to this that Thaddeus heard, but did not understand. He had never been good at catching emotional context. That had been Betsy's strength, and she would have known how to coax this boy's worries out into the open, so that they could be confronted and dealt with. But Betsy was no longer here.

"I need to go back to Kingston," Luke suddenly announced. "I need to buy a pair of boots and I need to look for a missing relative. It remains to be seen what I discover beyond that, but at least I have somewhere to start. Would you like to come with me?"

"Me?" Thaddeus was surprised, but on reflection found it a tantalizing suggestion. He had always found it easier to clear his head when he was on the way to somewhere. "I'd have to speak to Mr. McFaul."

"It was Mr. McFaul who suggested it," Luke said. "He figures you need to get up out of that rocking chair."

Chapter 22

Luke wanted to check on Sister Bourbonnière first, so as soon as the packet steamer docked at Kingston's main wharf, he and Thaddeus walked along Brock Street toward the Hôtel Dieu hospital.

The upriver flow of emigrants had finally slowed. Although the hospital was still full to overflowing, most of the patients were in beds, with only a few here and there lying on pallets in the hallway. Luke and Thaddeus were greeted by a nun whom Luke didn't recognize.

"I expected to find one of the Sisters of Hôtel Dieu," Luke said. "I volunteered here over the summer, but was called away on family business."

"I am from Les Religieuses Hospitalières de Saint-Joseph in Montreal," the nun said. "We were sent to assist, as all of the Sisters here have been ill. They are recovering," she hastened to add when she saw the expression on Luke's face. "All except Sister McGorrian, who is still quite acutely ill. One of the priests is very ill as well."

"Not Father Higgins?" Luke realized that his hands were shaking slightly.

"No. One of the local priests, Father Phinney."

They thanked the nun and walked down through Stuartsville. Luke had expected to see people he recognized — those he had treated for minor ailments, or those who had gathered around the stoop in front of his lodging house while he read newspaper articles to them. But only twice did someone call to him as they passed. The flimsier structures appeared deserted. There were signs of habitation in the more substantial of the shacks and in the lodging houses, but it was too cold that day for anyone to be sitting in the dooryards.

There was no sign of Mrs. Shanahan and her unlikely brood. When Luke and Thaddeus entered her yard, a pale and sullen-looking man pulled aside the piece of canvas that served as a door to the tiny hovel.

"Don't know no Shanahans," he said. "I just got out of hospital and was lucky enough to find this. It'll do for over the winter, 'til I'm feeling better in the spring, and then I'm off west to look for work."

There were huge gaps where the sides of the building didn't quite meet, and a large hole near the peak of the roof. Luke had lived rough while homesteading with his brothers, but he thought he would be unhappy, indeed, to have to winter in such a makeshift shelter.

***

The general hospital was still a bedlam and full of far too many patients, but Luke could see that an order of sorts had been imposed on the chaos. Many of the patients appeared to be in a convalescent state, although there were still many who moaned in the grip of the acute phase of the disease.

"Luke! Welcome back!" It was Mrs. Thompson of the Benevolent Ladies. She confirmed that the peak of the crisis appeared to have been passed. "And not before time, I might add. It will take all of our resources to look after the patients who are recovering. Most of them are still too unwell to leave. And there are few places for them to go even if they could."

"How will they fare over the winter?" Thaddeus asked.

"They've begun to winterize some of the sheds," Mrs. Thompson said, "and part of the cellars at City Hall has been made available, as well. It's not ideal, but it's better than letting people freeze in the streets. I don't think any of the emigrants have any idea of what a Canadian winter is like."

They finally located Sister Bourbonnière in one of the hospital sheds. In spite of the fact that she was still ill, she continued to doggedly tend to her duties. She smiled when she saw Luke.

"I understand you've got some extra help now," Luke said. "Shouldn't you be lying down some- where?"

She shrugged. "There is nowhere. We do not 'ave as many to look after as we did, but still every bed is taken. I will survive."

"And Sister McGorrian?"

The nun's face grew more serious. "I am afraid that Sister McGorrian's life is in God's 'ands," she said. "She 'as been far sicker than the rest of us. We shall just 'ave to wait and see."

"This is my father, Thaddeus Lewis," Luke said. "Pa, this is the Sister I told you about."

Sister Bourbonnière grew more solemn at the introduction. "I am so sorry to 'ear about your good wife, sir," she said, "although I know that God will 'elp sustain you through these troubles."

"I have no doubt of it," Thaddeus said. "Thank you."

While his father spoke with the Sister, Luke scanned the shed anxiously. He knew he would have to face Father Higgins at some point, but he was not ready to do so. Not just yet. As his eye swept up and down the rows, he happened to notice a man who was past the critical stages of typhus, but still pale and thin and not yet ready to leave the fever shed. Luke wasn't sure why he remembered the man, until he turned to look the other way, his gaze falling on the bunk where John Porter had died. It came back to him then — the convalescent patient was the other Mullen brother.

"I know Dermot's in good hands now," Pierce Mullen had said to Father Higgins. Dermot Mullen. Luke had forgotten about him. There had been no reason to remember him particularly, except in connection with John Porter. Luke wasn't sure there was any reason to remember him now.

They checked the other sheds, both at the hospital and at Emily Street, but they found no sign of Anna Porter or Bridie Shanahan until they reached the cellars of the City Hall. They had been confused at first, approaching the imposing building from the market side, but were directed around to Ontario Street, where several doors opened onto steps that led to the building's subterranean depths.

Mrs. Shanahan was not hard to find once they reached the basement. She was perched on the Porters' trunk, which she had padded with a filthy piece of carpet, and her seven charges were clustered around her feet.

"We heard that they were opening the doors, and I sent Anna quick to get us a spot," she told Luke.

He could well imagine the ghostly Anna slipping in ahead of everyone else and staking out a spot until Mrs. Shanahan could move her brood and belongings holus bolus into the cellar.

"It's not so convenient as the other place," she continued. "We all have to share the stove, but it's a lot warmer and the privy is nicer."

"Mrs. Shanahan, everybody, this is my father, Mr. Lewis," Luke said.

"Oh, fathers and sons, fathers and sons, always in a lather about something they are. That's why I only have girls, you see," she said, peering at Thaddeus. "There have to be seven, though. Seven gets to heaven."

"I agree," Thaddeus said. "I always got along better with my daughters, although I have to say that this particular son has caused me little grief."

"Oh, Dr. Luke, yes he's a good boy. He fixed my thumb."

"May I sit for a moment with you and your excellent girls?" Thaddeus asked. "My old legs don't hold me as well as they used to."

Luke had warned his father that the children with Mrs. Shanahan were not her own, and that she was a little peculiar about the exact relationships.

"Sit down, sit down," the woman said. "Make some room, girls."

Luke sat down as well, but said nothing. His father seemed to be striking the right note with Bridie Shanahan, adopting a bantering tone that held no challenge. What Thaddeus did next, though, astonished him. His father produced a length of green ribbon from his jacket pocket, a ribbon that Luke was sure he had lately seen in his niece Martha's hair. Thaddeus made no reference to it; he merely began twisting it around his hand, then untwisting it, as if this were an unconscious and soothing habit of old.

Luke watched Anna closely. She noticed the ribbon — after all, she noticed everything — but did not appear to react.

It was Bridie Shanahan who became agitated.

"What do you want to bring that here for? Haven't we had enough of green ribbons? Leave them all behind in Ireland, I say. What do you want them here for?"

Thaddeus continued twisting it through his hands, while Mrs. Shanahan watched with repulsion on her face.

Finally, he said, "Why do they leave green ribbons, Mrs. Shanahan? Who do they leave them with?"

"Ribbonmen," she spat. "They bring nothing but trouble, when troubles are all we have. Too many died anyway. Put it away."

Thaddeus rolled the piece of ribbon into a ball and stuck it in his pocket.

"You're quite right," he said. "We have no need of green ribbons here, do we?"

She muttered and mumbled after this, and Luke judged that she would provide no more useful information for the time being.

His father apparently agreed. He stood, smiled at the children, and held out his hand for Mrs. Shanahan to shake. "We thank you for your time, ma'am, and I hope you find that your new home continues to be cozy."

She looked confused at the outstretched hand, but when Thaddeus bent into a slight bow, she smiled and shook it.

"Well, that was interesting," Thaddeus said as they walked away.

"Yes, it was," Luke said. "It certainly confirmed what Mr. McFaul told me, but I'm not sure that it had much to do with anything else. I'm not sure where we go from here."

"I think it's time to have a look at some records," Thaddeus said.

"If they exist."

"Oh, don't worry, there have to be records. You don't dump a hundred thousand people on the far side

of an ocean and not keep some sort of record. Let's
start with the emigration agent. Perhaps his lists have
something to tell us. Where would we find him?"

"At the brewery wharf. It's a long walk, I'm afraid."

"You know, I do believe Providence has conspired
to make my old age nothing but a plague of long
walks," Thaddeus grumbled. "All right, let's be off.
Let's just not go too fast."

"Dr. Luke!" A voice called out. "You're back!"

They had just reached the parade ground on King
Street, and Luke turned in the direction of the voice.
It was Mary, and she carried a bundle of rags that
was making a low mewling noise. It could only be
Deirdre Doyle.

He glanced around. "Where's Rennie?" he asked.

"Gone off, and she's never come back, this whole
time you've been gone." Mary sounded annoyed.

"But where did she go?"

"With Pierce Mullen. On the boat. She was supposed to come back in a couple of days." Deirdre
began to wail. "There, there, Deirdre." Mary jostled
the bundle, but it failed to have any sort of soothing
effect on the baby.

"On the boat?" Luke asked. "You mean on the
steamer?"

"Yes. Flea got him a job with Captain Bellwood.
The boat has gone back and forth every few days up
until now, so when Pierce asked Rennie to go to Toronto
with him, she thought she'd be back in a couple of days.

But she's been gone a long time, and I've been stuck with Deirdre."

As if to give substance to Mary's complaint, Deirdre's cries turned into an ear-splitting screech.

"I'm at my wit's end," Mary said, raising her voice to be heard above the cries. "She won't stop screaming."

Luke took the bundle from her and unwrapped the rags. His face deepened with worry as he examined the child. He handed her back and said, "You need to take her to the hospital."

"No. It isn't, is it?" Mary was wide-eyed.

"I don't know for sure," Luke said. "But she should see a doctor."

"I'll take her straight there," Mary said, "but what should I do about Rennie?"

"I'm not sure there's anything you can do," Luke said. "All I can tell you is that there is far less steamer traffic than there was. It may just be a case of the boat not coming back as soon as she thought."

"I wish Rennie had never set eyes on Pierce Mullen. He's caused her nothing but trouble. And now because of him, she's not even here for Deirdre. We need to find her, Dr. Luke." And with that she rushed off toward the hospital.

"It's amazing how often the words *need* and *we* end up in the same sentence, isn't it?" Thaddeus remarked after Mary left. "I'm beginning to understand why you constantly find yourself in difficulties when it comes to promises."

But Luke didn't appear to hear him.

"What is it?" Thaddeus asked.

"I'm not sure," Luke said. "It just seems odd to me that once again a Mullen pops his head up in the middle of strange circumstances."

"Who is this Rennie?" Thaddeus asked.

"Mary's sister. It's Rennie's baby. Both girls are pretty flighty, but they do seem to look after Deirdre."

"Do you think the sister has eloped with Mullen?"

"Oh, I don't think it was anything as firm as that. I suspect she just went off to have a bit of fun. Pierce and Rennie are from the same part of Ireland and knew each other from before. Someone told me Rennie always had eyes for Pierce and now that she's a widow she has hopes in that direction."

"Enough to abandon her child?"

"No, I don't think so," Luke said. "I'm sure it's just a matter of the steamer not coming back when she thought it would. I'm sure it will sort itself out in time."

"Ah well, in any event, I think it's clear that we're on the right track regarding the green ribbons, although I'm not sure what bearing they have on where the Porter girl has gone, or this Rennie woman either. Mrs. Shanahan's reaction was very telling, but I don't think the little girl with the strange skin knows anything about vigilantes and green ribbons."

"Don't be so sure," Luke said. "She's an odd little thing."

"Why did Mrs. Shanahan go on about there being seven?" Thaddeus asked.

"Apparently, she had seven children that she lost, and she's replaced them with seven children that she's gathered up from the sheds. I have no idea if they're genuine orphans or if they're like Anna and have just lost track of their relatives."

"Interesting," Thaddeus said, and then he lapsed into silence while they walked over a particularly rutted part of the street. "Did you tell me that John Porter was a Protestant?"

"Yes, that's what drew my attention to him. He heard me say I was the son of a Methodist minister and asked if you could visit him, although it turned out that he wasn't a Methodist. He belonged to the Church of Ireland."

"And Mrs. Shanahan?"

"I don't know," Luke said. "I've never asked her."

Chapter 23

The sorting point for emigrants arriving in Kingston had always been the brewery wharf. As a result, a tiny room at the east end of the brewery office building had been set aside for the use of the emigration agent and the assistants who had been hired when it became evident that the current season would see large numbers of Irish pouring in. Luke had witnessed the arrival of enough steamers to know that the agent kept records of some sort. He had seen the assistants scribbling away in ledgers while new arrivals were assessed. He had no idea what kind of records they were, or even if he would be allowed to look at them, but he judged that the office was a logical place to start.

The clerk behind the desk rolled his eyes when they made their request.

"We're trying to find the last known relative of a young orphaned girl," Thaddeus said. "I'm an ordained minister in the Methodist Episcopal Church. It's possible that she belongs with members of my meeting. I'd appreciate it if you'd at least let us look."

This story was plausible, Luke thought, but not very probable. Thaddeus had stretched the truth to the breaking point, but if it gained them a look at the agent's records, he supposed it was worth it. And then he realized that his father had told no lie. He had merely made statements that were, of themselves, true, and let the clerk infer that there was a connection between them. It was sophistry of the worst kind and Luke made a mental note to challenge his father on this later.

The clerk's face softened a little at the mention of an orphan, and he shoved a pile of ledgers at them. "It would help if you had a rough idea of the dates involved."

Luke had arrived in Kingston during the last week of July. "Somewhere between the twenty-first and the thirty-first of July," he said. This would cover a period that spanned several days on each side of his arrival.

"Try these," the clerk said, and he picked out two heavy leather-bound books.

"We also need the first records of the season, if that's possible," Thaddeus said, and was rewarded when the man showed him which one it was. "Don't forget we have more than one person we're looking for," he said when Luke cast him a questioning look. "Our green friends may be related in more than one way."

Luke opened the heavy cover of the book and found that the first page was dated July 20. The agent had kept far more complete records than he had imagined possible, given the crowds of emigrants that had arrived in Kingston each day, and the pressure to process and dispose of them as quickly as possible in order to make way for the next shipload. The name of the head of the household was listed down the left-hand column of each page, and beside it, in some cases, the name of his spouse. Children were not listed separately; just the fact of them, their number, and their gender. But to Luke's surprise, there was also a column that detailed the emigrants' final destination. And over on the right-hand side, what had happened to them. Many of them had been quarantined and Luke wondered how many had ultimately ended up on one of the wagons he had helped unload in front of the burial pit. Too many. Others had travelled on. Some of them had stayed in Kingston. Some of them had received assistance — a few pennies, at the most a shilling or two, in order to find a night's lodging or to procure a meal.

It was evident that the information had been entered in a great hurry. Some of the entries were nearly illegible, the agent scribbling down whatever information he could glean from emigrants resentful of being asked anything at all. He knew first-hand how suspicious they were of questions, how quick they were to conceal and confound.

Regan, Cleary, Murphy, Miller, O'Malley, O'Shea. Luke was struck by the sheer numbers in each family. In one case, he found an entry for a Gerald McCrea, aged fifty-two, who appeared to have in tow no fewer than sixteen children, their ages listed like stair steps, from a son in his twenties to a baby girl of two. What had happened to them all? Luke wondered. Did they have a destination in mind when they decided to cross the ocean, or had they just trusted their luck by choosing a town at random? What had happened to the matriarch of the family, for no mother had been listed? Were there even more children who had died in Ireland, succumbed on the voyage over, or been held back at Grosse Isle or Montreal or Prescott and died alone, snatched away from the secure bosom of a boisterous, lively family? The tragedy of the past summer became all the more poignant when he began attaching names to it.

Suddenly, one entry leapt out at him: Margaret Porter, aged eighteen. No other Porters listed that day, and the timing was right — the day before John Porter was quarantined in the hospital shed.

Poor Maggie, chasing down a battered piece of luggage, the contents of which were probably worth less than the cost of the steamboat ticket, unaware that the last members of her family would stop here in Kingston.

She had gone sailing on, but to where? His finger followed the row across the page, all of the spaces left blank except for one — destination. And there it was: Cobourg.

He made note of the name of the steamer she had boarded and then waited while his father continued running his finger down the long lists of names. "Ah," he said at one point, then continued through the next two or three pages before he closed the book and handed it back to the clerk with a comment of thanks. They both waited until they were outside the office before speaking.

"Maggie Porter passed through Kingston on July 25, the day before Anna's parents were detained here," Luke said. "So that gives us a specific date to work from. And the agent indicated that she was headed to Cobourg."

"Excellent," Thaddeus said. "You thought the uncle was in Bewdley, Beverly, or Bexley, correct? Our best bet is Bewdley. It's a little north of Cobourg."

"I knew you'd know the place."

"Been there many times. Preached at a fine three-day camp meeting there in 1841," Thaddeus said. "Rather marred, though, by the appearance of a mob of rowdies. I had to wrestle one of them to the ground."

"Is that allowed?"

Thaddeus shrugged. "Someone had to do it. So … would you like to hear what I found?" His father seemed almost jolly, and Luke reflected on how excellent Archibald McFaul's advice had been. Thaddeus's mind, "one of the finest in the Province," was apparently fully engaged in solving this Irish puzzle.

"There was no sign of anyone named David Porter."

Luke was disappointed. He had been sure that the green ribbons were related somehow, but he could make no case for it if David Porter had, in fact, stayed in Ireland or gone to England or America or the West Indies or anywhere but Canada.

"I did find two names that were of interest, however," Thaddeus said. "The first was Florence Mullen. Travelling alone, apparently, as no other family members were mentioned. He was listed as a passenger on the steamboat *Bellweather*, which departed from Kingston on May 21."

The Bellweather. Captain Bellwood. Flea Mullen loading empty barrels at the nearby wharf. Luke was a little surprised by this. He had assumed that Flea had been in the country far longer than a month or two. Every Irish emigrant to Canada was looking for work, but in the very short time he had been here Mullen had somehow managed to make connections and find employment with both Captain Bellwood and a boss called Hans.

"What was the other name?" he asked.

"Charley Gallagher."

"But that's not possible," Luke protested. "Charley Gallagher was shot down. He's dead. Unless it's a different Gallagher with the same name. There are probably a lot of Gallaghers in Ireland. It must be someone else entirely."

"You could be right," Thaddeus said, "but I find it intriguing that someone named Charley Gallagher was on the same steamer as Mullen."

"They must have been on one of the first ships to cross the Atlantic this spring," Luke said. "I wonder if it was *The Syria*?"

"What makes you ask that?"

"According to his brother, that was the ship Gallagher was expected to arrive on. I wonder if he had the ticket in his pocket when he was shot."

Thaddeus finished the thought for him. "And when it looked like he was dying, someone decided to make use of it in his stead."

"David Porter, travelling as Charley Gallagher?"

"Possibly," Thaddeus said. "Although I don't see

how he could have got his hands on the ticket. You can hardly shoot someone down and then run over and rifle his pockets while a dozen or more people stand and watch. And I doubt that any of Gallagher's friends or relatives would have handed it over willingly. Not to a Porter."

"Flea Mullen?"

"Much more likely, I think. Mullen travels on Gallagher's ticket and finds himself on the same steamer as a sworn enemy. If a green ribbon is a mark of revenge, I think we can conclude that our drowned man didn't fall off the boat accidentally."

"But if the drowned man was David Porter, why would he take Mullen's name? And why put on a dress and masquerade as a woman?"

"I can only conjecture at this point," Thaddeus said, "but what if Flea Mullen took Gallagher's ticket and followed David Porter? And what if David Porter knew he was being followed and decided to disguise himself as a woman? He wouldn't be able to use his own name."

"But why use Mullen's? Wouldn't that give him away?"

"I don't know." Thaddeus said. "I'm just pointing it out as a possibility. Maybe it was the first name that came to mind. And Florence is such an odd name for a man. Anyone here would assume it was a woman's name."

That was true enough, Luke realized. He himself had found some of the Irish names strange and unfamiliar, their gender unclear to his ears. The emigration agents had little time to inquire into anything too closely. They scribbled down whatever information they were given and moved on. And if David Porter was as fair and pale as his brother John, he would have had little beard to give him away.

"I think we need to talk to McFaul's priest and find out exactly what happened when Gallagher was shot," Thaddeus said. "If it turns out that Flea Mullen wasn't there that day, then our theory falls apart. If he was, then it's as good as anything else to go on."

"I've already talked to Higgins," Luke said. "I doubt he has anything more to say."

He didn't want to talk to the priest, didn't even want to see him. Whenever he thought about Higgins he got a sick feeling in his stomach and his mouth went dry. But he would have to act normally when they met again; otherwise Higgins might well read more into their encounter than was warranted. Or maybe it was warranted. Luke didn't know anymore. All he knew was that his father must never, ever find out about that night at the shore.

"I'm not sure I can get him to tell us anything else," he repeated.

"Well, I'll have to ask the questions then, won't I?" Thaddeus said. "In the meantime, let's have a look at that loading dock. If we do it now, it will save me walking all the way back here again."

There was little to see at the western end of the brewery other than a locked loading door. There wasn't even a window to peer through.

"I don't think there's anything here to see," Luke said. "But I'm sure there was something strange going on that day."

"I agree," Thaddeus said. "Otherwise I don't understand why a brewery in Kingston would have a barrel from a distillery in Toronto. Our Captain Bellwood is running some sort of racket, and I suspect that's why he wouldn't let Father Higgins aboard his boat that day. And you think Flea Mullen is mixed up in all this?"

"I'm sure of it," Luke said. "And now Pierce as well. Whatever connections Flea has have been expanded to include his brother. I wonder, though, what all this means for poor Rennie Doyle?"

Chapter 24

They caught up with Father Higgins in front of the general hospital.

"Luke!" Higgins said when he saw them. "And this is your father, is it not? How pleasant to see you again, sir." Then he turned to Luke. "You had some troubles when last I saw you."

Luke's face flushed. It was perfectly obvious to Thaddeus that something had gone wrong between the two. Luke's letters had been so full of praise for Higgins's dedicated service to the emigrants, and his delight in the other man's friendship, but now something had soured and Luke seemed uncomfortable in the priest's presence: an argument over some trifle, no doubt, and both of them too stiff-necked to make it up. Higgins's words, however, were obviously in reference to Betsy's last illness, and so he made an appropriate response.

"I'm afraid Luke's mother has gone to her Maker," he said. "Fortunately, Luke was with her in her last moments, and I'm sure that was a great comfort to her."

"I'm so sorry to hear that," Higgins said. "Please accept my condolences."

"Thank you. Mrs. Lewis had been ill for a number of years, and although I'll miss her sorely, we all know she's gone to a better place." The niceties dispensed with, Thaddeus came straight to the point. "And now, Luke and I wondered if we might have a word with you, if you would be so kind. We're intent on solving a puzzle."

"Of course. I'm just on my way to Hôtel Dieu if you'd like to walk with me."

Thaddeus felt that he had walked quite far enough that day, but the priest had already set off, so he had no chance to object. He hurried to catch up. Luke stayed a few paces behind, where he wouldn't have to join in the conversation. From this angle, he realized that Higgins had lost weight since he'd seen him last, and that although he still walked at a furious pace, he stumbled a little after every few steps.

As soon as he was in step with Higgins, Thaddeus said, "We're trying to find what's left of Anna Porter's family, and we understand that they came from your district."

"Anna Porter? The little ghostly girl that everyone thinks is a spirit of some kind? Yes, the Porters lived in my neighbourhood, but they weren't of my flock."

"I understand that," Thaddeus said, "but we're looking for information that at first glance might appear unrelated, but which we think might be helpful. What happened the day Charley Gallagher was shot?"

He had hoped to catch Higgins off balance and expected him to be taken aback or to hesitate before he answered, but the priest immediately replied, "Of course. What is it you want to know?"

"Everyone believes it was David Porter who fired the shot that killed Gallagher, but that's only what they've been told. Did you see it happen?"

"Yes, I did. There were several shots fired. No one knows for sure which bullet hit Charley, but yes, the generally accepted version of events is that David was in the best position to do so."

This was news to Thaddeus, the fact that more than one gun had gone off.

"What happened after that?"

"Charley fell to the ground and several people ran over to him."

"Who in particular?"

"What difference does it make?" the priest asked. "He was dying regardless of who knelt beside him."

"I'm not sure it makes any difference at all," Thaddeus said. "But in the interests of being thorough, I'd like to know, that's all."

The priest's brow furrowed as though trying to mentally recreate the scene of that day.

"Well, there was David himself of course."

"David Porter? He ran to the man he had just shot?"

"Yes. And Bridget Sullivan. That's Mrs. Shanahan's mother. She was Charley's cousin, you see. Flynn Murphy. Connor Doyle. Florence and Pierce Mullen."

"But not the other Mullen brother?" Thaddeus asked. "What is his name?"

The priest looked puzzled at this. "Dermot? No, Dermot wasn't there. Why?"

"What happened then?" Thaddeus asked. "What did everyone do besides sit there while Charley Gallagher died?"

"Well, Bridget ran to get a cloth, I suppose, to see if she could staunch the wound. Flynn ran off to find Mrs. Cleary, an old woman skilled with potions and such. Pierce jumped up and began shouting at David Porter."

"There was an argument?"

"Not so much argument as accusation. Pierce was about to go at David with his fists, but Connor grabbed one arm and I grabbed the other."

"No one went for a constable or some other authority?" Thaddeus asked.

Higgins looked impatient. "Of course not. Had the law been summoned, everyone there would have melted away long before it arrived. No one needed that kind of trouble on top of everything else."

"Even though someone had been killed?"

"Even so. There would have been an inquiry and the Porters would have been exonerated. It was a legal eviction. The Porters were defending themselves and it wasn't their fault that poor Catholic Charley Gallagher got in the way of a bullet. End of story." There was a bitter edge to Higgins's voice born of chronic injustice.

"What happened then?"

"David Porter ran off. Connor and I made sure that Pierce didn't follow him, then I went to Charley and administered the Sacraments. There was blood everywhere and his breath was laboured. It was evident he was dying, but at least he didn't die unshriven."

"And there were no consequences whatsoever for the Porters?"

"No legal consequences whatsoever," Higgins said. "David Porter disappeared that night, which everyone took as a sure sign of his guilt."

"Where do you think he went?"

Higgins looked impatient. "He could have gone anywhere. All of Ireland was on the move, the starving walking the roads looking for work, for food, for a roof over their heads. There were thousands of evictions, thousands of homeless families. David Porter could have gone to any other district in the country and no one ever would have remarked on the presence of a stranger."

"Could he have come to Canada?" Thaddeus asked.

"I suppose," Higgins said, and his eyes narrowed. "Why, do you think he's here?"

"We don't know. Maybe, maybe not. We're just going down as many twisted paths as we can follow." He gave Higgins his best smile, one that he had used many times to disarm. "We're just not sure whether there are any Porters left at all, you see, and then there would be the question of whether or not any of them would be in a position to look after the little girl. Were they a wealthy family?"

They had reached Hôtel Dieu, and Thaddeus half-expected Higgins to brush them off and go inside, but the priest halted at the front steps while he answered.

"They had a number of acres in wheat. Not wealthy, but not desperate either." He shrugged. "They probably sold their crop and used the money to buy passage. It's not a popular thing to do, when your neighbours are starving, but it would have been typical of the Porters."

Higgins took a step toward the door, and Thaddeus judged that little more information would be forthcoming this day.

"I just have one other question and then I'll let you be about your business," he said. "Do you know what this is? Luke found it on John Porter's body." He held out the scrap of green ribbon.

Higgins's eyes widened for a moment, but he said quickly. "It's just a scrap of ribbon." And with that, he disappeared into the hospital.

Thaddeus turned to Luke. "Let's walk on a bit," he said, "and then let's find a place to sit for a moment." His knee was throbbing from all the unaccustomed walking.

There was a low stone wall in front of a building just down the street, and when they reached it, Thaddeus lowered himself onto it with a barely stifled groan.

"Are you all right?" Luke asked. "I guess we shouldn't have walked so far."

"Never mind," Thaddeus said. "It was worth it not to interrupt the priest's story."

"What did you make of it?"

"There's something he's not telling us."

"You think he lied? But he's a priest."

"No, I don't think he lied." Thaddeus rubbed his knee as he thought about what he had been told. "But there were some things he deliberately left out, and some things he was hoping we would infer. Fortunately for us, he isn't very good at obfuscation. I don't expect he's done it often."

"But —"

"Just shush for a moment, boy, while I think this through."

Luke sat by his father and waited until he was ready to speak.

"First of all, Higgins knew perfectly well what the green ribbon meant."

"I agree," Luke said. "I couldn't see his face for most of the conversation, but he was startled when you showed him the ribbon."

"He didn't, however, seem to have any idea where David Porter went. Or how he got there."

"Someone took Charley Gallagher's ticket. And someone used it."

"It couldn't have been David Porter," Thaddeus said. "Pierce Mullen pushed him away. Higgins and the man named Connor intervened to prevent them getting into a fistfight. Who else was there?"

"Mrs. Shanahan's mother ran to get a cloth."

"Another man ran to get the old woman who was skilled with potions."

"That leaves one person sitting by Charley Gallagher's dying body."

"Florence Mullen," Thaddeus said. "And everyone's attention was on the scuffle happening a few feet away. Mullen could easily have reached into Gallagher's pocket and taken whatever was there. I think my idea that it was

Mullen travelling on Gallagher's ticket is reasonable. I just wonder why Higgins told us a tale about the Porters selling their wheat."

"What do you mean?" Luke asked. "How do you know it's a tale?"

"Think about it," Thaddeus said. "When was John Porter quarantined?"

"In the last week of July."

"And I wonder, on average, how long it takes a ship to cross the Atlantic?"

"Weeks and weeks. Probably two months or so. He had to have left Ireland in late March or early April. Oh …" Luke's eyes widened as he realized the point his father was making. "You don't harvest wheat in March."

"Precisely," Thaddeus said. "So why would Higgins spin us a tale about it?"

"To explain how the Porters could afford to emigrate?" Luke asked.

"It's not that expensive to come to Canada," Thaddeus pointed out. "That's why so many of them have come here, instead of going to the States. Higgins said the Porters were comfortable enough, and they'd been planning to emigrate anyway. Maybe they saved it up, or the uncle who was already here sent them money."

"I don't think so," Luke said. "His letters were full of boast, but he didn't seem to have accomplished much."

"In any event, families far poorer than the Porters found a way to get on a ship. So the question is, why did Father Higgins attempt to confuse the issue?"

"Is he protecting someone?"

Thaddeus considered for a moment before he replied. "Maybe. Or it may be a matter of something that was told to him in confidence — something that he considers privileged information. Perhaps he knows who fired the shot that hit Charley Gallagher and wanted to steer the conversation away from any further questions." He shrugged. "Or it may be something else entirely."

"I don't follow," Luke said. "It was David Porter who killed Gallagher."

"No," Thaddeus said. "Everyone *believed* it was David Porter. That's a different thing entirely. You know, it would be helpful if we could get someone else's version of what happened that day. So far, we've really only got one account."

"The problem is that there are so few people to ask now, and no one wants to talk about it anyway. We might try to make sense from Mrs. Shanahan's ramblings, but with her it's hard to tell what's real and what isn't."

"What about the girl?"

"Who? Anna?"

"No. The girl with the baby. The one we met on the way to the Emigration Office."

"Mary? Rennie Doyle's sister?" Luke said. "I hadn't thought of her. And apparently Rennie's husband was there that day, which I hadn't realized before. But I'm not sure how much Mary could tell us, other than what her brother-in-law told her."

"She may not have any new information about the shooting of Charley Gallagher," Thaddeus said, "but she might very well be able to tell us where to find the Mullens."

Chapter 25

Mary had taken the baby to Hôtel Dieu, either because she had greater faith in the nuns than in the Benevolent Ladies, or because the other hospital had no room for her, although Luke thought that little Deirdre must have been easier to accommodate than most patients. All she required was a cradle, which had been tucked into a corner at the far end of the hall. She was not difficult to locate — her fractious cries were audible from outside the front door.

Mary brightened when she saw Luke and Thaddeus, but her face grew guarded when Luke said, "Come outside for a minute and talk to us."

"I shouldn't leave Deirdre," she said.

It must be hard, Luke thought, to look after a seriously ill child that wasn't even your own. No wonder Mary was so anxious to locate Rennie. Then he thought of Mrs. Shanahan, who had gathered up seven helpless children, and of his parents, who had taken Martha in and treated her as their own.

"It's all right," he said. "The nuns are here if she worsens."

Thaddeus was waiting for them at the stone wall. Luke and Mary joined him there, sitting a little apart, so that his father would be close enough to hear what was said, but not so close that it seemed like he was part of the questioning.

"You and the Mullens and Mrs. Shanahan are all from the same place in Ireland, is that right?" Luke began.

"Yes, that's right. Banesalley. We all knew each other."

"Mrs. Shanahan said that Rennie always had an eye for Pierce Mullen."

Mary sighed. "Sometimes Rennie is such a silly girl. She was madly in love with Pierce, and Connor Doyle was madly in love with her. She couldn't get Pierce to settle down, so she married Connor instead."

"What happened to Connor?"

"The fever. We were all sick by the time we came here, although it turned out that Rennie and I didn't have ship's fever — just some other kind of fever. We were better after a few days, but Connor didn't even wake up long enough to say goodbye to Deirdre." She choked up a little as she said this.

Father and child, both in the same jeopardy, Luke thought.

"So when Pierce came waltzing into Kingston, the way was clear?"

Mary's eyes widened at this. "You mustn't think ill of Rennie. She would never have been disloyal to Connor. She made her vows and she intended to keep them. But you have to understand — two women and a baby by themselves in this strange country. It's a sad, lonely thing living on charity. So when Pierce turned up, Rennie thought maybe it was a chance at something better, and she liked him anyway, so who's to care? I know it seems wrong, with Connor so short a time in his grave, but there's no use pretending he's going to come back either."

"Don't take me the wrong way," Luke hastened to say, "I'm not judging anyone. I'm just trying to understand what happened."

"Rennie knew Pierce was here. She saw him at the sheds when he was visiting Dermot. She said he had changed, that he'd realized what he'd lost when she married Connor, and that he wanted to settle down. Flea got him a job on one of the boats, so he had ready money to spend. Rennie said she was just having a fling, but I know she hoped it would turn into something more."

"Would she leave the baby behind if she thought there was a chance with Pierce?"

"Never. I know Deirdre's difficult, but Rennie loves her. Something bad has happened, and now Deirdre's sick and Rennie may never see her again." Mary began to cry.

"Deirdre may be fine yet," Luke said, although his experience told him that this might not be so. "And I'm sure Rennie will come back for her. If Pierce has truly changed his ways, he'll bring her back." This only served to make Mary cry harder, and make Luke wonder if Rennie Doyle had herself fallen ill with typhus, and even now lay insensible in a fever shed somewhere.

Thaddeus silently handed over his handkerchief. Luke reflected that they should have brought a more ample supply. Handkerchiefs were items that seemed in great demand among the emigrant population of Kingston.

After the girl's sobs had subsided a bit, Thaddeus spoke for the first time.

"This has nothing really to do with you or your sister," he said, "but we're curious. Do you know anything about the day Charley Gallagher was shot?"

Mary blew her nose and she looked at Thaddeus suspiciously.

"Why do you want to know about that?"

"Because it might help us find Flea, and if we can find Flea, we might also find Pierce."

Conflicting reactions chased across Mary's face. Thaddeus waited without comment until she was ready to speak. Finally, concern over her sister seemed to trump whatever reluctance she had.

"It was Bridie Shanahan and her family who were being evicted. There was a fight and Charley was killed."

"Do you know who shot him?"

"No. I don't think anybody knows for sure. Most people seemed to think it was David Porter, the uncle of the strange little merrow that Mrs. Shanahan looks after, but Connor said it could as easily have been one of the other Porters."

"John Porter?"

"Or the son, Jack. He was there as well."

"There was trouble with the Porters before that, wasn't there?"

"Yes. They were always a quarrelsome lot. And nasty."

"In what way?"

"Well, for example, David Porter was a carter, and he'd undercut everyone else. Work for less, just to get the job. It was all right for him, he didn't have a family to support like the other men."

"So David Porter wasn't a farmer like his brother?" Thaddeus asked.

"No, John was the farmer. But they were both happy enough to sign on as destructives whenever they could. Most hated the work, but they enjoyed it. They'd be laughing and joking the whole time they tore a cabin down."

"Were there a lot of cabins torn down in Banesalley?"

"Yes," Mary said. "But we were luckier than most. We didn't have to go to the workhouse. The landlord offered to send us here. He said it was cheaper than paying the poor rates. Death or Canada, that's what they said to us. We didn't know it could be both."

Luke wondered if the Porters had been offered the same opportunity. It seemed likely, and would explain why they had emigrated before they'd had a chance to harvest a crop. But why had Higgins lied about it, if other tenants on the estate were being encouraged to come to Canada?

"Did anyone ever do anything to the Porters because they were upset with them?" Thaddeus asked.

"Of course not. Anna is a merrow. No one would dare. Although," she said, her brow wrinkled in thought, "she doesn't seem to have been much protection against the fever, does she? But that's the way with fairies, isn't it. Sometimes they bring great fortune, but there's always a price to pay."

Mention of the fever seemed to remind Mary of her obligations. "I really need to see to Deirdre," she said, standing up abruptly. "I've been gone a long time."

"Deirdre's fine," Thaddeus said.

"No, I have to go. I can't talk to you anymore." But when she was but a few steps away, she turned to them. "You'll go after Pierce, won't you? And you'll find Rennie?"

"We'll go after Pierce," Thaddeus agreed. "And we'll look for your sister while we do it."

After Mary disappeared into the Hôtel Dieu, Thaddeus turned to Luke. "Has our theory about the ribbons just fallen apart? And what on earth is a merrow?"

"It's a fairy spirit. From the sea. You've seen Anna, with her strange skin. Everyone in Banesalley believed that Anna inherited her … I don't know … *merrow-ness* … from her grandmother, and that she protected the whole family."

"It's a benign spirit, then?"

"No," Luke said, trying to remember what he had been told. "A merrow can be held against her will when someone takes her red cap. She can bring fortune, but she can be a harbinger of disaster as well. Father Higgins said that everyone believes that Anna Porter is a merrow and that Flea Mullen is a cluricaune, and that all the evils in the world are caused by the fairies fighting each other."

"Interesting," Thaddeus said, "although it's all nonsense, of course. Still … if the Porters were protected by a fairy, what would be the only thing that could touch them?"

"Another fairy," Luke said. "Flea Mullen."

Chapter 26

Luke wanted to make a stop in Wellington, in case there had been an answer to his letters to George Harliss, but Thaddeus argued that this was unnecessary.

"We already know that Margaret Porter was headed to Cobourg. We'll check the lists there, and if she got off the boat we know Harliss is in Bewdley. With any luck Margaret will be there as well."

"But what if she didn't?" Luke said.

"Beverly and Bexley aren't that far apart. If we have to go on, we can easily go to both."

Luke wondered if his father's reluctance to return to Wellington stemmed from an unwillingness to be reminded of Betsy's death. It would be hard for Thaddeus to return to the empty cabin, although Temperance House itself would be full of life — Francis, Sophie, Martha, all the guests. Still, there would come that moment when Thaddeus must go home — cross the yard and open the door to no one there. Luke didn't blame him for putting that moment off.

There were few other passengers on the packet steamer that ran between Kingston and ports west, so they had a corner of the cabin to themselves while they talked.

"I don't think there's any question that David Porter is our Wellington corpse," Thaddeus said, "but we can confirm that at Cobourg. The body had to have gone overboard somewhere between there and Kingston. If the name Florence Mullen is absent from the list, that will be a good indication that we're correct."

"And if 'Charley Gallagher' went on, we'll know we're right about Flea Mullen taking his ticket."

"Yes. But the only thing that would tie him to murder is the green ribbon. He certainly had motive enough, and opportunity, but without the ribbon, who's to say that David Porter didn't get tangled up in his skirts and fall overboard?"

Luke shifted uncomfortably in his seat. "There's one question we haven't addressed yet."

"What's that?" Thaddeus asked.

"Even if we do find out that the Mullens are responsible for the Porter deaths, what are we going to do about it? The evidence is all circumstantial, based on hearsay from witnesses who are just as likely to deny it all if asked again."

"Yes, I know. And it's equally likely that no one would do anything even if the witnesses could be per- suaded to repeat their stories. Who cares if two more

Irishmen die? And I certainly have no intention of standing in front of a constable and telling him about fairies. But it's not a question of bringing anyone to justice. It's question of knowing the truth."

"And what good will that do?" Luke asked.

"It will allow you to keep a promise," Thaddeus said. "You'll be able to tell Charley Gallagher's brother what really happened to him." He cast Luke a shrewd look. "I'm not sure the whole story is really all that important to Mr. Gallagher, but I have a suspicion that for some reason it's vitally important to you."

Luke's hands began to shake a little and he folded his arms so that it wouldn't be noticeable. His father was right, it was important to him. He couldn't be such a monster, could he, if he kept his promises? There was no bargain he could make that would be acceptable to God, he knew, but he could at least try, like his father had, to become a better man. He realized that Thaddeus's words were an invitation to confide, to share what was troubling him, but he held to his resolve — his father must never know what Luke suspected about himself.

Thaddeus broke the silence, which Luke was aware had stretched out far too long. "In any event," he said, "Providence has a way of taking care of things, even if the law won't. We'll discover what really happened, and then we'll have to wait for a higher court to mete out its justice."

The emigration agent at Cobourg was far less cooperative than the clerk in Kingston had been. It was a smaller port, for one thing, with fewer people landing, so the agent was the only man in the office. Not even Thaddeus's sad story about being a minister looking for someone from his lost flock was enough to melt his stone-faced refusal to let them look at the lists.

But they had the luck of timing to help. Just as they were turning to leave, a whistle blew. It was an emigrant steamer chugging into port, and it served them well as a distraction. The agent rushed hurriedly through the door, the latest record book tucked under his arm.

"He'll be a few minutes, don't you think?" Thaddeus said, reaching across the desk for the pile of ledgers that lay in a neat stack to one side.

They quickly located the books that held the dates in question, Luke scanning the lists from the last week of July, Thaddeus opting for the first of the season.

Luke ran his finger down a column and there it was: July 26, Margaret Porter. And a notation to the far right of the page — "trunk sent to Toronto by mistake."

Poor Maggie, chasing her family's luggage across a strange land. And unless she had enough for steamer fare to get herself back to Cobourg, she and her trunk were probably still in Toronto. The sorry crowd of Irish he had met earlier that summer had been forced to walk miles to claim their belongings. "They'll pay one way, but not the other," the old man had said.

"She was here and went on," Luke said to Thaddeus. "Hurry up before the agent comes back."

"*Mmm,*" was the reply. Thaddeus appeared to be reading everything twice.

Luke was about to replace his ledger when it slipped out of his hand and fell to the floor, its pages splaying open. He picked it up and smoothed out the pages, brushing the dust from them as best he could. And then his mind registered a name: John Porter. Travelling alone. Disembarked at Cobourg. Given a shilling for lodgings until he could meet up with his relatives.

But John Porter had died in Kingston. Luke had buried the body himself. And then he realized what the entry meant: not the John Porter he knew, but his son. Anna had called him "Jack" and said that he was ill and had been quarantined at Montreal. Perhaps his illness wasn't typhus, but something else from which he had recovered in a few days. It happened often enough, he knew, this mistake in diagnosis, and Montreal was worse than Kingston in terms of the numbers of typhus victims they were treating. Even if Jack Porter had the dreaded ship's fever, he might have recovered enough to have been sent on his way as soon as possible, so that his bed might be used for someone else. He checked the date in the ledger: August 6.

He was bursting with what he had discovered, but he waited until his father finally shut the other ledger with a bang and then they replaced both books, as far as they could tell, in the order in which they had found them. After a quick look out the door to make sure the agent was still fully occupied, they slipped outside and walked away as fast as they could.

Luke let his father speak first. "I could find no listing for Florence Mullen," he said. "Charley Gallagher spent one night in Cobourg and presumably boarded another steamer the next day. Our dead man is almost certainly David Porter."

"Margaret Porter's trunk was mistakenly sent on to Toronto, and she followed it there."

"Could she have returned with it in the meantime?"

"I doubt it," Luke said, "unless she had some money with her. They don't pay for them to come back."

"Then it's off to Bewdley," Thaddeus said. "Either she tracked down her luggage and came back to her uncle's, or she's still in Toronto."

"I did find one other name of interest," Luke said. "John Porter. It can't be Anna's father, so it must be her brother Jack."

"Her brother? You didn't tell me there was a brother involved," Thaddeus said. "Honestly, Luke, if you expect me to help you solve puzzles, you have to give me all the pieces."

"He was quarantined at Montreal. I just assumed he was either dead or still there. He must have recovered from whatever he had and come to Cobourg to find his uncle."

"And now we'll find him," Thaddeus said. "Let's see if we can hire a couple of horses and we'll make a ride to Bewdley."

They rode west for six or seven miles to the town of Port Hope before they turned north. Bewdley was situated at the tip of Rice Lake, Thaddeus said, and although he had preached there on occasion, the Wesleyan Methodists, a denomination at odds with his own Methodist

Episcopals, had made great inroads in the area. He did allow, however, that the Church of England appeared to be the most popular in the township.

Bewdley was a very small town indeed, and Luke wondered how his father had ever gathered enough people together for the meeting at which he had wrestled a heckler to the ground. There was a sawmill, a general store, and an inn, along with a scattering of houses, none of them particularly imposing. It would be the timber trade, he supposed, that kept Bewdley going, and he wondered how the town would fare now that Britain's railways no longer needed Canadian wood.

When they asked for directions at the general store, the storekeeper directed them along a road that led northwest. As the man was also the postmaster, he handed them two letters and asked if they would mind delivering them, "seeing as how Mr. Harliss hasn't been in for weeks, and you're going there anyway." Luke recognized the letter he had himself sent, and, with a sinking heart, suspected that the other one was from John Porter. He tucked his own letter away in his pack. If this was the George Harliss they were looking for, there was no point in delivering it. If he wasn't, there was even less purpose in doing so.

They found the Harliss farm down a narrow road that was overgrown with grass and weeds. They might have gone right past the cabin, it was so hidden by gnarled lilac and sapling trees, but the sound of an axe slapping against wood made them stop and take a closer look through the bushes. There was only the faintest evidence of a path, and when they found it, it was deep in fallen leaves. It was clear that few people had walked from the cabin to the road in recent days, nor had anyone ventured down the path to the clearing.

The cabin, when they found it, was tiny and lopsided, a settler's shanty, built many years ago and unimproved since then. They followed the sound of the axe around to the back, where perhaps two acres had been cleared, the scanty crops harvested. Beyond that, there were only trees.

"Not much has been accomplished here, has it?" Thaddeus remarked.

"No. And it doesn't look much like the fine farm he described in his letters." Harliss had apparently been here for several years. Luke thought of the many acres he had chopped and burned, and the progress that his brother's Huron farm had seen in much the same amount of time.

They crossed the field to where a thin young man was attempting to fell a large oak, his axe pinging off the dense wood. With every stroke he made, the axe head tangled in the branches of a stumpy cedar close by, hindering the effectiveness of his effort. Not far away, an older man was digging at a stump. They stopped when they saw the Lewises and waited while they crossed the field.

"Are you George Harliss?" Thaddeus asked, and when he received a nod in affirmation, he turned to the boy. "And are you Jack Porter?"

"Who wants to know?" The reply was surly, the boy's face narrowed in suspicion.

"We have news of your family."

"My family's dead, as far as I know," Jack said. "They died of being Irish."

"Not all of them," Luke said.

At this, the older man spoke up. "Who are you anyway? Why have you come here?"

"I'm Luke Lewis, and this is my father, Thaddeus. I've come from Kingston, where I was helping in the fever sheds. I wrote you a letter."

Harliss spat. "Haven't been to town since spring."

Luke wasn't sure how to proceed. He was about to tell these men that nearly all of their family was dead or missing, and yet he had to do it in such a way that he could offer them some hope as well. After all, there were still Anna and Maggie to think of. He was grateful when his father spoke, addressing Jack directly.

"Your sister Anna is in Kingston. She's being looked after by a very kind woman, but she's anxious to find her family. We have every reason to believe that your other sister, Margaret, is alive as well, and we were attempting to find her when we discovered your name on the passenger lists in Cobourg."

Jack Porter was very still as he asked, "And Ma and Pa?"

"I'm afraid they died of the fever. I'm sorry."

Jack's shoulders sagged. "Yes. I was sure that was the case, otherwise they'd have been here by now."

"We'd best go up to the cabin and you can tell us what you know." Harliss walked over to Jack and took the axe from his hand. "C'mon boy, you should go sit down."

There was a bench at the back door by the well, and Jack sat down heavily. Harliss lowered himself down beside the boy and looked expectantly at the Lewises, but instead it was Jack who spoke.

"They took me off the boat at Montreal," he said. "The doctor there said I had fever, and it's true, I was burning up. The others were told they had to go on without me. Pa told me that when I got better I was to stop at a place called Cobourg, as that was the nearest port to Uncle George's farm, and that he would leave word with the emigrant agent there that I was expected. He'd leave a little money, he said, and directions on how to reach Bewdley and the farm."

These must have been comforting words to Jack's ears, Luke thought, this notion that he would get better and join the family again. John Porter must have believed that he was saying a final goodbye to his oldest son, but he had hidden it for the boy's sake.

"My fever went away in a few days," Jack said. "It comes back now and then, but it wasn't the same fever that was killing everyone else. When I got better, they stuck me on a boat and sent me on. They said they needed the bed for someone else."

Luke nodded. "Yes, they would have done. The hospitals have been overflowing with sick."

"I got off at Cobourg and went to the agent like Pa said to, but he had no message for me, and no money either. I didn't know what to do. They fed me a little and tried to make me get on another steamer, but when I said I wouldn't go, they gave me money for a bed for the night. The next day I asked the way to Bewdley. I thought maybe Uncle George could help me look for the others, but of course I thought Uncle George had a fine, working farm and all kinds of money to spare. I didn't expect this." He looked around him in disgust.

Harliss said, "It will be one day, my boy. I'd been counting on your father to lend a hand, mind you, and the others to work as well. But even if it's just you and me, we can build it up."

Not unless you manage to clear your land a little faster, Luke thought.

Jack looked at his uncle. "You don't even know how to cut the trees down," he said. "At the rate we're going, it will be a hundred years before you have a farm."

"Be that as it may," Thaddeus said, "we have some other issues to deal with first."

Luke was glad that his father had interjected with this. Jack Porter was obviously profoundly disappointed in his uncle and spoiling for a fight over it.

"Perhaps Luke, here, would be the best person to tell you what happened to your father. He was there at the time."

"By the time they reached Kingston, your parents were both showing signs of infection," Luke said. "They were quarantined there. Your mother died. And although your father survived the fever, and appeared to be getting better, he died a few days later. I'm sorry."

"He was getting better? But he died anyway? And how does that happen then?"

"It happens," Luke said. "Sometimes the fever leaves a person with congestion, or it affects the kidneys.

It's not that uncommon." Except that John Porter was also left a green ribbon along with his pneumonia.

"And Maggie? What happened to Maggie?"

"Some of your luggage went missing, and no one was sure where it was sent. Your parents and Anna went one way and Maggie the other in an attempt to track it down."

"Da would have told her the same as me," Jack said. "She would have asked the agent at Cobourg if there was any message for her."

"There was, of course, no message, but she did find out that her trunk had been sent on to Toronto. We think she followed it."

Jack sighed, but suspicion had returned to Harliss.

"Why are you botherin' yourselves about this anyway? There's hundreds of missing Irish. Are you going to track them all down?"

"My son's initial motivation was to try to find what is left of Anna's family," Thaddeus said. "She is being looked after, but her current situation is less than ideal."

Jack snorted. "There is no situation in the world that would be ideal for that whelp. They say our grandmother was a merrow, and I believe it, for Anna's inherited all the traits. She brings good fortune in one hand and carries it away with the other."

So even her own family considered her something strange. Poor Anna.

"There are some other considerations," Thaddeus said. "There are some things that have happened that are a puzzle. As I find myself in need of diversion, I offered to help Luke try to solve it."

"What things?" Jack asked.

Luke brought the green ribbon out of his pocket. "I found this with your father's body."

Jack leapt to his feet. "I thought you said Pa died of fever," he shouted at them.

"I'm almost certain that he did," Luke said. "He certainly had typhus. And in all probability that's what killed him."

"Do you know what the green ribbon means?"

"Someone told me that when it's found with a body it signals a vigilante killing. What we don't know is whether it was placed with him, or if he intended to leave it with someone else."

"The green ribbon is left by Catholics," Jack said. "If you want to know how it ended up with my father, you should ask them, since they're the ones that murder people in their beds." He stopped for a moment as if to consider the import of what he had just been told. "So my father was killed."

"I don't know that," Luke replied. "Sometimes patients die just when you think they're getting better. I can't be certain this wasn't the case with your father."

Again George Harliss interjected. "And just how many fever victims have you found with green ribbons?"

Luke ignored him. "Do you know what happened that day? The day of the eviction?"

Jack sat down again and cradled his head in his hands. "What difference does it make?"

"Leave him alone," Harliss said. "He's just found out that his parents died. Why pester him with questions?"

"Because we're looking for the truth," Thaddeus said. "The truth … and Margaret."

"I was there," Jack said.

"At the eviction?"

"Yes. The bailiff knew there was going to be trouble. Too many people had been turned out, and they all blamed us. We were just doing a job and happy with the extra money we were being paid to do the teardown. Pa was uneasy when the guns came out, but we were making plans to emigrate and every penny was welcome, so we could hardly refuse." He sighed. "You have to understand — our potatoes turned black too. Even once we'd sold our corn, there was going to be barely enough to feed us all and pay the passage as well."

"What happened?" Thaddeus asked.

"We were just about to pull down the roof beam when a mob came along the road, yelling. They shouted at us for a few minutes and then some of them started throwing rocks." He shrugged. "Some shots were fired, and then Gallagher fell over."

"Do you know whose shot hit him?"

"I don't know," he said. "It all happened so fast. Uncle David, maybe. Da was on the roof. I'm not sure if the bailiff fired or not. Suddenly everybody was running toward Gallagher, but then Pierce Mullen went after Uncle David and the priest tried to stop him. The priest and Connor Doyle."

"And what happened after that?"

"Everybody ran. The mob, Uncle David, me. I went home and told Ma what had happened, and she was in a state until Da came in. She was sure he'd be murdered."

Thaddeus frowned. "Why was she worried about your father? Everyone was convinced it was your uncle who had fired the shot."

"I didn't know that at the time," Jack said. "All I knew was that there had been a killing. By a Porter. And our name was Porter, and we'd share the blame. It looks like Ma was right to be worried, doesn't it? Only they waited until he was in Canada to get him."

"We don't know that for certain," Thaddeus pointed out. "Where did your Uncle David go?"

Jack shrugged. "I don't know. He just went away."

Luke was sure that Jack wasn't telling the whole story. Higgins had said that no Protestant would ever be convicted of shooting down a Catholic under the circumstances. After all, the Catholics had attacked first.

"Didn't your uncle have Anna's protection?" he said. "I was told that no one dared touch a Porter because she's a merrow."

"That's such a load of nonsense," Jack said. "Da always said she was like his mother, and that our good fortune was due to her. If that's the case, the effect must have been diluted over the generations, because our fortune was never very great. As far as I'm concerned she's just a strange wee thing who makes everyone nervous because of the way she looks."

"What has this got to do with anything?" George Harliss said. "This is ancient history. Ancient Irish foolishness. It should be left in Ireland where it belongs."

Thaddeus ignored him. "Can you think back for me, Jack? On the day of the shooting, who ran to Charley Gallagher first?"

"The priest and the Mullens." Exactly as the priest had said, Luke thought. At least he hadn't lied about that. Then Jack's eyes widened. "Do you think the Mullens had something to do with Da? How could they from Ireland?"

"They're here in Canada," Luke said. "They were in Kingston."

"Well, there you have it, don't you? If you think Da was murdered, you needn't look any further than the Mullens."

"I'm not making that assumption," Thaddeus said, "nor should you. We don't know what happened. It could well be as Luke said and your father died as a result of the fever. But in the meantime, we need to find out what happened to your sister. We'll go on to the next port after Cobourg and see if we can trace the records."

"I'm coming with you," Jack said.

Harliss protested. "You can't go off and leave me now. I'm counting on you, boy."

Jack spun to face his uncle. "And we were counting on you. A lot of good that did us, you old liar!"

Harliss began to whine and looked to Thaddeus in the hope of support. "I had no help. And I don't know how to chop. I don't know how to do anything. I thought it was such a grand thing that I could have my own land, but no one told me the state it would be in. I didn't know there could be so many trees in all the world."

"As far as I'm concerned, you can make the personal acquaintance of each and every one of them," Jack said. "And you can do it without me."

Chapter 27

Maggie Porter's trail ended at Toronto Harbour. As they moved along the north shore of the lake, each port's records became more chaotic, the names scrawled in hurriedly. The great flock of emigrants had been pushed ever westward until they spilled out over Canada's hinterland looking for somewhere they could light for an hour, a day, a week, anytime at all as long as there was a mouthful of food in it.

The fact that she had been allowed to disembark was unusual. Luke had witnessed the assessments that had taken place in Toronto — the sick shunted to the sheds, those with relatives herded up the street, everyone else directed back to the steamers, where they would be taken on to the next port.

"She had no relatives here, and no job to go to, so why was she allowed to stay?" Thaddeus asked.

"Someone must have vouched for her at the dock,"

Luke said. "The day I was here there was an official of some sort picking girls out of the crowd, although he didn't appear to be connected with the emigration agents. They were taken around the corner to where Flea Mullen was waiting with a wagon. I wonder if that's what happened to her?"

"She would never have gone with Flea Mullen," Jack said. "She would have run as fast as she could in the other direction."

"Yes," Luke said, "but Flea wasn't the only carter in Toronto. It could have been someone she didn't know. And a couple of weeks after I saw him, Flea wasn't driving anymore. He was working as crew on one of the steamers."

"So where would these girls have gone?" Jack asked. "Were there some sort of jobs for them to fill? Domestic servant or something?"

"Yes, I'm sure it was something like that," Luke said quickly. He had his suspicions that it was nothing so innocent, but they had no evidence that Maggie had been picked out of the crowd, or boarded a stranger's wagon. But as they walked along Front Street they saw signs in many windows — NO IRISH NEED APPLY. It seemed more and more unlikely that Toronto's affluent families would countenance an unskilled Irish girl in their households, not even to do the laundry or carry the slops.

"Maybe she kept walking in the hopes of finding farm work farther north," Luke said.

"She's just a wee thing," Jack said. "She'd never be strong enough to do much in the way of heavy work. She'd be passed by in a moment for someone bigger."

"So how do we find her?" Luke asked.

"Let's start with the simple solution," Thaddeus said. "We could put an advertisement in the paper."

"And even if she saw it, how would she find us? We have no address to leave other than Wellington."

Thaddeus had to think for a moment before he could answer. "We could ask her to contact the emigration agent. We'll leave word with him."

"You can do whatever you like," Jack said, "but I'm not going to sit and wait for her to get in touch with us. I'm going to look for her."

"As are we," Thaddeus replied, "but we'll cover all the eventualities that we can. Let's search the obvious places first, and if we find nothing, we'll go to one of the newspapers."

They began their search at Reese's wharf. It had been here that the steamers had disgorged their gaunt passengers all summer, but now, at season's end, it was nearly deserted. They made their way north to King Street, where Toronto's fever sheds had been built, twelve long structures that had housed thousands at the height of the crisis, but here they were informed that convalescent patients had been transferred to the hospital at the western end of the city limits, near the old fort.

They continued west along King Street, Thaddeus grumbling at the distances involved.

"The city's grown too much since I was last here," he said. "It used to be that you could walk across the whole thing in a few minutes."

They soon found the Convalescent Hospital and a nearby stable that had been converted to accommodate

extra patients, but they could find no indication that a
Margaret Porter had ever been there. As at Kingston,
the hospital was staffed mostly by volunteers, the
Toronto equivalent of the Benevolent Ladies, Luke
supposed. Thaddeus stopped to speak with a woman
who was carrying a bucket of water down the hall.

"Where do the patients go who have recovered?"
he asked. "Or at least the ones who are healthy enough
to be discharged?"

The woman shrugged. "A lot of them don't wait
for permission to leave. They just walk away, although
they're not supposed to go into the city if they show
signs of fever. If they aren't herded out into the country
to look for work, they find a shack somewhere and live
off the charity of the soup kitchens. The New Town
Extension just over there is full of them, and they tell
me Corktown, down by the Don River, is nothing but
Irish shacks. Those would be the most likely places to
look for someone."

"Should we go east or west?" Luke asked as they
stood on the steps outside the hospital.

"Let's try to the west," Thaddeus said. "It's closer."

The area around Fort York and Garrison
Common was rapidly being encroached upon by the
expansion of the city, but the architecture of the New
Town Extension was a jumble of wooden sheds and
unpainted houses. Small groups of thin, ragged men
and women sat in front of these, while their similarly
thin and ragged children darted here and there, chasing one another or throwing rocks with no particular
aim in mind. These urchins descended on Jack and

the Lewises as soon as they came into view, crowding around, asking for pennies.

Thaddeus chased them away with a word. Again, Luke wished he had that kind of command over people. If he had been alone, he knew that he would have been marked as an easy target, and that the children would soon have relieved him of most of his pennies. Jack just scowled at them, and they seemed to find him unapproachable, for he walked along as though there were a wall that enclosed him, protecting him from unwanted contact.

No one they asked seemed to know anything about a Margaret Porter.

"Try along the wharves," one man said. "That's where most of the whores are."

Jack's fists balled up and he was about to lunge at the man, but Luke and Thaddeus each grabbed an arm to hold him back. "He means nothing by it, Jack" Luke said. "He doesn't know her." But again he had the uncomfortable feeling that Maggie might well have fallen prey to the last resort of desperate women.

"I always choose the wrong way," Thaddeus grumbled as they turned east again. "Now we have to walk all the way back and then some."

Luke knew that the constant travel of the last few days had aggravated the pain in his father's knee. As they reached Front Street again, he hailed a passing horse cab.

"You're free with your money," Thaddeus noted as he sank gratefully into the seat. "But I won't complain about it."

Soon they were at the eastern end of the city, which was bounded by the course of the Don River. Discouraged from settling in the city, the emigrants had hunkered down along the banks of the river. Everywhere they looked there were wooden shacks and sheds; sometimes little more than pieces of board propped against a fence served as shelter.

Again, as they approached, they were bombarded with requests for money, for food, for any kind of benefaction. Rather than chasing them away as he had done before, Thaddeus took a coin out of his pocket and fingered it without offering it. "Does anyone know where we can find Margaret Porter, sometimes known as Maggie?" he asked.

The beggars eyed the coin, but no one answered, until finally one of them stepped forward, in size like a child, but a child whose face was lined with the worries of a hundred-year-old man. "We can find a girl for you, if the price is right."

"I don't want just any girl," Thaddeus said. "I'm looking for Maggie Porter."

"There's a Maggie over in the next alley," a boy said.

"There's a family moved in the end of my row. I'm sure their name is Porter," said another.

"Me sister's name is Maggie."

"Our cousins are Porters."

"I seen them on King Street."

They would say anything for the money, Luke knew, anything that anyone wanted to hear.

Thaddeus put the money back in his pocket. "If you can find the real Maggie Porter, I'll give out the money," he said. "But I have to see her with my own eyes first."

The crowd of beggars muttered and moved away.

"It was worth a try," Thaddeus said.

"Not with the Irish."

They continued walking amongst the shacks, picking their way through the muddy ruts and malodorous refuse that had accumulated in what passed for streets. Jack stayed a few paces behind, as if to deny any connection with them.

They were well into a haphazard collection of huts, where no attempt had been made to allow for paths of any kind, when Luke stepped into a pile of muck and his foot slid sideways. Thaddeus caught his arm as he fell, only just managing to forestall a headlong tumble into the slime.

"Are you all right?"

"I'm fine, Pa, thanks. I nearly went in though."

"Dr. Luke?"

Luke spun around at the sound of the voice.

"Is that you, Dr. Luke?"

The call came from under an overhang of three planks that had been shoved up against the side of one of the shacks. Luke walked over to the low opening that served as a doorway and peered in.

"Rennie? What are you doing here?"

"I'm stranded," she said. "Can you help me?"

"Come out, so we can talk to you."

"I can't. I don't want you to see me like this."

Luke looked at the other two and shrugged. He ducked under the overhang to find Rennie shivering against the wall of the adjacent shack. She appeared to have little on but a dressing gown, which she clutched tightly around herself.

"How did you end up like this, Rennie? This is dreadful."

"I told you. I was stranded. Then I got away, but now I have to hide."

"Hide from who?"

She began to cry, sobbing so much that Luke could hardly make out what she was saying.

"I went off with Pierce on the boat," she said.

"I know. Your sister Mary told me. She's been terribly worried."

"Is Deirdre all right? Mary has her, doesn't she?"

"Yes, Mary has her." Luke didn't want to add to Rennie's distress by telling her that Deirdre was in hospital. Time enough for that later, when he could break it gently. "What happened?"

"I went off with Pierce just for a bit of a good time. I always fancied him, you know, even after I persuaded myself that I was in love with Connor. I know that's wrong, but I couldn't help how I felt, could I? And now Connor's gone."

She glared at Luke, as if challenging him to dispute this sad fact. "Any road, Connor's dead and Pierce wanted me to go with him on the boat. He said we'd be back in Kingston in a day or two. I didn't think there was any harm in it, me having a day or two to have some fun for once."

Again, she looked to Luke, seeking some sign of approval. He merely nodded his head, neither confirming nor rejecting her argument. It would be easy enough, he supposed, to condemn her on moral grounds, if he were a different man. But Luke's own moral ground was decidedly shaky. He let the statement pass. "So you went on the boat?"

"Oh, aye, and it was grand. I got to ride in the cabin, away from all the rest. And then we got here and went to a big brick house and had a meal where there was more than I could eat and it was wonderful. Pierce said he had a good job with Hans and we could go back and get Deirdre and Mary and find a nice place to live and it would all be fine."

Hans. The mysterious Hans, who shorted the constable at the Toronto docks and dared the man to complain about it. Hans, who would be unhappy if someone in Kingston made a mistake and there weren't more barrels in a couple of weeks.

"Just who is this Hans?" Luke asked.

"Not Hans, *Hands*." Rennie hit the final *d* hard when she said it, so that Luke would understand what the name was. "I don't know who he is, but he's called Hands because he has his hands in everything, or so they say. There's not a cutpurse or a harlot in the city but owes part of their takings to Hands."

"So Flea, and now Pierce, are mixed up in all this?"

"I didn't realize it until I got here. I swear."

"But that still doesn't explain how you ended up here." He wanted to add "half-dressed" to the observation, but Rennie was embarrassed enough as it was, he judged.

She wiped her streaming eyes on a corner of the

dressing gown. "Hands runs most of the whores in Toronto. He's been picking young girls off the boats all summer, promising them work. The prettiest ones would be put in the brothels — he's got four or five on the go — and the others would be sent out to work the wharves."

So Luke's suspicions had been on the mark. He wished now that he had intervened when he saw the girls in the wagon with Mullen. In all honesty, though, what could he have offered them in exchange? Another journey on another boat to another strange town where no one wanted them?

Rennie went on. "After a few days, I started to realize what was going on. These gentlemen in fine suits would come to the door and go upstairs, but they wouldn't stay long. I tried to get Pierce to leave right then and there, but he wouldn't. He said there was nowhere else he could make as much money as working for Hands."

That was probably true enough, Luke thought. Every emigrant in the city was looking for work.

"I kept asking when we would be going back to Kingston, and Pierce said that was up to Hands and Captain Bellwood. And then one day Hands came in and told Pierce he had to leave that night, he had a job for him."

"Where did Pierce go?"

Rennie shrugged. "I don't know. It could be any-where. But as soon as he was gone, Hands lived up to his name. He had his hands all over me. You see, when I arrived with Pierce, Hands assumed that I was

just another girl — as soon as Pierce was done with me,
I'd be put to work. My dirty old rags were long since
burned, and I was given this dressing gown to wear
instead. They promised a new dress, but I never saw it.
When I told Hands to leave me alone or I'd bolt, he just
laughed at me. He said he had every constable in the
city in his pocket and if I ran away, I'd be arrested for
stealing the clothes they gave me. That's how they keep
the girls there, you see, by threatening them with jail."

"What did you do?"

She looked at Luke as though he was dim and half
mad. "I let him do what he wanted, of course," she
said. "And then I went to Flea and asked him to help
me. He said Hands won't abide anyone defying him
and that he'd hunt me down to the ends of the earth if
I crossed him. He said one time a girl ran away and she
ended up floating in the river."

Murder, fraud, theft, rape. Up until that moment,
following the trail of what had happened to the Porters
had seemed like a simple enough thing to do. Now it
had suddenly become far more dangerous than Luke
had ever imagined.

"That night I went upstairs," Rennie continued.
"Flea and Hands had gone off somewhere. The doors
were all locked, but I knew that the older woman who
looked after the girls had the keys on her belt. I thought
if I could get all of the girls to come with me, we could
knock her down and take them. The one girl I talked
to wouldn't even listen to me. She was in a right state, I
tell you." Here she stopped and wiped her nose on her
tatty gown. "One of the other girls had just swallowed

three bottles of Fowler's Solution and they were in fear for her life."

"Fowler's Solution? That's arsenical based."

"Yes, each girl gets a quarter teaspoonful every day, so they won't get … um … diseased, you know … from what they're doing."

Luke didn't know, but Rennie blushed furiously as she said this, so he assumed that Fowler's Solution warded off some ill-effect of harlotry.

"Anyway, this girl got hold of all the Fowler's that was in the house and drank it straight down. The old woman was in a lather and most of the girls were clustered in one of the rooms around the body. I tiptoed in and had a peek, and it gave me a start, I'll tell you, when I saw who it was."

Luke felt his stomach heave as he asked, "Who?"

"Maggie Porter. She was having some kind of fit and heaving and rolling and shaking and the old woman was trying to hold her down while the girls clustered around weeping and wringing their hands."

Anna had said Maggie was dead, and Luke had dismissed her words. But that had been days ago. She had predicted the same for her brother Jack, however, and he was still alive. Luke vowed to keep a close watch on him. Jack was far too ready to solve problems with his fists.

"The old woman had the keys on her belt and I didn't dare get close enough to try to take them," Rennie said, "but everyone was making such a racket that I figured no one would notice a little more noise. The lock on the back door was pretty flimsy-looking, so I took a poker and pried it open. And then I came here. But I'm afraid to go anywhere else. Hands will find me and kill me."

"When was this?"

"Last night."

Luke rocked back on his heels as he tried to think what to do. He wanted to reassure Rennie that she was safe now, that Hands wouldn't find her, but he realized that he had no idea if that was the case. He needed to talk to his father. And he was going to have to tell Jack Porter that his sister was probably dying, if not already dead.

"Wait here," he said to Rennie. "And don't worry, we'll sort something out for you."

He stepped outside the lean-to and motioned to his father to join him as he moved away from where Jack was standing.

"What's this?" Jack shouted after them. "Keeping secrets from me, are you? I demand to know what's going on."

If the rest of his family had been anything like Jack, Luke was beginning to realize why the Porters had been so disliked. "I'll just be a moment," he said, "and then I'll tell you everything I know. I just need to consult with my father to see who might be able to help the poor girl inside."

But Rennie had heard them and poked her head outside. She hadn't realized Jack was with them until then. He had hung back when she'd first called to Luke.

"Jack Porter?" she said. "You have Jack Porter with you? What's he doing here?" Dislike and suspicion were apparent on her face.

"It's all right, Rennie, he just came along to help us find his sister," Luke said.

"Well, he's out of luck, isn't he? She's dead by now. And worse than that, she died a whore."

Luke had stepped back to stand by Jack's side as Rennie began to speak. Even so, he was nearly too late to stop Jack as he lunged into the lean-to, dislodging one of the planks.

"That's not true! Take it back," he yelled at Rennie, his fist raised to strike her. Luke caught him by the arm and held him off while Thaddeus grabbed the boy's coat, then gave him a hard push to the ground.

"You're not helping anything, Jack. None of this is the fault of this woman," Thaddeus said in a quiet voice.

Jack rolled over to a sitting position, his head in his hands. "I wish I'd never come to this accursed place. Bad as it was, we'd have been better off in Ireland."

"You might be right about that, Jack, but there's nothing you can do to change that now," Luke said. "In the meantime, we don't know for sure what's happened to your sister. We need to find her. And the only way we can do that is if Rennie helps us."

Chapter 28

Rennie, draped in Luke's jacket, the dressing gown flapping beneath, led them out of Corktown and back toward the city.

Luke, never having been to one, had thought that a bordello would be very grand, ornate like a palace, moustachioed guards with swords standing at the entrance, and that one would glimpse rich hangings and draperies inside whenever the huge, brass-knockered oaken door swung open. He was disappointed when Rennie stopped at an ordinary-looking brick row house just north of Queen Street. There was a brass knocker on the door, to be sure, and the structure boasted three stories, but otherwise it seemed little different from the other buildings in the row.

"Well, what do we do now?" Thaddeus asked Luke. "We can scarcely barge in the front door and demand the girl."

"I guess we watch, and see if we can figure something out. Unless, of course, you'd like to pose as a customer?"

Thaddeus's mouth opened to utter a protest before he realized that his son was teasing him again. "You're the one who smells like rosewater," he said. "Maybe you should go."

"I'm going in the front door," Jack said. "I'm not going to stand around in the street while my sister's dying."

"And what are you going to do when they deny all knowledge of her existence?"

"I'll force my way in."

Luke caught his arm just as he was about to cross the street and climb the steps to the house. "Idiot," he said. "That's the best way to make sure we never find her."

"Dr. Luke, come with me," Rennie ordered. "You two wait down the street a bit and watch the front door. And try not to look so out of place. Pretend you're having a conversation about the weather or something."

She led Luke around the corner to a small lane that ran behind the row of houses, a narrow alley where the dustbins were kept, the coal delivered, and tradesmen knocked diffidently at the back doors. Rennie counted out the houses as they tiptoed along until she judged they had reached the right one. The backyards on both sides of the lane were fenced with board. Luke tried the gate that led to the brothel, but it was firmly locked. Other gates along the lane had not yet been locked for the night, and they slipped behind the one that stood two doors down.

"If Maggie died, and I'm pretty sure she must have, they won't have done anything with her until Hands got back," Rennie whispered. "The old woman just followed orders. She won't have arranged anything without being told."

"But what if Hands came back and they've taken her away already?"

"Even if he came back during the day, he'd probably wait until dark before he moved her. I would, if I had a body to get rid of. This looks like a fancy street. He wouldn't want the neighbours to notice anything unusual, would he? And he'd be sure to use the back door, so it would look like just another tradesman's call."

Luke couldn't fault her logic. The sun had just set in the autumn sky, twilight gathering shadows around them. He hoped they wouldn't have long to wait. He was cold without his jacket.

The approach of the wagon nearly took them by surprise. Rennie heard it first and pulled Luke farther behind the fence. As the cart creaked past them, a last lingering ray of sun illuminated the driver's face. It was Flea Mullen.

"They'll want to get the business done before the customers start arriving," Rennie breathed into his ear. "Evenings always seemed to be the busiest times."

As soon as Flea had tethered the horse and disappeared inside, Luke turned to Rennie. "You keep watch here. I'll run around the corner and tell the others to be ready to follow."

"But what if they see me?" Rennie said. "I'll be a dead woman. Let me go instead."

Luke debated for a moment. If anyone was liable to attract attention in a street of dignified houses, it would be Rennie, dressed as she was with her odd skirts trailing below a man's jacket. But he understood her concern.

"All right," he said. "Just tell Jack to be quiet and not make a scene."

"I'll try," she said, and then she was gone.

It was only a few minutes later when Luke heard the back door of the house swing open. He slid down to the ground on his belly, so that he would blend into the shadows on the ground but still be able to peer around the fence.

There were no obstructions between his line of sight and the tiny back dooryard. Flea Mullen and a tall brown-haired man emerged from the house, each toting one end of something that had been rolled in canvas.

"If you weren't such a midget, Flea, you could carry her by yourself," the brown-haired man said.

"Shut your gob, Badger."

For some reason Luke had expected the other man to be Hands. But it stood to reason, he supposed, that Hands would have any number of henchmen he could call on when there was work to be done. In spite of his name, Hands would never get actually get his hands dirty.

The men drew close to the side of the wagon, and then they heaved their bundle up into the bed. The canvas wrapping they had used had not been secured, and just before the bundle landed, Luke was sure that he saw a small hand slip out from between the folds.

So Rennie had been right. There had been little chance for Maggie after such a large dose of arsenic. And now she was being loaded into a wagon with as little ceremony as any of her fellow countrymen who had perished of fever.

The brown-haired man returned to the house and Flea climbed up to take the reins. This would make it more difficult for them to follow the wagon. Luke wasn't sure that Mullen would know him again — their paths had only crossed twice — but he would be instantly suspicious if he saw Jack or Rennie on the street.

Luke waited until the wagon reached the end of the laneway and turned south, then ran around the corner to where the other three were waiting.

"This way," he said.

"Did you find Maggie?" Jack asked. "Is she all right?"

"Not now," Luke hissed. "Be quiet and keep your head down. Come on."

They raced along the street in the direction that the wagon had taken, catching a glimpse of it just as it rounded a corner.

"Stay back, stay back," Thaddeus said. "Don't let him see us."

They were very nearly caught out. Just as they passed beneath a street lamp, Flea happened to turn around and look behind him. Thaddeus pulled Jack out of the illuminated arc of the gaslight, effectively concealing him in the shadows. Rennie did the most unexpected thing — she grabbed Luke and embraced him, turning her back on the wagon.

"Just play along," she hissed, as Luke, surprised by her action, struggled to pull away. "Pretend we're kissing and he'll just think I'm a whore plying my trade."

Luke did, as best he could, but he found Rennie's closeness distasteful and the smell of her unwashed body repugnant.

Finally, after what seemed an eternity to Luke, Thaddeus called, "He's gone on."

Rennie disengaged from her impromptu embrace, but not without casting Luke a puzzled glance first. Then she shrugged and they continued down the street, taking greater care to stay away from the light of the lamps.

After travelling three blocks farther, the wagon turned into the yard in front of a low-slung wooden building whose gate had been left open. Flea stopped the horses, climbed down from the wagon, and closed the gate.

"What place is this?" Jack asked. "And where's Maggie? It's time you told me what's going on."

They had crept close enough to read the sign on the gate — FRASER & HESS CABINETMAKERS — and as Luke peered over the gate, he could see a number of plain pine coffins sitting on trestles. The cabinetmaker must be under Hands's power, too. By far the easiest way to dispose of a dead body, he realized, would be to place it in a plain pine coffin and pretend it was just another fever victim. No doubt Flea would drive the wagon to the convalescent hospital as he normally did, then plod across the city again toward the burying ground at St. Paul's Church. No one would think anything of it. There had been so many of these journeys over the summer that it had become a routine sight.

"I don't know for sure what's going on, Jack," Luke said. "I think there's a body in the wagon, but whether it's Maggie or not, I have no way of knowing."

Just then, a door opened and Flea came out. Luke heard Rennie's sudden intake of breath as Pierce Mullen followed his brother into the yard. The two hopped up into the bed of the wagon and picked up the shrouded figure that lay there, Pierce at the head, Flea struggling at the feet.

Suddenly the bundle shifted and slipped through Flea's hands, spilling to the ground. The loosely wrapped canvas fell open, revealing the figure of a slender young woman with a halo of whitish-gold hair framing a face that, paradoxically, was a darkish brown in complexion. In spite of the damage that had been done to her skin from the arsenical mixture, the family resemblance was clear — Luke knew without a doubt that this was the body of Maggie Porter.

Chapter 29

Thaddeus felt sudden movement beside him, but he wasn't fast enough to keep Jack from clambering over the fence.

"Maggie!" Jack screamed as he dropped to the ground and ran across to the body that now lay in a crumpled heap. Startled, Flea jumped out of his way while Pierce stood open-mouthed on the back of the wagon. With a sob, Jack knelt and cradled his sister in his arms.

Flea recovered himself first. "Well well well," he said, "if it isn't another Porter spawn. I thought we'd got rid of the worst of them, but the young ones keep springing up, just like a nest of vermin. Doesn't matter how many you kill, there's always another one nosing around."

"Shut up," Jack said, his head still bowed over Maggie's lifeless body.

"No, I won't shut up," Flea said. "I've had enough of shutting up just because somebody like you thinks I ought to. This is a different land, young Jack, and you don't hold the whip hand anymore."

"Shut up," Jack said again, his head still bowed.

"I've taken such pleasure in seeing the misfortunes of the Porter family come raining down on their heads," Flea went on. "Let me see, what on earth has happened to you all? Oh yes, of course, the fever. It has no favourites, does it?"

Thaddeus could see that Jack was breathing heavily with anger. The boy would spring at Mullen, he knew, if pushed much farther.

"And then your uncle accidently drowned, didn't he? What a shame. And such a beautiful man he was, too, all decked out in his finery."

Jack looked up at Flea for the first time. "What are you talking about?"

"Why, your poor Uncle David. Or should I say your aunt? It was hard to tell which he was with his skirts on."

So they had been right, Thaddeus thought, as he crouched behind the fence with Luke and Rennie. The drowned man at Wellington had been David Porter.

"What did you do to him?" Jack demanded.

"Me?" Flea said. "I did nothing. I did nothing when he ran off that night, except to follow him. I did nothing but sit in the foul hold of a timber ship watching the rats gnaw on dead bodies while he slept in the cabin above me and dined with the captain. I did nothing when half the souls around me were taken off the ship and sent to purgatory on some God-forsaken island. And because I did nothing, he very nearly got away with it. I very nearly lost him at Quebec. And then someone called out "Florence" and I realized what he'd done. The bastard had disguised himself, and had stolen even my name from me. He'd seen me. And then, like it was the biggest joke in the world, he donned a dress and called himself Florence."

"What did you do?" Jack asked again.

Flea went on as if Jack hadn't spoken, lost in the reverie of his mad chase across the Atlantic Ocean. "I couldn't get close to him, you see, not until we got past Kingston. I was bottled up with a hundred others on the prow of the steamer, while he sat his lily-white arse down on a bench in the ladies' cabin. But Providence rewards those who wait, eh, young Jack? And sure enough your darling uncle made a mistake."

"What was that?" Jack's voice was low, almost a hiss, and Thaddeus had to strain to hear the words.

"Miss Florence had to go outside to take a piss. Such a lovely dark night it was, and the wind blowin' so no one could hear him hit the water. A ribbon in the pocket, a good shove, and over he went."

"I'll see you hanged for it, Mullen."

"Oh, I don't think so, young Jack. You see, I made a mistake, too. I was seen. By Captain Bellwood of the good ship Bellweather. I thought that was that, I would be hanged, but of all the steamer captains on all the great lakes, I managed to pick the one that's crookeder than the wake he steers. Bellwood didn't turn me in, he turned me over — to Hands — who is a fine, upstanding member of the Orange Lodge and has half the Toronto police in his pocket. My punishment, young Jack, was not to hang, but to land the best job I've ever had. I tell you, young Jack, pandering and pilfery suits me better than growing black potatoes any day. And then, as if fortune hadn't smiled on me broadly enough, it sent sweet young Maggie my way. She was tasty, Jack, she was a delight. It's too bad she didn't see it that way, I'd liked to have tried her a few more times."

Thaddeus expected Jack to rise to the bait Flea had dangled before him and attack, but instead his mouth twisted into a sneer.

"You're not the one with the last laugh after all, Mullen," he said.

For the first time since Jack had dropped so unexpectedly into the yard, Flea looked uncertain.

"You chased my uncle halfway across the world in the name of revenge," Jack said, "but you've missed a few important facts. There were three Porters and three shots. Which one found its mark? The bailiff fired over everyone's heads. Uncle David aimed at the mob all right, but he missed. Me Da was on the roof — not a good angle to shoot from — but then he couldn't anyway. He'd laid his rifle against the cabin before he climbed up the ladder. It was waiting there, for whichever man was brave enough to use it. You sent the wrong man into the water, Mullen."

"You? It was you?"

Luke climbed over the fence and dropped into the yard, reaching behind him to unlock the gate so that Thaddeus could slip through. From his vantage point on the back of the wagon, Pierce saw them immediately and shouted a warning to his brother. But before Flea could move, Jack lunged forward. Thaddeus caught only a flash of metal and then Flea toppled backward, Jack's knife buried in his chest.

Pierce scrambled down from the wagon, Luke rushed to Flea's side, and Thaddeus ran forward to grab Jack. But none of them moved fast enough, and before any of them could intervene, Flea had reached into his pocket and pulled out a small brown pepperbox pistol. He fired once, and it was Jack's turn to fall back.

The bullet struck Jack in the throat, and a spray of bright red blood spewed across the yard. Thaddeus reached the fallen boy first and tried to staunch the flow, but it gushed around his hands in spurts, and he knew that the injury was dire. Jack's eyes were glassy and his mouth opened and closed in wordless protest.

Luke left Flea and knelt by his father, jamming his handkerchief into the wound in a futile effort to stop the lifeblood from draining away into the dirt. A few moments later, although it seemed like years to Thaddeus, Jack Porter died.

"Pierce, quick!" Both Luke and Thaddeus turned at the words. "Quick, the gunshot will bring Hands running."

Pierce had been standing by the wagon, his mouth hanging open in surprise at the carnage that had erupted in the small yard. Now he hurried to his brother's side.

Flea reached into his pocket, and Thaddeus tensed, ready for another round of violence, but Flea pulled out a large roll of banknotes and handed it to his brother.

"What do you want me to do with that?" a bewildered Pierce asked.

"Take it ... take it ... go get Dermot," Flea gasped as he spoke, his breathing erratic and laboured. "I'm done. Forget about the girl ... just get Dermot and get out. Go to the States where no one knows you."

Pierce just stood there looking foolish as his brother panted instructions at him. Neither of them noticed Rennie as she strode into the yard. She marched over to Pierce and snatched the roll of money, peeled off the majority of the notes, and stuck them in the pocket of Luke's jacket.

"You big lummox," she hissed at him. "Go on, then. Go off to America and don't come back. I never want to see you again."

She flung the remaining notes at him. They hit his chest and then fluttered to the ground. As they landed, Luke saw one that appeared to be only half there. He snatched it as Pierce scrambled to pick up the rest of the money.

Just then the back door slammed open and a voice boomed out, "What in the name of God happened here?"

Pierce ran for the gate and disappeared down the street.

"Hands," Flea gasped. "I've been stabbed."

For some reason, Thaddeus had expected Hands to be a large man, blond and ruddy-faced perhaps, but that could have been because of Luke's confusion over his name. One would expect "Hans" to be Dutch or German, with a physical presence that matched the extent of his power. "Hands," on the contrary, was of medium height, with medium-brown hair and a medium build, a figure surprisingly nondescript for a man whose influence reached so far. He was accompanied by two large men who towered over him. They stood with their fists balled up, ready to start swinging at whoever their boss told them to.

"You need to send someone for a doctor," Luke said.

Hands looked at the butchery that had taken place in the yard and laughed.

"There's no point wasting good money on an Irishman. Looks to me like Flea's dying anyway — we'll just wait 'til he goes. He's so small we can pop him in the same coffin as the girl. Two for one, eh boys? Just like we did before."

"This man may well recover if he gets medical attention," Thaddeus said. "And at the very least you should call the police."

"The police?" Hands laughed even harder. "There's no point in calling them either. They'd just reach the same conclusion that I believe I've come to. This is nothing but a case of two drunken Irishmen killing each other over a couple of whores."

There was a sharp crack from somewhere behind Thaddeus, and Hands suddenly swayed as a red bloom of blood spread down his right shoulder. His hands clutched at the wound before he crumpled to the ground. Astonished, Thaddeus spun around to see Rennie, still pointing the gun, with a look of grim triumph on her face. Hands's henchmen rushed to his aid. Thaddeus pulled Luke by the arm.

"Come on, run!" He headed for the gate, grabbing Rennie's arm as he went by. He knew they had only a few moments to disappear into the shadows. At least one of Hands's men would soon give chase, and Thaddeus knew that they could never outrun him. Their only chance was to find someplace to hide. He stopped only long enough to snatch the gun out of Rennie's hand and toss it back into the yard.

Their unfamiliarity with the neighbourhood put them at a disadvantage, and the light spilling from the gas lamps made them far too visible. They needed to get away from the main thoroughfares and lose themselves in the maze of lanes and paths that led behind the houses.

Thaddeus nearly ran right past the lane, but at the last moment he saw it and veered into it, calling softly to Luke and Rennie to follow. He hoped that there was an exit at the end of it.

There wasn't. The houses had been built in such a haphazard fashion that the lane ended at a brick wall.

Thaddeus gasped as they turned to retrace their steps. The bed of the laneway consisted of gritty sand covered with a layer of coal dust. Their footprints were clearly visible, even in the dim light thrown by the waning moon.

"Let's hope we haven't been followed too closely," he said as they ran back down the lane. But just as they reached the end and were about to run back into the street, they saw one of Hands's men walking along, peering carefully from side to side. They shuffled back into the lane and Thaddeus tried to figure out what to do.

Just then they heard a low growl, and Rennie let out a muffled shriek. A huge dog advanced stiff-legged toward them, ears back, tail stiff. A watchdog, set loose at night to keep the lane clear of thieves and picklocks.

The dog sniffed, then growled again. Thaddeus realized that the front of his jacket was covered in Jack Porter's blood and that for some reason this aggravated and confused the dog. It would only be a matter of time before it sprang at them.

Luke was dragging his foot back and forth through the sandy grit of the lane. Thaddeus wanted to caution him to stay still, but then Luke slowly stooped and picked up a stray piece of coal that lay in the dirt. The dog's growl grew louder. Luke reached into his pocket and pulled out a bloody handkerchief. He must have shoved it back into his pocket, Thaddeus realized, after he had used it to try to save Jack. Luke tied the bloody cloth around the chunk of coal.

"Get ready," he said in a low voice, and Thaddeus tensed himself to move.

Hands's man had reached the laneway. Startled, the dog turned and at the same moment Luke let loose the package. The bloody missile flew through the air and struck the man in the chest just as the dog leapt at him, slavering and barking furiously.

"Now!" Luke yelled as he grabbed Rennie by the arm. They dashed out of the laneway, past the man, who was beating at the dog with his hands, trying frantically to keep the beast's gnashing teeth away from his face.

Thaddeus felt a stabbing pain in his knee as they ran. He was out of breath after two blocks and began to fall behind; Luke and Rennie slowed to allow him to catch up.

"I don't think Hands's man is in any condition to follow us," Luke said. "We can stop running."

"Good," said Thaddeus. "I can't run anymore anyway." He glared at Luke. "You do realize that I'm far too old for this."

"Would you rather have faced the dog?"

"No. But where are we going? Wherever it is, I'm not going to be able to get there very quickly."

"Do you think we should go back to Corktown?" Luke asked. "Rennie was able to hide there."

It would have been the safest choice, but Thaddeus knew he couldn't walk that far. An inn was out of the question, given their appearance. Both he and Luke were covered in blood and Rennie's odd apparel and Irish accent would draw far too much attention.

"We need to get out of the city," Thaddeus said. "And we need to do it right away, before Hands gets a search organized. They'll be watching the harbour."

"What if we took the stage as far as Whitby and caught a steamer from there?" Luke suggested.

"We're far too conspicuous even for that. We'll have to find somewhere to shelter for tonight and get ourselves cleaned up in the morning."

"We are going back to Kingston, aren't we?" Rennie asked. "I need to get back to Deirdre."

Luke was about to answer her, but Thaddeus caught his eye before he could speak. Now was not the time to tell this woman that her child was ill. Better to leave it until there was something she could do about it.

"Yes," he said, "we should go back to Kingston."

They turned and walked south toward the city centre, Thaddeus limping and leaning heavily on Luke, Rennie trailing along behind. They had not gone far, though, when Thaddeus said, "Here we go."

They had arrived at a stone church whose congregation seemed to be in the process of adding a shed-like hall to the rear of the building. The walls were still open to the elements, but it was partially roofed and would provide adequate, if not comfortable, shelter for the night.

Rennie sat apart from the two men, sniffling and wiping her nose from time to time with the muddied skirts of her gown.

Thaddeus was exhausted, and in pain. All he wanted to do was to lie down, go to sleep, and dream away the violent events of the evening, but he was too aware of the young woman's distress.

"Are you all right?" he asked her.

"No," Rennie replied. "I've never shot anyone before. Do you think I killed him?"

"I doubt it," Thaddeus said. "You just winged him. He won't be writing letters anytime soon, though."

"Oh. That's too bad. I meant to kill him."

"You needed a better gun."

He could feel Luke shaking beside him, as much, he suspected, from shock as from the cold. Rennie noticed as well. She slipped her arms out of the sleeves of Luke's coat.

"I'd better give this back."

"No, it's all right. You ke-keep it for tonight," he said, although his teeth were chattering.

"I don't think this is the time to observe the usual standards of propriety," Thaddeus said. "We'll make both coats do as a blanket and we'll all get under them. I know it's a little unseemly," he said to Rennie, "but it's better than freezing to death."

"It was closer quarters than this on the way over the ocean," she said, as they huddled together, "and the men weren't nearly so gentlemanly." And then after a moment, she said, "Do you think Flea is dead?"

"I'm afraid he may be," Luke said. "The knife went in close to his heart."

"He killed David Porter, didn't he?"

"Yes, he did. He took Charley Gallagher's ticket and chased Porter all the way across the ocean. For no reason, if Jack Porter can be believed."

"I'm not sure that he can," Thaddeus said. Although he desperately wanted to sleep, every time he closed his eyes his mind played out the scene that had ended with two men dead. "He claimed to have fired the shot, but it doesn't really make any sense. Why would John Porter have left the gun leaning against the cabin, if everyone knew there was going to be trouble? Anyone could have picked it up. If it were me, I'd have kept it near me."

"But why would Jack lie about it?"

"I think Jack was striking back at Flea by making him think he'd killed the wrong man. After all, Flea was really rubbing Jack's nose in it, gloating about the deaths of all the Porters."

"But the Porters aren't all dead," Rennie pointed out. "There's still Anna."

"Anna can't be touched because she's some sort of fairy being," Luke said. "Flea might have been able to do something about her because he's a cluri … whatever … but no one else would dare, isn't that right?"

"Only if you believe in fairies," Rennie said. "I know Pierce wouldn't dare go near her. He's a big cowardly lummox with no more backbone than a lumper potato." She hesitated for a moment. "I'm not sure what Dermot would do. Not if he knows that her brother killed Flea."

"But Flea told Pierce to leave the girl," Thaddeus said. "Leave the girl and go to the States, that's what he said."

"But which girl was he talking about leaving?" Rennie asked. "Anna or me?"

Chapter 30

Luke walked down to the city's market stalls the next morning wearing his father's shirt and the jacket he reclaimed from Rennie. There was a well beside the church, and he had sluiced as much blood from the clothing as he could, although a brown stain still marred his shirtfront. Thaddeus's coat was in a sorry state, as well, but with repeated scrubbing the stain became nearly invisible against the dark fabric.

Luke needed to find something to cover Rennie with, however, before they could hope to board a stage unnoticed. He had little experience of women and their dresses, but he was under the impression that they usually made them at home, or had a seamstress sew them to order. He didn't know if it was possible to buy anything ready-made.

His question was answered quickly at the market. There were several stalls that offered used clothing.

These had likely been passed to servants by the more well-to-do ladies of the city, used for a time, then sold to ragpickers.

He found a skirt that she could use to cover the bottom of the bedraggled gown she wore, and a plaid shawl that she could wrap around her. There were grease spots on the skirt, and the edges of the shawl were frayed, but the discarded clothing was still in better repair than the clothing Rennie had been wearing when she arrived in Canada.

He was about to turn away, well-pleased with his purchases, when his eye caught a pair of boots tucked under the trestle table the ragpicker had set up in the stall. They had been of good quality originally, and although the leather was now cracked, they were still serviceable and had no holes. Luke negotiated a price with the picker that was more than he could afford to spend, but he reminded himself that he had made a promise to Mary.

His other promises had led him only to disaster, he reflected as he walked back toward the church. He had promised that he would look for Anna Porter's remaining family — he had done so, only to find one already dead and the other rushing headlong on a path to destruction. He was still profoundly shaken by what had happened to Jack Porter — he could not have imagined that so much blood could spill out of one body in so short a time. He spared a sorry thought for Flea Mullen, and David Porter as well. Was there not enough dying already, without making more corpses in senseless acts of revenge?

It had been too dark under the church shed to check whether or not the half-note that had fluttered to the ground matched the half that Henry Gallagher had given him, but now he stopped and fished both of them out of his pocket. Although the cut edges were a little worn and bent from wear, it was clear that they belonged together. The numbers and the images lined up perfectly. He would have to return the mutilated note to Henry, along with an explanation of what had had occurred. He would have to get it straight in his own mind first, before he could commit it to paper, but as he thought about the sequence of events, he felt a profound despair at the thought of having to relate such a depressing tale. Time enough for that later, he decided, once everyone was safe.

Rennie looked, if not distinguished, at least presentable in her new finery. They could be mistaken, Luke judged, for two gentlemen of modest means travelling with a servant girl. They walked east until they found a staging inn and boarded with two other people, a farmer and his wife, who continued with them until Whitby, severely limiting their opportunity to discuss the events of the day before.

Thaddeus, as the least recognizable of the three of them, strolled past the Whitby wharves by himself, keeping a sharp eye out for anyone who seemed too interested in his movements. He was relieved to see that the steamer that was waiting at the dock was not *The Bellweather*, but a packet ship that ran a regular route between the Lake Ontario ports. After he reported that all seemed normal, he returned and bought three tickets, and Luke and Rennie clambered aboard the vessel just as the final whistle was blowing.

There were only a few other passengers aboard. It was late in the season and the autumnal storms caused heavy swells on Lake Ontario, making travel uncomfortable and more perilous. There was a well-dressed family with five children who were huddled by the stove, and three businessmen with warm wool chesterfield coats and tall hats conversed amongst themselves, commenting on the weather and the lack of business in Canada. At the other end of the cabin were five more modestly dressed men who had pulled their flat old-fashioned hats low over their brows as they stretched themselves out on the benches. Two of them had wound woolen mufflers around their faces in anticipation of the creeping, damp cold that would soon pervade the cabin in spite of the stove.

Thaddeus, Luke, and Rennie claimed a corner of the passenger cabin for themselves, and by the time the packet had reached the swell of the lake they had all fallen asleep.

Chapter 31

As soon as Kingston Harbour was in sight, Luke went to sit beside the still-drowsy Rennie.

"I have some bad news to tell you," he said, "although there is no reason to think the worst. Just before we left Kingston, Deirdre appeared to have come down with the fever. Mary took her right away to the hospital. I'm sure she'll be fine, with Mary and the nuns looking after her."

Rennie looked at him with wordless astonishment for a moment, and then she jumped up from the bench and began yelling at him. "Why didn't you tell me this before?" she shouted. "You heartless piece of bog peat! My baby lying on her death bed and you only get around to tellin' me about it now?"

Luke rose and she began slapping and hitting his shoulders and arms, backing him into the corner of the cabin as he tried to get away from her. "Honestly! You're thick as manure but only half as useful!"

"But —" Luke said. That was as much of a response as he was able to make as Rennie continued to rain insults down on him. These included a number of Irish terms that he was unfamiliar with, as well as long, disconnected phrases that included something about Molly Malone and her nine blind illegitimate children.

The altercation drew a great deal of attention from the handful of other passengers, but Thaddeus judged that it didn't matter at this point. If anyone on board the steamer had been looking for them, they would have made their presence known long since. He supposed he could intervene, but he reflected that it would do his son good to learn the value of saying nothing in the face of a woman's wrath. It was practical experience that should prove useful when he married. And suddenly, Thaddeus remembered that Betsy would no longer be there when he finally went home. He wouldn't have believed that it was possible for him to have put it out of his mind for so long, but in the rush of the events of the past few days he had forgotten that she wouldn't be in their little cabin, stirring up a pot of tea to warm him and listening raptly to his news of the outside world. He wished then that the steamer would sail on forever, taking him to all the far-off places he had always wanted to visit, never to return to Wellington and The Temperance Hotel.

As soon as the ship touched the public wharf, Rennie leapt down onto the dock and ran off in the direction of the Hôtel Dieu, after having delivered one last hard blow to Luke's upper arm.

"You'd better pray that the baby is all right, otherwise I wouldn't want to be in your shoes," Thaddeus remarked.

Luke suddenly realized that he had forgotten to give Rennie the pair of boots he had found for Mary. "At the very least, I'd better deliver these personally," he said, holding them up. "Make amends any way I can."

"You go ahead," Thaddeus said. "I'll be with Anna and Mrs. Shanahan." His knee was still sore and he felt stiff from the hours of travelling. He would be happy enough to sit guard over the girl for a little while. He hoped that nothing had happened to her in the time it had taken them to travel to and from Toronto.

Thaddeus hadn't forgotten Rennie's hesitation when they had talked about whether or not the Mullens would attempt to harm Anna Porter. She had seemed sure about Pierce, but less so about the other brother, Dermot.

Pierce had had a head start, and he hadn't needed to be careful. Hands's men would be looking for Rennie, not Pierce, and there was nothing to stop him from openly boarding the first packet that was leaving Toronto Harbour. Still, there were not so many of those now that winter threatened, certainly not the daily excursions that were offered during the summertime. Suddenly, Thaddeus wished that he had taken a closer look at the muffler-wrapped men at the other end of the cabin.

Perhaps he was being too cautious. There was no real reason to believe that the Mullens would do anything at all. Flea had urged Pierce to retrieve his brother and make for the border, and surely Hands's Toronto gang could survive the defection of a minor member without exacting revenge. And yet, Rennie's words returned to him: "Hands don't like being crossed. If you run away, he'll hunt you down and kill you." This would certainly be true for poor Rennie. She had shot the boss, and even if the wound proved to be fatal, it was a transgression that was unlikely to be forgiven by the boss's flunkies. He wondered where she would go.

He sighed as he limped down the steps to the cellars of the City Hall. Revenge was a nasty business, and there had been far too much of it already.

When Luke reached Hôtel Dieu, he walked in on a three-sided argument between Rennie, Mary, and Sister Bourbonnière.

Rennie was jouncing Deirdre up and down on her arm in an attempt at comfort, but, as usual, the child was whimpering.

"You should not take 'er," Sister Bourbonnière was saying. "She will recover, yes, but she still needs care, and you 'ave no place to take 'er to."

"I'm sorry, Sister, but we have to go. It's not safe for us here."

Sister Bourbonnière turned to Luke. "Tell them, please, Luke, that they cannot take the child yet."

"I'm sorry, Sister, but the mother is right. It's not safe for them here."

The nun threw up her hands and muttered something in French, then added, "Very well. Go then."

Rennie and Mary pushed their way toward the front door. Only at the last moment did Luke remember his errand.

"Mary," he shouted. "These are for you." He ran to her and thrust the boots into her hands. She gave him a puzzled look, and then followed her sister down the front steps of the hospital.

"Foolish girls," Sister Bourbonnière muttered, and then she said, "I'm glad you are 'ere, Luke. It's Father 'iggins. 'E's been taken with the fever, but much worse than the rest of us."

Luke's heart raced at the mention of the priest's name.

"Follow me. 'E kept going as long as 'e could, but 'e 'as 'ad to give up and rest for a time. I know 'e will be cheered up if 'e knows you 'ave returned."

She led him down the hall to her closet dispensary, where Higgins had been given a pallet on the floor. It was a sign of respect, he supposed, that Higgins had been afforded this small token of privacy.

He looked ghastly. His face was lined and grey with a sheen of sweat that indicated a spiking fever, although he had not yet taken on the masklike appearance that was sure to follow. He had, however, already developed the racking cough that usually came later in the progression of the disease, and Luke caught a glimpse of bright-red blood in the wadded up piece of newspaper he was using as a handkerchief. The disease had ambushed him with frightening speed and alarming fury.

Luke's misgivings about facing him again faded away in the surge of pity he felt for the man. Whatever wrong had been between them, it had been on Luke's part, not the priest's, and he realized how unfair he had been to blame the man for his own frailty. He could not voice this to the priest. Not now. And, it appeared, not ever.

"Luke," Higgins said in a low voice. "It finally got me."

"You'll be all right yet," Luke said, kneeling beside him. "I know you're not nearly as strong as the Sisters, but even you should be able to fight it off."

He was rewarded with a weak smile. "Poor puny Irishman that I am," Higgins said, and Luke remembered what it was that he so loved about this man. "You went away," the priest said, wrinkling his brow as if trying to remember.

"Yes, I was looking for Anna Porter's family."

"And did you find them?"

"Yes. But it didn't turn out well. Margaret Porter is dead. Flea Mullen killed David Porter, and then Flea and Jack Porter managed to kill each other."

Higgins was seized with a paroxysm of coughing. Luke helped him sit up so he could catch his breath again, then the priest fell back onto his pallet and closed his eyes. When he finally opened them again, he said, "I'm going to hell, Luke."

"What are you talking about? You're a priest."

He shook his head. "I have sins to account for and I thought I could give a good accounting, but everything I've tried to do has turned to dust."

"Do you want me to fetch one of the other priests?" Luke asked. He didn't like this talk of sin. He would have his own accounting to do some day.

"I know who shot Charley Gallagher."

"Yes, I know," Luke said. "It was Jack Porter. He told Flea as much. He took the gun his father left against the cabin wall."

"No. John Porter had the gun beside him, although I don't think anyone else could see that. I was standing to one side, on a little knoll of grass, and I could see him on top of the roof."

So Thaddeus had been right, Luke thought, when he pointed out that he'd want the gun close by if trouble was expected.

"The bailiff fired up into the air, as a warning shot," Higgins went on, "but both David and John fired straight into the crowd. I don't know for sure which bullet struck Charley, but both the Porters aimed to kill. David ran away that night, and I let him go without saying a word. I hoped he would get away cleanly. There would be no more blood spilled, you see, if David was gone and no one knew about John."

It made sense, Luke thought. What were the chances that Flea Mullen would ever catch up with David Porter?

Higgins began coughing again. "Do you want me to get the Sister?" Luke asked, but the priest shook his head.

"I have a confession to make, Luke."

"You need another priest for that."

"No, I'll make it to you. No one else would understand it, and so it wouldn't be a true confession."

Luke steeled himself, but the sins that plagued the priest seemed to have nothing to do with the night by the shore.

"I was in the fever shed the night John Porter died."

"You didn't … you didn't kill him, did you?"

"He had pneumonia like I have now."

Luke nodded.

"He was taken with a fit of coughing that threatened to shake the shed. He tried to sit up, to catch his breath, but he was too weak. I didn't help him. I let him cough his life away. There was no one else there to see, so when I was sure he was gone, I laid a scrap of green ribbon between his shirt and his vest, as a sign that justice had finally been done. So God help me, Luke, no, I didn't kill him, but I might just as well have. I'm not sorry. But now I'm going to hell."

Luke knew there was nothing he could say to comfort this man. He would take his sins with him to the grave, and forego eternal grace on account of it.

Higgins beckoned to him to lean closer. "Don't let the Mullens get the little merrow," he said in a low voice. "There's to be no more blood spilled over this. It's done." He closed his eyes again and whispered, "And now you could fetch a priest, if you would."

"Why, it's Dr. Luke's father!" Mrs. Shanahan was standing by the small stove in the middle of the room, stirring something in the old tin pot she used for cooking. Several children were nearby, playing a game with small pebbles, but Thaddeus couldn't have said with certainty which girls were attached to Bridie and which were playmates from the other families who had taken refuge in the cellars.

"Where's Dr. Luke? He hasn't come to check my thumb in a long time."

"He's just off running an errand," Thaddeus said. "He'll be along soon." He eased himself down to sit on the small trunk that Mrs. Shanahan used as a chair.

"You can't sit there," she said with a sharp tone in her voice. "That's mine now. Anna gave it to me."

"I'm sorry," Thaddeus said, although he had no idea for what. "May I sit beside it?"

"Sit wherever you like," Mrs. Shanahan said, "just not on the trunk. It's not right that you sit on the trunk."

"Where is Anna?" he asked. He knew from what Luke had told him that there was no point in looking around the cellar. She could be standing right in front of him and he might not notice her.

"Why, she's doing the same as Dr. Luke, she is," Mrs. Shanahan replied. "Running an errand. Off to find us some bread to go with our soup. Gone down to the sheds, she has, where they're giving it out."

"How long ago did she leave?"

"Oh, it's been years. When you're hungry it always seems like years, doesn't it?"

Thaddeus wondered if he should hoist himself up again and go after Anna. It was possible that one of the mufflered men on the steamer might well have been Pierce Mullen. Or was it just his imagination that made him think it possible? But it wasn't Pierce who would be a threat, it was his brother Dermot. Luke said he was still recovering from fever, but Thaddeus couldn't remember if he had been in one of the sheds or one of the hospitals.

"Where do you go to get bread?" he asked.

"Oh, I don't go at all. I send Anna. It's such a long walk all the way down to the lake, you see, and I have all the girls. I can't leave the girls you know. Seven makes it right again. Have to look after them."

That was enough for Thaddeus. With a groan he pushed himself up from the floor. "I think I'll just go and see if she's all right," he said.

He had just reached the top of the steps when he heard shouting. Just down the street he saw Pierce Mullen and another dark-haired man, who had a hold of Anna Porter's arm.

"Let her go, Dermot. It's not worth it," Pierce said.

"Her brother killed Flea!" Dermot yelled. "Are you going to let that pass?"

Thaddeus could see that Dermot was holding Anna very gingerly, as if a part of him still believed that she was possessed of some supernatural power, and that if he held her too closely, his own skin in turn would become covered in scales. One good push and the girl could wiggle free, he judged, but she appeared to be unconcerned that she was being held. She simply stood there, motionless and insubstantial.

Thaddeus knew that he if rushed Dermot, Anna could easily get away, but he had no way of knowing if the men carried any weapons. Flea had unexpectedly carried a gun, Jack Porter a knife, and neither had hesitated to use them. Thaddeus didn't know if the surviving Mullen brothers were as ruthless.

"Let her go, Dermot," he said calmly, approaching the men. "There's been no harm done here. You and

Pierce can walk away from this. Go to the States like your brother wanted you to."

"And just who are you?" Dermot demanded. "How do you know my name? And how do you know what my brother wanted?"

Just to the far right of his field of view, Thaddeus caught a glimpse of Rennie and her sister running down the street toward them. He would keep the Mullens talking in the hope that Rennie's ultimate arrival would distract them enough so that he could make a grab for Anna.

"I was there when your brother died," Thaddeus said. "It's true that Jack Porter stabbed your brother, but Flea pulled a gun and shot him down in return. I think you're even, don't you?"

"It's true," Pierce said. "I don't know who this man is, but he was there. Let's just go, Dermot."

"You're a cowardly bastard, Pierce. You'd let a Porter go free after everything they've done?"

Before Pierce had a chance to reply, the air was filled with a high-pitched, ear-splitting screech. Both Mullen brothers turned in the direction of the noise and Dermot was so startled that he nearly let go of Anna's arm. Thaddeus did not turn to look — he launched himself in Dermot's direction and hoped that the tackle would be enough to bring him down. Just as he went smashing into Mullen, he realized that Anna was no longer there.

Luke hurried out of the hospital and headed down Brock Street, spurred by the priest's words. Ahead of him, he could see that Mary and Rennie had nearly reached City Hall. Suddenly he saw them stop, then break into a run, disappearing down Market Street. They could only be headed for the cellars.

He ran after them, but stopped before he reached the entrance, flattening himself against the side of the building. He saw that both Mullens were there, and that Dermot was holding Anna by the arm. His father was talking to the men and gesturing, with Mrs. Shanahan behind him, holding, for some reason, her tin pot. None of them appeared to notice Mary and Rennie until Deirdre let out a shriek that would have deafened them all had they been inside. The Mullens turned toward the unearthly sound, and at that moment Thaddeus launched himself at Dermot. Luke ran forward and grabbed Pierce, wrenching both of the man's arms behind him so that he was unable to go to his brother's aid. Mary and Rennie added their screams to Deirdre's and the din was enough to start drawing a crowd from up out of the cellars.

Had Dermot Mullen been well, Luke thought, Thaddeus would have been no match for him. But he was obviously still weak from his struggle with fever, and the unexpected tackle had knocked the wind out of him. He lay on the ground gasping while Thaddeus pinned him down with one knee. Suddenly, Luke realized that he didn't know what had happened to Anna. She must have pulled away from her reluctant captor when he was knocked over, but Luke hadn't seen her move, and he didn't know where she had gone.

Suddenly Bridie Shanahan pushed her way past

the onlookers who had crowded the entrance to the cellar to watch the scene. She stalked over to Dermot and began banging his head with her tin pot. The thin soup she had been preparing flew in all directions, not a little of it landing on Thaddeus.

"No more ribbons! Do you hear me, Dermot Mullen? There will be no ribbonmen here. Enough! Go away!" she shrieked until Luke, judging that Pierce was no threat, went over and gently relieved her of her tin weapon.

"There's been too much already, Dr. Luke," she said, although she let him take the pot. "Too much. No more!"

Dermot Mullen had recovered his breath. "You stupid woman, I'll get you for this." Thaddeus dug his knee into the man's chest, and whatever else he might have said was lost in a grunt.

Bridie Shanahan drew herself up to her full, albeit diminutive height. "You will not, Dermot Mullen! The merrow lives with me now. And I didn't take her, I didn't. She gave me her red cap all on her own, and seven gets to heaven, she knows that. You'll not lay a finger on me. It stops here."

And suddenly, Anna reappeared beside Luke and fixed Dermot with her basilisk gaze.

"Yes, it does," Pierce said, stepping forward. "Come on now, Dermot. We're done here. We're going across to the States. Just like Flea told us to."

"Well, if that doesn't beat all. Pierce Mullen has finally grown a backbone." It was Rennie. She moved toward Pierce, chin jutting out in challenge.

"Come with me," he said, turning to her.

"Why should I?" she asked.

"Because you want to. And I want you to."

She looked at him for a long moment, her eyes narrowed in calculation. "What about Deirdre?"

"From now on, she's like my own."

"Prove it," Rennie said. She marched over and thrust the baby into his arms. Deirdre looked up into Pierce's face with a puzzled frown. She had continued her whimpering until then and now Luke expected another deafening shriek, but to his surprise she stopped mewling and looked into Pierce's face with a peculiar intense stare that was not unlike Anna Porter's.

"Well, that settles Deirdre," Rennie said. "Now what about Mary?"

"What about me?" Mary said. "I'm supposed to just trail along behind you? I followed you across the ocean, Rennie, and now you want me to follow you across the border?"

"You know there was no choice, Mary. We would have starved. And there's no choice now either. I shot a man. And sooner or later his friends will come after me if I stay here."

Mary had been clutching the boots Luke had given her. She looked down at them, then over at Luke.

"Just answer me one thing, Dr. Luke," she said. "Is there any chance at all for the likes of me?"

It took Luke a moment to understand what she was asking him. When he finally did, his response must have shown in his face, because her face fell. "Oh well, thanks for the boots, anyway."

He longed to tell her why he didn't want her, that it was nothing to do with her, or being Irish, or being poor; that there was no woman who had claimed his affections ahead of her. Instead, all he could say was, "Are you going with Rennie?"

She surprised him. "Do you remember the night Rennie left the baby with Mrs. Shanahan and I was frantic to find her? You never asked me where I was that night, and why Rennie didn't leave Deirdre with me." She blushed a little. "I was meeting a man — a soldier from the fort. He fancies me. I'm not sure what I think of him, but if there's no chance with you, he'll do as well as anyone."

Luke thought his heart would break for her, but there was nothing he could do to make it better, nothing at all.

"If you're not coming, Mary, then we'd better be on our way. We've got company." Pierce gestured toward the wharves.

A steamer was in the harbour and coming in to the public dock. It wasn't one of the regular packets — it was far too late in the day for a scheduled arrival. Luke was sure that it was *The Bellweather* and he was certain that Captain Bellwood would have a contingent of Hands's friends on board.

Thaddeus gave Dermot one last hard poke with his knee. "If I let you up, do you promise to do what Pierce says and not cause any more trouble?"

"C'mon, Dermot," Pierce said. "You don't want to tangle with Hands. He'll do a lot more than knock you down."

Dermot nodded, and Thaddeus let him up. "Go east," he said, "and find someone to take you across the river."

Rennie ran over to Luke and planted a kiss on his cheek.

"Thank you," she whispered. "And thank your father, too." She hugged Mary for one long moment, and then she ran after Pierce. Mary watched until they disappeared down the street, and then she melted away into the shadows of the gathering twilight.

Chapter 32

"Maybe we should go inside," Luke said. "I doubt that Captain Bellwood could recognize my face again, but I don't know who else is aboard."

"You'll have to help me up first," Thaddeus said. "That flying tackle was not a good idea."

"It got the job done, though. Now I know why Mr. McFaul thinks you're such a useful man to have around in a crisis."

Thaddeus grunted as Luke pulled him to his feet, and then they went into the cellar and gathered around Bridie Shanahan while she tried to salvage her interrupted meal.

"You're staying for supper, are you?" she asked, looking at them as though they had just dropped in for an unexpected visit, and the scene in the front of the cellar had never taken place. "We'll have to put another potato in the pot."

"Anna, come sit beside me for a minute," Luke said. The girl seemed unaffected by Dermot's aborted kidnapping, although his grip had left a red mark on the peculiar skin of her arm. "You should wring out a cloth in cold water and wrap it around that," he said. "That way it won't swell up so much."

She nodded, and then waited, as if she knew that Luke had more questions for her.

"The day your father pulled down Mrs. Shanahan's house — you were there, weren't you? That's how you knew it was him."

"No one saw me," she said. "No one but the priest. You and him and Bridie. You can see me even when other people can't."

A priest, a sinner, and a lunatic, Luke thought. Was it only those who lived on the fringes of the normal world who could see into the supernatural one?

"What do you want to talk about that day for?" Mrs. Shanahan said. "Talking doesn't bring them back, does it?"

"Where did the letters come from, Anna? The ones in the trunk."

"That's my trunk now," Mrs. Shanahan said. "She gave it to me."

"From the priest," Anna said.

"He gave them to you?"

"No, but he saw me take them. He took his jacket off and they were in his pocket."

Henry Gallagher had sent money to his brother in several different ways, Luke recalled. He had arranged Charley's passage through the Canada Company, but

he hadn't trusted them with the money part of it. He'd
sent that through the church. Others must have done
the same, and Father Higgins had their letters in his
pocket to deliver.

"You gave the money to your Uncle David, so he
could get away from the people who thought he'd shot
that man."

"So that's why the priest lied," Thaddeus said. "It
was to protect Anna."

"And David Porter. If David wasn't there, no one
could harm him. He hadn't counted on Flea Mullen
taking Charley's ticket."

"There must have been a lot of money if Porter
could afford a cabin passage."

"They were all dead," Anna said. "They couldn't
go across the sea no matter how much money there
was, could they? I didn't take their money unless they
were dead."

Luke had no doubt that Anna had been right
about the fate of her neighbours. She had predicted her
own father's death, hadn't she? And her brother's and
sister's as well. But for some reason not David Porter's.
He tried to put his next question into the same words
that she had used when making her predictions.

"Why didn't you know that your Uncle David was
dead?"

For the first time since he had met her, Luke saw
emotion on Anna's face. "I don't know," she said. Her
brows were pulled down slightly, as much expression as
her thickened skin would allow, Luke guessed. "There
was a lady dead. I didn't know who she was."

Luke was stunned. Whatever prophetic skills Anna possessed had been confused by the simple circumstance of David Porter donning a dress.

"Don't know why you want to bring all this up again," Mrs. Shanahan was muttering to herself. "It won't be bringing Mr. Shanahan back, will it? Nor Bridget, nor Dorey, nor Sheena, nor Eileen, nor Lucy, nor Maeve, nor Tessie, nor Ma, nor Pa, nor half of Banesalley, will it?"

"Were those your daughters?" Thaddeus asked.

"Seven girls there were, now there are seven more. Seven gets to heaven and one of 'em is a merrow."

"Aren't you afraid of her?" Luke asked. "A merrow is a messenger of doom."

"I've already had all the doom a body can have in a lifetime. And I didn't steal her red cap, she gave it to me. Now I'll use her gold for seven girls. Seven gets me to heaven and I'll see my girls again, I will."

It was beginning, almost, to make sense. "The letters in the trunk — that's what you gave to Mrs. Shanahan, isn't it Anna?"

She nodded. "Da found them. He was mad. He said I should have saved some of the money for us and not given it all to Uncle David."

"Why didn't you?"

Anna shrugged. "They were dead. All of them. Then Da said we couldn't take Gran's red cap with us, but the letters were like the same thing. He said I was to see them all safe across the ocean, and then he'd give them back."

And she had, Luke thought. All of her family had crossed the ocean, only to perish in Canada. He was beginning to understand the nature of bargains with the otherworld.

"And once you got the letters back, you gave them to Mrs. Shanahan?"

"Me Da pulled her house down and she lost her seven girls," Anna said. "I don't want any more green ribbons either."

"Just one more question," Luke said in a soft voice. "Father Higgins?"

"He's dead too."

Chapter 33

The next morning, Luke and Thaddeus parted ways, Luke aboard a coach that would take him to Montreal, Thaddeus on his way back to Wellington astride a bay mare that he rented from the livery. It had been a long time since Thaddeus had been on horseback. His knee still hurt, and he felt bruised and shaken from his exertions of the last few days, but the wind in his face and the gentle rhythm of the horse's gait soothed him as he headed west toward Bath. He had ministered to this circuit once upon a time. He would ride slowly and stop often, visit old acquaintances, share meals with old friends. Maybe then he would be ready to go home.

He and Luke had talked for a long time the previous night, stitching together the things they knew, guessing at the things they didn't. It was a sorrowful story, and one that was not yet ended. Thaddeus still didn't know who had left the ribbon with John Porter's body. Luke would not share this intelligence.

"It was told to me in confidence," he said. "And I'll take the information with me to the grave." By which Thaddeus guessed that it must be something to do with the priest. There was still a reserve when Luke spoke of Higgins, a warning that the subject must not be pursued too far. Someday, Thaddeus hoped, his son would be ready to tell him about it.

They decided that it would be Thaddeus who would write to Anthony Hawke, the man charged with investigating the shameful fraud that had taken place in Toronto. He would tell Hawke what they knew about Captain Bellwood's role in the disappearance of brandy that had been earmarked for fever patients, and about Hands's comprehensive network of criminal activities in the city. He had little hope that it would do much good. Hands, as Rennie said, had his hands in everything, and this apparently included much of the local law enforcement.

It would fall to Luke to tell Henry Gallagher that his brother would not be joining him in the Huron Tract. "I'll give him the gist of what happened," he said. "It's enough that Charley is dead. He doesn't need to know who shot him."

Thaddeus concurred. "The last thing you want to do is start a new round of reprisals. It can end here."

Which brought them to Bridie Shanahan and her strange atonement: seven girls lost, seven girls gained, in the hope that she could appease her way to heaven, a strategy with which Thaddeus was all too familiar.

And to Anna Porter, whose concept of justice derived not from ordinary precepts of right and wrong, but from some strange fairy otherworld beyond the ken of mortal man.

Luke had taken the two halves of Henry Gallagher's pound note and presented them to Anna before he left. "Go steal some glue," he said to her. "You can put them together to help Bridie look after the girls."

Thaddeus suddenly realized that he still had a length of green ribbon in his coat pocket. It was Martha's by rights; he had only borrowed it. But now he felt compelled to toss it away in a gesture that he hoped would mark an end to the cycle of violence and revenge and regret, that, in the words of Bridie Shanahan, "It stops here."

He rode to the edge of the road, where it sloped down to meet the lake, and held the ribbon out so that it trailed in the northeast wind. And then he let it go.

Acknowledgements

Although this is a work of fiction, a number of historical personages have made their way into my story, most notably Thaddeus Lewis, who laboured for the Methodist Episcopal Church during the 1800s, supported by his wife Betsy. This story has, however, departed radically from the events Lewis detailed in his autobiography of 1865.

Many sources were consulted regarding the dreadful emigration of 1847. Of inestimable value were Donald MacKay's *Flight From Famine* (Dundurn, 2009) and *Les Religieuses Hospitalières de Saint Joseph and the Typhus Epidemic, Kingston, 1847–1848* by Nancy McMahon, National Archives of Canada, as well as information provided online by the Ireland Park Foundation of Toronto, the Irish Famine Commemoration Association via the Kingston Irish Folk Club, archived copies of

The British Whig at OurOntario.ca Community Newspapers Collection, and Transactions of the Kingston Historical Society, Volume 1 to 10 (Mika Publishing Co., Belleville, 1974).

Kingston: Building on the Past by Brian S. Osborne and Donald Swainson (Butternut Press Inc., 1988) provided information on 1840s Kingston; James Scott's *The Settlement of Huron County* (Ryerson Press, Toronto, 1966) contains a wonderfully detailed history of The Huron Tract; and numerous websites have chronicled the changing nature of Toronto's streets.

Many thanks go to the Robert Lecker Agency; my editor, Allison Hirst, my publicist, Karen McMullin, and all the folks at Dundurn; Colleen Johnson for not showing up for coffee too often; Books & Co., Picton, for their continuing support; and most of all to Rob, who displays patience beyond all understanding.